One Big Mess
Dan Fitzgerald

One Big Mess TM & © 2022 Dan Fitzgerald & Markosia Enterprises, Ltd. All Rights Reserved. Reproduction of any part of this work by any means without the written permission of the publisher is expressly forbidden. All names, characters and events in this publication are entirely fictional. Any resemblance to actual persons, living or dead is purely coincidental. Published by Markosia Enterprises, PO BOX 3477, Barnet, Hertfordshire, EN5 9HN.

FIRST PRINTING, June 2022.
Harry Markos, Director.

Paperback: ISBN 978-1-915387-13-4
eBook: ISBN 978-1-915387-14-1

Book design by: Ian Sharman
Cover art by: Paul Houston

www.markosia.com

First Edition

Part One

Chapter 1
Lester

Lester squatted on top of a refrigerator-sized, anvil-shaped rock in the center of Umed's backyard. It was almost midnight and the moon was full. He could have been compared to a wolf if he didn't already look so much like a weasel. Lester was five-foot three, a good four inches shorter than average for a kid entering the tenth grade. He had dark, home-cut, frizzy hair, slicked back and a handful of freckles dotted around his pointy nose. He was hunched in a defensive posture. Lester's father liked to drink and smoke and sniff and whatever else a degenerate ice cream truck driver could do in his spare time. He liked to hit, too. Lester's mom wasn't around anymore.

Mark sat at his bedroom window; he was curled up in the dormer watching Lester on his stage. Mark and Lester shared a fence in the backyard. He used to share this property line with Umed, but as Mark had already learned, life's condition changed, often with little warning and grave consequences. Mark wondered why Lester chose that particular perch. It seemed to Mark that any of the unnecessary scraps peppered throughout Lester's yard would do: Either of the two tire-less and broken-down cars, or the stack of roofing shingles of varying color and grit. The rusted wall of the empty pool. Even the delimbed dining room table could platform such a creature. But Lester had chosen the rock. Mark supposed that it suited him. Rocks were natural, and Lester was definitely a part of nature.

"You son of a queer. Get back in here!"

Following his own garbled threats, Lester's father stumbled out of the house and into the backyard. He propped himself up with a screen door that had been dangling on its last hinge for the better part of the summer.

"Come and get me, fuck nut!"

Mark had seen this act before. It came with the drinking and the smoking and the lack of regard for life in general. Lester's dad didn't have a chance. Even if he wasn't drunk or huffed out, Lester was quick. Mark had never seen anyone glide on air quite like Lester. He was lithe, Mark thought. Then Mark shut his eyes and winced before refocusing his attention on Lester's passionless father.

To look at him, Lester's dad wasn't out of shape. He was built just like his son: skin, bones and sheets of compact, near-massless muscle. But he had way too many miles on his tires. Twenty years ago he could walk on air, too. Now his lungs just struggled to secure it.

"Fuck nut? I'll fuckin' you... Fuck it."

Lester's father slammed the backdoor. The screen door surrendered its last tack and collapsed to the grassless lawn. The deadbolt turned. He had found a way. It was a psychological punishment that partnered the damp night air with an endless assault of vampiric insects under a blanket sewn of disregard. Lester's dad hadn't been able to physically hurt his son in two years. He would have to be able to catch him first.

Mark knew Lester could get back into his house. At least he thought that he knew this. Mark felt no obligation to invite his neighbor over, neither for hot soup nor for a warm bed. Besides, Mark *couldn't* invite him over, literally. Anyway, fuck Lester, the kid was pure trash.

Mark looked to his bedroom door and shuddered as he envisioned what waited for him on the other side. He looked back down at Lester. The weasel had abandoned its squat. Instead, Lester lay on his side, in a ball, on top of the rock.

It was bedtime for Mark, too.

Chapter 2
Ashley

Mark holed up at a different window in the morning, the window facing east, the window facing Ashley. The setup was different this time. The blinds were drawn. The only vantage of Ashley's back yard angled through a cleverly fabricated slant in one of the slats. From Mark's bed, if he put his head where his feet belonged, he could see Ashley's deck and right into the pool. It was a nice setup. Every Saturday morning, weather permitting, Ashley would lie in the sun before taking a dip. Ashley was beautiful. In a two-piece, she was a goddess.

Mark never felt guilty about this. It was his house, his room, and his window. He could choose his own view and do whatever he wanted to himself in his own room looking out of his own window. He did, however, agonize over his conflicted thoughts: impure fantasies of entering Ashley's back yard. Hostile dreams involving the bottom part of Ashley's bathing suit, a quick look and a two fingered touch.

"Christ," Mark thought aloud, "she's right next door."

Didn't that mean anything? Was there a law of proximity, a code between neighbors that permitted him access? All of his efforts seemed wasteful considering she was so close.

After Mark finished with himself he thought about before. He recalled two years earlier when he and Ashley were dating, or whatever eighth graders did awkwardly between classes and after school. When there was an unlocked gate between their yards that he used daily. And a second gate, in the same corner, that led to Umed's yard which Mark had used just as often. If you were to go out there now, in the corner of Mark's property, you would find a bungee cord tying the two gates together and holding them closed. It was arranged so that if you pushed on one gate you would be denied egress and the added stress on the bungee would force the second gate to shut tighter. No one had pushed on either gate in a while.

The gates were locked, Umed was back in India with his parents, and Ashley hated Mark. She hated him with all her beauty. She hated him with her two-piece and everything underneath it. She hated Mark with all the love she had once held for her dead mother.

Chapter 3
Mark

Mark jumped out of bed and tossed his now unclean boxers in the hamper. He skipped to his dresser, where all his neatly folded clothes were meticulously shelved in chromatic order. The aligned garments went from whites, right into Roy G Biv, followed by the grays, then the blacks. Mark selected a comfortable outfit: shorts he didn't care much about and a plain white tee. He threw on his knock-around Nikes and then made his bed.

Mark stopped to look around his bedroom. Everything was in its place. Everything had a place and everything had a purpose. Mark was certain of this. His chamber substantiated the minimalist dream. Its design was neat, orderly and functional. He had even brushed up on feng shui to make sure his room had the proper flow. There were no posters on the walls; the flat screen, mounted on a swivel bracket, doubled as his monitor. Additionally, or in

Mark's mind subtractionally, the remainder of his living space contained only a dresser, a hamper, a desk with a chair, a love seat, and a bed. What else did a 16-year-old need? His Xbox fit into a desk-side compartment complete with a siding rack. He had a handful of games stacked neatly in alphabetical order in a lower drawer. Mark had stopped buying software when he recognized that he could download whatever he wanted and store all his apps furtively within the cloud.

Mark had fixed a body-length mirror to the back of his door. He routinely gave himself a once-over before leaving his room. Mark liked what he saw. He understood fashion like few in his school. It was simple, actually. Mark carried a non-complicated style with a mix of t-shirts and dark, slim-fit jeans and a black pair of Chuck Taylors to bring his trappings to heel. If you dropped a few bucks at the right store it was easy to look at least decent. You needed a clue, but it didn't require a fashion degree from FIT to dress like you had a purpose. This nugget of urbane wisdom had been passed down to Mark by his father at the start of junior high. It seemed like sound advice at the time, so Mark stuck with it.

After approving of his reflection, Mark grabbed his phone from its charging base. He didn't bother to look at the display. Mark knew there were no snaps, streaks or texts that required a response.

Mark took a peek out the window overlooking his back yard. Lester had scurried away, of course, but the weasel's whereabouts had little to do with his observations. Mark broke ground on the construction of a koi pond a few weeks prior and the project was nearly completed. He didn't know if he would buy any fish, but amphibian lodgings had never been the point. It looked nice. Like everything in his room, it served a purpose. In this case it made his yard aesthetically pleasing. Sometimes that was purpose enough.

Mark slid his phone into his back pocket. He had all day to fix his pond. All weekend to make his yard look even nicer than it already did. Mark walked to his bedroom door, grabbed the knob and paused. He wished for a lot of things in that moment, scattered and imperceptible thoughts on how his world should be along with the usual fragmented regrets and worries. Recognizable shame rooted in his stomach. Most of all he wished that his dad was around. That would seem to fix everything. Maybe then he wouldn't hate his mother with all the love he had given his dead father.

Chapter 4
It

It started as soon as Mark stepped out of his bedroom. It being just that, it, a thing. It had no form, no identity, and no readily discernible characteristics. Some would call it stuff. Others named it junk or garbage. Many referred to it as crap. Those in the know labeled it a sickness. Mark simply called it, it. And it lived everywhere. Stacked right outside of his door, there it was. Look east down the hallway and a trail of it, on both sides of the corridor, piled to the ceiling, led to an inaccessible bedroom filled with it. Any dresser, bed or nightstand that had previously shaped and given purpose to his dad's former bedroom long ago ceased to be anything but shelf space for it. Then the stuff on top of the shelf space became shelf space for more of it. Each new shelf neatly stacked on top of itself, until it reached the ceiling in every direction.

Mark was proud of his shelving ability. At first it lay scattershot throughout the room. Messy piles of it taking up valuable space for more of it by not being squared away. Now there existed a method to it all, like a warehouse or shipping container. The trick entailed saving the package that it came in. If the packaging arrived both square and sized to fit what it contained, he scrapped the shipping box. Mark was skilled at corralling cardboard. He could break down and tie up ten boxes of varying size in half as many minutes. A few of the oversized boxes were saved and left open in the nearest functioning part of the house so that Mark could add to those boxes any new item that materialized without a properly sized and squared home. That was the key, Mark knew: right angles to maximize storage and prevent messy pockets of air from occupying its space.

To the west of Mark's room a pig trail led to a once-grand staircase. Preceding this staircase there remained one accessible room, Mark's bathroom. This bathroom, like Mark's bedroom, remained both empty and immaculate. Not a single stray hair in the drain nor a crooked bristle on any brush. The room bred neither soap scum nor moldy grout. Mark's bathroom contained the bare necessities: sterilized tile, polished porcelain, a pristinely white shower curtain and a newly purchased royal blue bathmat.

It never made its way into Mark's space. He had that much control. It was strong, ferocious, inexorable, seemingly ubiquitous, but not infinite. It had its limitations. It could be viewed, coveted, carted, purchased, packaged, shipped and delivered.

But after that it was organized by Mark. And Mark would not allow it to beat him.

Chapter 5
It

Mark passed it in the stairwell, on each step, on his way downstairs for breakfast. Mark made sure to look at his feet when he navigated the treads. This was in part to ensure that he didn't trip on any of the boxes. But its main function was to avoid an elevated view of the landscape he was forced to wade through just to get something to eat. It was painful to take in all at once.

The entire first floor was little more than homage, a grand and exalted altar, to the patron saint of hoarding. It was everywhere.

It had buried the living room, and the dining room crawled with it. It jammed the playroom and stuffed the closets. It was crammed in the guest room and packed into the pantry. It had engulfed the den and enveloped the laundry room. Praise be to Sanford, the sacrifice was nearly completed.

It made its way into the garage but it hadn't filled that space yet. Mark had a long-standing dream of owning a vintage cherry-red Iroc Z, circa 1990. He would refer to her as his Ironic Iroc, and she had to be parked indoors. Last spring he realized that it would never let him. If he had sooner discovered his system of right angles, air pockets and packaging, maybe then he could have utilized the basement properly. But no, that was the first place he started hiding it. Before he understood its endless want and need Mark had haphazardly tossed everything he touched down the cellar, as quickly as it arrived, in heaps and piles. The basement reminded Mark of the garbage dumps he used to pass by as a kid when he and his parents would drive upstate to visit his cousin. Mark could only pray that it didn't smell as badly.

There were only two clear pathways Mark could take from the landing at the bottom of the basement steps: One led to the breaker box, and the second led to the furnace. Mark researched and studied everything he needed to know about repairing each of them. Mark could replace any size breaker and he could charge three hundred dollars an hour to work on any Rheem modulating furnace. No one would be invited into the house to service either of these fixtures. Mark would let it all burn before he allowed that to happen.

The kitchen was okay. It was at least functional. Mark wouldn't be hosting any dinner parties, but he kept the stove, sink and a few cabinets clear. The fridge remained accessible and Mark maintained a tablet-sized space at the kitchen table where he kept his placemat. Mark preferred to eat in his room, but every so often he dined on spaghetti or some other messy meal and he refused to stain his carpet. The rest of the kitchen was filled with it.

It was not worth mentioning what it was. If it shipped in a stackable, sized-to-fit box, it stayed in that box, never to see the light of day. If it arrived in over-sized or irregular packaging, Mark found a new box that could accommodate it.

In the beginning many of the boxes and bags read Home Goods or Marshalls. That's when she still went out, when she still could go out. Now most of the packages were labeled by Amazon or the HSN.

It didn't matter what the boxes contained, Mark never cared to look. That wasn't true. He cared in the beginning. Then he grew angry. What upset him most was opening boxes filled with organizers: desk organizers, drawer organizers, closet organizers, cabinet organizers, pantry organizers. It was absurd. By virtue of entering Mark's near formless and positively functionless home, any item in a box immediately lost its pre-specified utility and therefore held no value. In turn, for Mark to categorize or classify the contents of any package would be an exercise in futility. Sisyphus would be proud.

Mark stuffed his head in the fridge. It contained, to the horror of Mark's GI tract, exclusively microwaveable, ready-to-eat meals. Mark knew most of what he ate was unhealthy but he had never been taught how to cook. He hoped to learn someday soon, when he was both less occupied and had a clear kitchen space to experiment in. For now he ate his processed food stuff and balanced it out by snacking on fruits and vegetables between meals.

Mark was poised to grab the clotted remains of last night's mac-and-cheese when his ears began to bleed.

"Mark? Mark? Sweetie, are you downstairs?"

And there it was.

Chapter 6
Miles in Nothing Determinate

"Fuck!"

Mark rolled his eyes and huffed audibly. This reaction was instinctual. Habitual. Every word out of her fat mouth pierced his eardrums. Every needy imposition uttered, and all her utterances were impositions, filled his mouth with bile.

"Whaaat? I'm eating breakfast."

"I need you real quick."

Mark shut the refrigerator door, his appetite gone. Instead, he grabbed a granola bar from the cabinet and jammed it by the phone in his pocket.

Mark sighed before he turned past the fridge and took his first step down the long dark hallway that led to her room. It used to be long, anyway. It used to end in a den that was furnished with a glorious home theater and stocked with hours of effortless relaxation. Mark's PS4 was still buried somewhere back there, ceasing to be anything more useful than a wedge among many.

The den was both ordered and filled to capacity. Mark already had his system in place by the time it made its way out of his father's bedroom. This former entertainment hub was stacked with floor-to-ceiling boxes that spilled out into the hallway past the downstairs bathroom. The door to this bathroom remained opened but the space no longer served a purpose other than storage, so Mark had cut the water to it last spring.

God, what would he do if a pipe burst in the basement? What could he do? Plumbing was a useful skill. Mark had considered buying a few yards of Pex just last week; maybe a pipe cutter and some adapters. Lord knew he couldn't sweat a pipe anywhere near the basement. Fire, solder and heaps of unconsumed consumables were best kept separate.

Directly outside of the bathroom, bordering the entrance to his mother's room, lay dozens of bolts of fabric. Mark didn't have a box for these. They stacked well enough right on top of each other with their inner cardboard tubes facing the kitchen, miles of neatly stacked fabric in varying colors and patterns. Each bolt was both useless and maddening. Mark prayed there would be no more fabric deliveries. His mom had been off that kick for a few months. A fabric kick? What does one do with fabric anyway? Doesn't anything that needs fabric come with its own fabric, prefabricated?

Mark made a quick left at the foot of the last purposeless bolt into the short corridor connecting to his mother's room. It was unfinished, a roughed-out passageway leading to both nothing and everything. At the end of the corridor hung a room divider, a row of dangling, plastic slats that parted upon entry. It was like the partition used in the freezer section of a supermarket. Mark had installed it himself after his mom insisted that her bedroom door remain open at all times.

It was a compromise. The reason behind the brokered deal was apparent the instant Mark split the curtain. The horrific smell that issued from her room offended more than Mark's olfactory senses. He was compelled to change his clothes and rinse with mouthwash after any prolonged session at her bedside. He could feel the beast take hold of him, corrupting everything exposed.

Mark took pride in his inability to get used to the stench. It became a cognizant effort on his part to avoid adaptation. He refused to let any of his senses be co-opted by it. Mark preferred his arms to tingle as their fine blond hairs stood on edge with every moment spent in her presence. Mark was sure this hypertension, the added stress of being in a response state of perpetual flight, shaved years off his life. But it was a small price to pay for his dignity at large.

Mark took one last gasp of air from the better side of the partition. He stepped into her room ready for battle, with his head held high and his chest filled with a deep pocket of breathable atmosphere. The contest was simple: How long could Mark remain in his mother's presence before he deflated completely?

Chapter 7
Fatty McWorthless

Mark loathed entering his mother's room. It ranked as the epicenter of it. Both the walls and the ceiling, like the connected corridor, remained unfinished.

Mark's dad had built this room explicitly for Mark before the accident. After framing out and roofing the extension, he had hung the sheetrock, but he'd died before he had a chance to spackle. So the room lay in a vulgar state of exposed joints and uncased outlets.

Had Mark's father finished the room, he would have set Mark up with a high-end entertainment center including an enormous television for his video games. Mark was supposed to move all his belongings downstairs and away from his parents so he could spend his teen years in relative privacy. As an added benefit, the TV in the den would have been freed from Marks endless stream of vlogs and videos allowing Mark's father to watch reruns of Seinfeld in peace.

Mark's swinging, pre-man cave, like the rest of his house, belied its intended purpose. Now it stood as nothing more than a cage holding a 395-pound woman who, in lieu of showering, bathed in piles of her own garbage.

Mark's mother's room differed from the rest of Mark's home. Mark could not direct its flow. His mother demanded that some boxes come her way as soon as they arrived. She had to see their contents, touch them, breathe them in and finally set them on one of her shelves.

She'd actually installed the shelving herself, canted, on raw drywall. To Mark, this act was egregious. It crossed an indelible line etched between coherence and insanity. No matter the amount of crap nor the severity of the sickness that coalesced to form one's reality, one could never hang pictures, install shelving, or furnish in any other way unfinished dry wall. Mark was certain, barring a divine error of omission, that this law had been scribed into the Holy Writ.

The cherry on top of her decorating transgression was that now those same shelves held no shape. Their topsides were fluid and free-formed in a precarious, jagged vein of tchotchke. It was sin on top of sin. Mark wondered if those two negatives made a positive. If somehow the shit on the shelf gave the shit shelf validity? Regardless, the interior design was the least of the problems in Mark's old new room.

Mark's mother never changed her bedding and kept her food wrappers in sorted piles scattered about the floor. On the rare occasion when she rolled herself into the shower in what was supposed to be Mark's personal toiletry space, Mark would sneak into her pen and throw out some of the trash. He would grab the wrappers smeared with globs of mayo first. Mark's mom loved mayonnaise. Its putrefaction supplied much of the odor. It was a limited solution inside of a dysfunctional system. Mark, In short time, learned how to be careful with what he considered disposable.

A nefarious deal had been struck. A year or so back, when the scope of Mark's Mom's disease became apparent, Mark had the inspired idea that he could simply throw out the boxes as they arrived. From doorstop to trash can. Mark's mother unearthed his betrayal early on when she made one of her semi-annual trips to the back yard for sun and fresh air. When Mrs. Brunson beheld her precious things in the garbage, she went berserk. Between her dread and grief she nearly hit Mark in a frenzy of sweat, rolling flab and expletives. Mark's mother swore she would check the trash every day. If she found any more of her cherished creatures in the garbage, she promised to order two of everything in staggered intervals.

Mark quickly relented. Not because he was concerned about her doubling the order, what did that matter at this point? He worried that she would be outside every day in the sunlight, where she could be observed and then promptly and righteously mocked. Imagine the daily spectacle of a big pasty blob, half clothed with shit-stained underwear, rummaging through her own filth. This singular, inescapable thought had left Mark paralyzed with inaction.

Now, standing before his mother, straining not to inhale (as the exposed screw heads, level and perfectly spaced every sixteen inches, watched him like an alien network designed to study humanity at its worst) Mark brimmed with a static disgust.

His mother was the worst. Mark couldn't stand what she had become. Fatty McWorthless - a wad of imposition and gluttony. What truly annoyed Mark was the metamorphosis that had taken place within the cocoon of the previous two years. Mrs. Brunson had been gorgeous. Mark's dad, when he lived, would tell one story over and over about how on their first date he witnessed her cause two accidents in a ten-minute span as city drivers craned their necks to get a better view of her backside. He called her "rubberneck" for years after that.

"I need you to fix my remote. It's only... It's not changing the channels when I press."

Mark took a step forward and over a pile of hamburger wrappers. He'd soon have to implement another clandestine garbage grab. Maybe, Mark thought, he could convince the delivery men to double pack each burger, two patties per wrapper.

It would be of trivial effect, but at this point Mark would take what he could get.

Mark and his mother had a deal set up all over town at her favorite shit shops: The Fish Store, Satellite Pizza and How May Kitchen, to mention a few. Mark's mom ordered over the phone, and they charged her credit card and added a delivery fee plus a hardy tip for themselves. The delivery person dropped the food off at the back door, no questions asked. It was an expensive arrangement, but it beat Mark having to cook for his inert mother five times a day.

Besides, money was not an issue. Mark's dad co-owned a lucrative commercial contracting business with Ashley's father. They had made a lot of money together, still did. Ashley's dad received the lion's share now, but he signed a hefty check to Mrs. Brunson twelve times a year.

Plus, Mark's father had a premium insurance policy in place in case what happened did happen. Mark and his mom hadn't touched it. They didn't need to. With what they received from Ashley's father each month they had yet to tap into Mark's father's savings, nor had they cashed out any part of his extensive and diversified investment portfolio. Mark calculated that his mother could continue spending for the next twenty years at her present rate. The house was paid off. They both had fantastic health insurance and a company car.

Anyway, Mark figured his mother had fewer wags left in her tail than the average neighborhood

Retriever. This morbid conviction allowed Mark to be an active participant in all of his mom's insanity. Between the horrific foods she inhaled and the burgeoning bed sores, Mark assumed her cantaloupe-sized heart would detach from its vine before he graduated. Mark would soldier along and allow inevitability to run its course.

"Mom, change the batteries your fat self."

"Mark Brunson!"

"What? Don't call me in here for stupid shit like this."

"Watch your mouth, sweetie. I just like seeing you."

"Well, I don't like seeing this. If you want my help, stop eating and clean yourself up."

"Don't be mean, Mark. I'm in mourning."

"Mom…"

Mark stopped himself. He had told her on multiple occasions how he felt about her issues. With tears in his eyes he had begged her to get help. She would listen to his pleas stoically before completely ignoring all of his sentiments and changing the subject entirely. Mark didn't try to reason with her anymore. He made snide comments and called her a fat slob or just ignored her altogether. It depended on his mood. But he did not engage. Not like he used to.

And for her part, Mark's mother accepted the insults with a smile and a dismissive nod. Boys will be boys, after all. And Mark was all she had left. Besides, she understood his frustrations. She at times was equally as frustrated. But he did not understand her. What she needed. What she had. When he finally recognized the significance, the axial nature in each of her actions, then he would back off. Things would get better. But now, right now, she needed her things and she needed Mark. Without either she would not be alive. So she put up with his belittling remarks, brushed them aside and enjoyed what she had to enjoy.

Mark, without comment, left the room. He hadn't the breath to expel his trademark sigh.

"Mark? The batteries! Mark!"

Mrs. Brunson was left sinking into her distressed mattress. She didn't have to use the bathroom and did not like to get up unless she did. She took care of all her little chores at once. Economy of motion was one of her strengths, and she took pride in it. Mark's mom looked over and through the piles that were consuming both the floor and shelf space in her room. Though to her they weren't piles, they were what was needed to function. She didn't see anything, actually. To Mark's mother the things around her were as air around a child, a core constituent of life, necessary and inescapable.

Before she got up to scavenge through her collection for some batteries, she thought of calling out to Mark one more time. An instant before saying his name, Mrs. Brunson pursed her lips together.

"I shouldn't burden him so much," she thought aloud.

As Mark's mom summoned the strength to shift her left leg toward one of the piles, Mark stomped back into her cage with four batteries in hand. He snatched the remote from the bed. Mrs. Brunson smiled. After replacing the batteries, he opened the drawer to her nightstand. Although he attempted to be gentle, a mountain of it slid off the top of her bedside stand, raining down like water from a pedestal fountain. Mark closed his eyes and took a deep breath before looking in the drawer. It was full of it, mostly food wrappers, but it none-the-less.

"Here, Mom."

He showed her the two extra batteries he held in his palm.

"I'm keeping these right…"

Mark slid a pile of it from one edge of the drawer as more of it spilled over the sides. It was almost liquid in its capacity to fill a space. Mark let out another sigh. Three double 'A' batteries rolled around in the corner of the drawer.

It all came back to him, his same fat mom asking for the same batteries just two months prior. The same trip to his room, through the same pig trails of it stacked to the ceiling, to grab his extra double A's neatly positioned in their proper station. It happened. Mark's mind was overwhelmed. All his efforts to keep a semblance of order in his life had failed. There was no system for it. His current actions were merely a facade, a fiction. The monster was too great. What would he do when the garage filled? It was only a matter of time. A flash of fire flitted through his mind. Just as quickly as it had flared, it extinguished. Anger flooded the space.

"You know what?"

Mark ripped the drawer out of its track. Any of it that lacked a secure footing atop the nightstand dropped to the plywood floor, followed by the loosed contents of the drawer. Mark watched crookedly as it spiraled down, a second fell wave of fluttering filth. It didn't matter; the floor looked exactly the same as it had before the crap from the nightstand found its way down. Like a drop of water added to a full bathtub, the former night stand pile became indistinguishable from the appointed floor pile.

"Here!"

When Mark shook out the last of it from the bottom of the drawer his mother's face, previously cinched in knots, began to relax. She did not appear angry or upset. Instead she observed Mark without emotion, like the partially subducted screw heads on the walls surrounding her, monitoring the action but not judging. Mark slipped the drawer back in its tracks.

"This is now your battery drawer. It's designated."

He placed the two double-A batteries in the center of the drawer and slammed it shut. The lamp and the remaining wrappers on top of the stand fell to the ground. The bulb popped. In that instant, Mark hoped for fire; his eyes widened and the corners of his lips curled up before he regained control.

Mark observed the top side of the naked night stand before him. It was beautiful. He turned to his fat mother. Her countenance was as bare as the stand. It was disgusting.

"See how easy that is, Mom?"

Mark turned his back and left the room. His mother, with a straight lipped and cheeky smile, looked at the newer mess on the side of her bed before changing the channel.

Chapter 8
The Pit

Mark left his mother's room in a fluster, violently swiping aside the plastic supermarket divider. The pit was there. The stem of anxiety that ran from his stomach to his heart, or maybe it was from his heart to his stomach. He could never tell. Mark felt his skin chaffing on his bones. He needed room, space, open air. Mark made a beeline for the front door. After stumbling over a box containing fifty sets of reindeer salt and pepper shakers, he grabbed the doorknob in a rage. As he yanked open the oak French doors, Fred – UPS Fred – stood at Mark's doorstep, deftly steering, with one hand, four cumbersome boxes on a dolly. His extended finger was poised, threatening, to ring the doorbell.

"Mark, my man, what's the word?"

Mark kicked the bottom of the stacked boxes as he shoved his way past Fred. Then he circled back and shouldered the top two boxes off the dolly. It annoyed him how much resistance he met. The boxes were bulky, weighty and full of it. They landed, one after the other, on the spacious slate walkway with a thud.

Fred was stunned. He saw Mark most every day, usually twice, since he had picked up this prime residential route nine months ago. Mark was nothing but a gentleman each time. He was consistently pleasant, jocular and kind. Fred used to kid with Mark about where he was putting all the stuff, but he quickly learned it was a sore point. He realized Mark was dealing with a disease and he let it be.

Mark's house wasn't Fred's only regular stop. There were three separate crazy cat lady stops on his route. But it had taken him a few trips to realize what was going on at the Brunson residence. The other stops were different from Mark's. You could see, smell, taste and feel the sickness at the other houses before stepping out of the truck. There were always telltale signs.

At one of the homes there was a car parked in the driveway that was loaded with shit from floor to ceiling, random useless shit. Nameless shit. Shit by association. Only the driver's seat was accessible. Fred assumed there weren't many acquaintances for the owner of the car to Uber around town.

There was an unkempt look to a hoarder's house. The sickness was too great, the rot was too deep. Not at Mark's house. Mark's home was not only nice for a hoarder's, it was nice for the expensive neighborhood it was located in. When Fred realized what was happening, he felt for Mark.

On the rare occasion, if there was only one package, he would send it back designated as undeliverable just to give Mark a moment of rest. Mark was always outside: edging, planting, trimming, fertilizing, mowing, painting or building. Fred figured it all out, put it all together, once he learned of Mark's father.

Part of Fred had been expecting this kind of blowout each time he rang the bell. He realized that although he was just the UPS driver, to Mark he was also the bringer of death. Unsure of how to respond, Fred decided to fiddle with the overturned boxes.

"Mark, it's cool, you don't need to sign."

Mark made it halfway across his perfectly manicured lawn when he came to an abrupt stop. He wouldn't turn around. He was crying, Fred noticed.

"I'll see you tomor-"

Fred stopped himself. Mark did not need to be reminded of tomorrow's delivery. The discomfort lasted for a heavy minute, Fred not knowing what to say, Mark not knowing what to do. Fred fought the urge to offer Mark a hug.

Fred finished stacking the boxes. He did not know whether to take them back to his truck or to leave them at their destination. He did know that either outcome was wholly inconsequential.

Mark stood silent, unmoving and indecipherable. Mark was torn. He knew Fred was just doing his job and that he helped to keep Mark's secret. Mark had a rapport with Fred, unlike the FedEx carrier or mailman, who both came with oversized boxes as often as Fred did. It wasn't Fred's fault that Mark's mother held no human value. Mark was ashamed of how he reacted. He was ashamed of how he treated his mother. He was ashamed of his mother.

As it turned out, Mark didn't need to make things right. His nose tackle corrected everything for him.

"Hey, Fag-a-tron, what's the problem? Your shipment of dildos came in the wrong color?"

Chapter 9
Dereliction

Fred tightened his grip on the dolly before snapping his neck to discover the source of the depravity. Fred was certain its origins resided in man. Study, at random, a sampling of one of its representatives and you were guaranteed to find corruption on a fundamental level. Fred wondered if humanity was a dereliction of its own anthropic principles.

He had seen a lot of people in his travels and a lot of horrible things: abuse, assault, abandonment, neglect, ignorance, gluttony, entitlement and litter. Fred hated litter.

Recently, while on his route, he witnessed some jerk-off driving in front of him throw a coffee cup out his window. A Styrofoam coffee cup. The rage he had felt. Not that Fred would ever ram a fellow human off the road with his big brown truck of death, but damn! If his brakes had happened to fail in that instant, he certainly would have worn a satisfied grin the moment of impact.

There were five of them standing in Ashley's driveway: Ashley, her boyfriend Todd, and three of his buddies. They boys were all laughing. Ashley was too, but her laughter was more constrained. She did not appreciate Mark's humiliation on the same level as her male counterparts. The contortions of anger behind her smile made it difficult to tell whether she enjoyed it either less or more.

Fred's initial reaction, his gut desire, was to walk over to them with his dolly in tow and politely, with neither warning nor hesitation, knock the biggest one's teeth out.

Fred could fight, but there was no misapprehension, he could not win this one. In his heyday, a rather formidable one before he discovered the library, he might have had a chance against two of these kids, maybe three. But that heyday had peaked around the same time as hardcover book sales.

There was a good chance they would all sprint from the bloody scene that unfolded before them. Most kids, even the bullies, did not have an answer to the violence contained in their threats. But every now and then their flight response lost out to the visceral thrill of fracturing another's jaw and the cathartic elation of spreading one's pain to the unacknowledged.

Fred had no way of knowing which one of these boys had already made his bones, but that was not the reason he ignored his gut. Sometimes he actually missed the sting of an unexpected left cross. Fred knew he would lose his job or go to jail if he assaulted anyone while on the clock. And with three kids of his own, three kids he was attempting to raise to be better than himself, an impromptu brawl was a luxury he could no longer afford.

Personal growth aside, Fred would be all smiles and cheers if Mark were to snatch the hand truck from him and smack the largest kid in the mouth with it.

Chapter 10
Leering

Seconds after the attempted emasculation, Mark was fully composed. He had managed to cram his frustration and shame into an unburdened crevice somewhere inside his ductile teenage frame.

Todd wasted little time doubling down on the initial insult.

"Mark, you coming to practice or is the locker room just too much for you? All that dick in your face."

Todd's boys, impressed as always with his humor, exploded with embellished laughter. Ashley wore a satisfied smile as she put an arm around Todd's waist. Mark ignored the dig and instead gave his attention to Fred.

"I'm sorry, Fred. Let me sign for these."

"Mark, if you want, I'll back you up. Fuck those guys."

Fred said what he had to say. If Mark hoofed it across the lawn hell bent on a rumble, Fred would be one step behind him. If he had to go to jail today, he would. That was Fred. Still, Fred was praying that Mark was bigger than his own sense of masculine obligation.

"Thanks, Fred. It's fine. As fun as it would be, I'm not sure it would do any good."

Fred was relieved. He only knew Mark a short while comprised of conversation snippets, electronic signatures and too many boxes. Nevertheless, he noticed something behind Mark's eyes. He feared that if Mark did think a difference could be made, Mark would have charged over to his neighbor's yard to take on four football players towing only a washed-up package mule as back up. Let the chips fall where they may.

Fred said goodbye to Mark, then ambled back to his truck. The entire time he stared down the boys. Todd's three teammates averted his gaze. Both Fred's glare and his forearms were intimidating to even the surest of men.

Todd never broke eye contact with Fred. He didn't blink. Todd had no fear of the forty-something box jockey and his Pullman Brown fitted shorts. He even had something to say.

"What?"

It was silent, but Todd was deliberate with his lips when he mouthed this taunt.

Without replying, Fred climbed into his vehicle and turned the key. Todd's eyes fixed on Fred until the brown and blue-collard truck rode out of view.

Fred snickered as he drove away, remembering a time when he would have wrecked Todd up and down the block and wouldn't have stopped until a frantic bystander called the cops. Or was he remembering a time when he was interchangeable with Todd? Either way, Fred missed part of his old life. Somehow hauling packages and being a father wasn't the end-all of fulfillment. There were still some stones that needed to be overturned. As Fred neared the freeway on-ramp, he realized that he was slightly disappointed at his inability to dig up those worms.

By the time both Todd and his teammates returned their attention to Mark, he was gone. He had walked around the back of his house to an unfinished koi pond. Only Ashley saw him leave. In fact, throughout the entire exchange, she never took her eyes off him.

Chapter 11
Undertakings

Mark didn't mind playing the martyr. He knew it was all bullshit. He knew his worth. Of course he harbored self-doubt, everyone did, but at worst Mark understood that although he might not be better than Todd, Todd certainly was not better than him. Not at football and not at life.

Mark wasn't gay. Ashley had sprinkled that rumor around Lake Side's campus last year. It had taken root and grown into a graspable branch for those who needed to support themselves with a low-lying limb. Mark didn't care for the most part. He didn't want to be gay, but he saw no problem with homosexuality in theory. Besides, being considered a fag by Todd and his friends was not the monolithic cock-block in Mark's life. Ashley had laid the sole claim to that obelisk.

Ashley vomited up scandalous stories about Mark on a weekly basis. She needed Mark to feel pain. Many of Ashley's extracurricular activities were in some way related to Mark's suffering. Since being gay didn't bother him, Mark never quelled the rumor. He couldn't have done much about it even if he wanted to.

Ashley had Lake Side High School under her thumb. She was entering tenth grade and dating a senior, the senior. She was by far the most attractive girl in the school, and it was not because Lake Side was light on pretty girls. Ashley blazed celestial in her radiance. She was both confident and easygoing. Ashley was nice to everyone, when she wanted to be, and everyone wanted to be nice to her. Even the senior girls, the popular ones who should have been dating Todd and reminding Ashley of her sophomore status, were enamored with both her beauty and presence. Ashley's wit sliced razor sharp, and she didn't suffer anyone's shit. These last two attributes she had inherited directly from her mother.

Before Ashley's mom had died she was an accomplished small-screen actor. She was beautiful but that wasn't the reason she'd found success on television. Ashley's mother cut her comedy teeth alongside her actual teeth. Growing up, her friends were forced to pack a second pair of underwear to serve as "tinkle insurance" during any overnight excursion. She graduated Harvard with honors as a comedy writer and excelled at her ordained profession. Before her death she had inked a deal with NBC to star in a sitcom she had created.

Ashley had signed on to play the role of her teenage daughter. The pilot was scheduled to air four months after the accident. Ashley missed her mom.

Any Lakeside resident who failed to succumb to either Ashley's looks or charm surrendered to the pity. Her mother had been the local celebrity, the center of the town's social structure, and she was gone. Everyone missed her. This left Ashley as the lone arbiter of trend and style in Lake Side. What was hot, according to Ashley, was making Mark miserable.

Keeping Mark down had not been easy. It was no geographical fluke that he and Ashley were a thing in middle school. He was the quarterback of the junior high football team, a skill he glommed from his dad, and an all-around stud. He had blond hair, brown eyes, olive skin and a perfect nose. For Mark the dating pool was an estuary. If Mark joined the football team, Todd sure as hell would no longer be the starting quarterback. Even as a tenth grader Mark would have beaten him out for the spot. Todd had an inch on him and maybe a dozen pounds, but Mark was ten-times the athlete.

Of course, hypothetical stock paid only hypothetical dividends. As Mark heard what should have been his teammates drive away in Todd's silver Jetta, he carefully placed one of the last chips of slate around his pond. Mark could have finished the job a week ago if he hadn't been so particular about each rock's placement.

Mark wasn't taking his time solely for the sake of aesthetic. He dragged out the pond's construction to avoid starting his next project. Mark may have enjoyed the swagger that came with managing the nicest yard in the neighborhood, but everything else concerning his landscape architecture had soured. Damn if he didn't want to go to football practice. Sure, he could start on the fire pit next week, but it all seemed so daunting; another time-consuming undertaking with which to waste away his weekend. A new construct to enhance the outside so no one could ever imagine what was happening inside.

"Fuck those guys!"

Mark turned toward the back corner of his yard. He had heard the words but he couldn't locate the lips that uttered them.

"I guarantee at least two of them smoke the pole."

Lester had climbed a tree in Umed's backyard. It was a large oak in the corner by the dual-gate connecting the three properties. Mark had climbed it often with his former best friend. Mark dropped the slate chip he was holding.

"I bet you'd know. Stop being all weaselly, Lester."

Mark, naked and unfinished, scuttled to his room. He left the weasel in his tree. He felt badly about what he'd just said to him. Lester took a lot of weasel shots at school. God-damn-it if he didn't look like one. Lester didn't need it from Mark, too. But there was no way, not any way, Lester and Mark could be friends. Lester was pure trash, inside and out. He lived too close to Mark. Everything about Lester was too close to Mark.

Chapter 12
The Weasel

Gliding from one branch to the next like a squirrel, the Weasel descended from his oak. It was effortless for Lester. Nothing seemed to faze him. Everyone in school ignored him, and those who did engage did so only to take their jabs. He let it all go.

Lester had moved into Umed's house last March. His uncle had died a wealthy man. A small portion of his portfolio resided in single-family rental units located in upscale neighborhoods. He had left the property behind Mark's house to both Lester and Lester's father. That was all that he left them, irrespective of the fact that Lester and his father were his only living relatives.

Of course they moved into the sprawling ranch the instant they were able to force the "Punjabis" out. God forbid they collected the rent money as Lester had suggested. Lester's father had been someone else's tenant for his entire life and he was tired of it, offended by it, and that was all that mattered. A quick fix to spite the solution. Umed's parents constantly spoke of returning to India with their medical degrees. A stubborn case of myopia forced them to do the right thing.

Lester was back on flat ground only an instant slower than what gravity could have accomplished with a free fall. He was back in his own disgusting yard. Lester liked how Mark's property looked, but he wasn't about to put in the time and effort needed to recreate the fantasy. His dad lacked the fortitude needed to keep himself from pissing all over it. Frankly, Lester lacked the grit required to get it done. All of Lester's resolve was already in hock.

Lester's life was one of survival. He'd been forced to steal from his dad to keep himself clothed. Considering his father could hardly afford to dress himself, this was no small task. And it resulted in a drubbing when Lester's dad was sober enough to account for his cash.

The beatings didn't bother Lester anymore. The math of it was simple: You can't hit what you can't catch. When Lester did fall asleep outside of his locked bedroom room, a rarity now-a-days, he strangely enjoyed the white shock of light that woke him up. It was only one shot, usually to the side of the head, and Lester was up and at 'em before his lowlife father could cock his arm a second time. Their relationship was a fun little game of "tag the abuser" which invariably ended in a volley of verbal f-bombs.

In the six months he lived in Umed's house Lester never once considered mowing his lawn. His only neighbor was Mark in the back. Lester lived on the dead end of a single road that crossed off Mark's road and looped around in front of his house. Encircling the court was nothing but unblemished forest. Lester supposed the rest of the road was scheduled to be developed at some point in the future. It depended on to whom Lester's uncle willed the land. Either way, a fancy yard didn't matter to Lester. There was no one around for him to impress.

What mattered was that Lester had his own woods to explore, a forest that began at his doorstep and ended in the mountains beyond. Lester loved every single branch and leaf that defined his personal Sylvania. The forest was where he was headed now, after Mark had called him a fag and a weasel.

It didn't bother him. Not from Mark. He could tell Mark didn't mean it. He wasn't prescient or amazingly self-aware. It was just that after years of being picked on, Lester could easily distinguish between those who truly reveled in making others feel pain and those who were just glad that it wasn't them taking the hit.

Eleven months ago, that minor distinction would not have made a difference to Lester. In the past he would have utterly destroyed anyone who messed with him regardless of intent. What Lester's new classmates at Lake Side didn't know, what they couldn't know, was that this Weasel had sharp teeth.

Lester's abilities stretched far beyond climbing trees and making a fool of his father. He had learned to take a punch before his sixth birthday. By nine he learned how to give one. It was sharp, quick and with a repetitive fury that few of his peers could withstand. Lester learned young that you either fight or you die, and he wasn't about to die. Not before his worthless father.

Lester studied hard and did his homework. His true passion was watching MMA fights on his phone. He had read dozens of books on self defense and digested whatever he could for free online. Between the moments in which Lester was struggling to survive, he worked over a torn-up heavy bag that his father had helped him hang in his basement. For a fifteen-year-old who weighed less than a fresh pile of steaming shit from the asshole of a Great Dane, Lester was lethal to anyone else his age.

Lester had not been in a single fight last semester. He'd been enrolled at Lake Side for only a few months, but he had ample opportunity to throw down. Lester encountered dozens of kids who enjoyed turning the knife; dick bags that thrived on human torment. But he couldn't afford to be expelled. He recognized the significance of where he lived and the opportunity that Lake Side afforded him. Plus, Lester didn't need to fight anymore. He had nothing left to prove. Besides, no matter whom he fought and for whatever reason he was made to fight, it would always be his fault. The destitute rodent with a foul mouth and a community-blight of a father consistently took the rap.

Lester had never once in his life willingly started a fight, yet he took a disproportionate share of the blame for every altercation. Many times his antagonist would avoid punishment altogether. This included not only the fights he was goaded into starting but any fight in which he strictly defended himself.

There was one instance, in his former school, when he didn't say a word and didn't throw a punch, yet he was suspended. That was the fight he learned from; the fight in which Mr. May got himself involved.

Mr. May had witnessed the one-sided affair and broken it up before it had a chance to escalate. Lester had been tying his shoelace in the hall when another boy, without provocation, kicked him in the face. By the time Lester got to his feet Mr. May had already pinned the instigator down. He reported the fight exactly as it occurred. The principal suspended Lester and gave the provocateur an extended detention, which he skipped without consequence.

The next week when Lester returned to school Mr. May pulled him aside the moment he stepped through the lobby doors. He explained to Lester what was going on and why it was happening to him. He spoke of economic inequality and profiling. He told Lester what his dad represented to the community and how Lester would never receive justice. He taught him how to behave and how to work the system to his advantage. Mr. May told him how and, more importantly, why to study. Lester learned that his raw test scores were among the highest in the school and that he had the ability to outperform everyone enrolled. Mr. May's words were revelatory, and Lester enthusiastically absorbed every lesson.

This was the first time in Lester's adolescent life that he was afforded an opportunity and that someone had believed in him. He was compelled to seize the moment and to never let his benefactor down. Mr. May offered Lester his phone number and told him to call with any questions or concerns. Lester was insatiable. He called nearly every day for the entire school year. When he told Mr. May that he was moving to an upscale neighborhood in a different state, Mr. May was ecstatic. It was a clean slate and a chance to get into college, for free.

Mr. May, a pragmatist, also informed Lester that both his white trash dad and the stigma of poverty would follow him. His new classmates would still treat him horribly. But now he had a chance to let it all go.

"Fuck them! Fuck your dad! Don't do what they expect you to do. Fuck 'em all!"

Lester entered the woods across the street from his driveway. He took two steps in before he turned to give the middle finger to his dad's house. He held his hand high and kept it there. He allowed for the gesture to bleed through his ramshackle home and past his garbage pit of a yard and he gave some of it, just a little bit, to Mark's house.

As Lester let his arm sink back to his side, a doe scampered off, only a chip shot away from where he stood. The deer was afraid of the Weasel. Lester smiled.

Part Two

Chapter 13
Kim

Mark had trouble concentrating. It was Lester. The weasel loitered by his locker, disregarded by anyone who passed. He portrayed a statue undeserving of a plaque. Lester's figure was cast in a white tee, dark blue jeans and a black pair of Chuck Taylors. His hair was slicked back. Roll up a soft-pack of smokes in his sleeve and he could have passed for a 1950's high school weasel. Lester, with a toothy smile and a hopeful spark in his eye, stared at Mark. Mark, in turn, made short and awkward eye contact with Lester before breaking it off with both a wince and a sigh. Mark instead pretended to give his attention to Kim.

Kim kept talking, incessantly, about what she had done over her summer break: one random non-event after the next. Mark didn't mind that she lived an uneventful life; everything Mark did was the definition of mundane. The issue was that she insisted on telling him all about it. Or maybe the issue was that she was fat.

Kim kept talking and Lester kept initiating eye contact with Mark. This normally wouldn't be a problem. Lester was a weird cat. Mark remembered three occasions last semester when they had made both unnecessary and prolonged eye contact. They were neighbors and neither of them had any friends. It only made sense that they would seek each other out. But there was something queer about this situation that unnerved Mark.

In the middle of one of Kim's fat, pointless anecdotes Mark realized what had been disturbing him. It was the sneakers. Mark always wore Chuck Taylors. They were his thing. Now Lester wore an old, beat-up pair on the first day of school. Mark didn't need that. He didn't need the biggest piece of white trash in the county, one he shared a property line with, developing some sort of man-crush on him. Mark wasn't looking for a protégé.

After a dreadful minute and a half watching Kim's lips flap, Mark took one more peek over her beefy shoulder. Lester had left. Mark was relieved. Maybe he was overthinking things. One, Lester wouldn't be the first kid in school to wear hi-top Converse. And two, Mark stared at Lester nearly as much as Lester stared at him. Maybe Lester was the one who should have been freaked out. Either way, even without a single friend to call his own, Mark would make sure he and Lester remained neighbors and nothing more.

"Mark?"

"Kim? What?

"Was that a question? You're so adorable sometimes."

Kim blushed at her own remark. Not that you could tell. Kim wore a lot of makeup. With his fingernail Mark could carve his name in the foundation she applied to each cheek. Actually, one cheek could spell his name and the other could read: I ♥ Twinkies. Kim's use of cosmetics was strange to Mark, even confounding. If she took the time to gussy up her face, that meant she cared about her looks. If Kim worried at all about appearances, her weight should have been her largest concern.

Mark wondered if he was a fattist. Kim and her carriage annoyed him. Well, Kim annoyed him because she was so obviously trying to get him on the cheap. He had been ostracized. No chick worth a look would dare to take on Ashley. She could make life too miserable for you. In such a small school with the undeniable and absolute patronage Ashley claimed, it wasn't worth it.

Ashley had little trouble seizing the reins at Lakeside High. At times Ashley was genuinely adorable as a person, kind and engaging, with actual empathy. And when she decided to give you her attention it was enchanting. Nothing at all in the world mattered in that moment. The way she made you feel, man or woman, when she chose you, it was a drug. Few were immune to her intoxicants. If Mark was a dick because Ashley said Mark was a dick, then Mark was a dick, period.

None of that mattered to Kim. She was a pretty cool chick in her own right. Not popular cool, but self-actualized cool. She had a core group of friends who kept to themselves and cared for one another. Kim and Ashley were neither friends nor enemies. They simply co-existed.

Even after Kim began scamming on Mark, it never got too real between her and Ashley. Ashley called her a desperate pig. Kim laughed, really laughed, before calling her a dipshit and walking away. Her impromptu performance had impressed everyone who witnessed the event. From then on Ashley left Kim alone to pursue what she felt she deserved.

Mark didn't know if Kim deserved him. On a purely aesthetic level, she was too big for Mark. And she had cankles. Cankles were a deal-breaker. Mark wondered: if Kim lost the twenty-five pounds she needed to lose, would the cankles remain? He imagined that hers might be a pair of those perma-cankles. Just thick bones where most of us have that little knob. But a fattist? Mark knew he didn't hate his mom because she was fat. He hated the fat because it was on his mom.

Kim was recounting one of her three affairs this past summer at her parent's rental in Delong, when the bell rang.

"That sounds great, Kim. I'll see you at lunch."

"Wait, what period do you have?"

"Ahh, sixth."

"Damn, I'm seventh."

"No big deal. I'll catch you in the halls."

Mark abruptly left Kim at his locker and made his way through the crowded corridors toward his homeroom. As he turned the corner he saw Todd talking to Ashley by her locker. His knees buckled. Mark regrouped and scrambled behind the locker bank before either of them noticed.

He doubled back toward the gym, intending to avoid Ashley's domain. He'd likely be late, but it was the first day of school, and no one gave out demerits on the first day.

Kim missed homeroom altogether. After the bell rang, she made a straight-shot to the guidance councilor's office. There was a problem with her schedule that needed immediate attention.

Chapter 14
Everyone Knew

After catching a glimpse of Mark at his locker, Ashley decided she would use the cafeteria entrance to begin her day at Lake Side High. The converging smells of quilted meat and vegetable paste nauseated her, but she refused to walk past Kim being all fat and clingy with Mark each morning. It annoyed Ashley that Kim talked to Mark. It annoyed Ashley that Kim refused to be bothered when she called her a pig. It annoyed Ashley that her mom had died with Mark's father's dick in her mouth.

Everyone knew what happened. The tabloids didn't report the exact details. It was left unspecified why Ashley's mother hadn't fastened her seat belt, but there was enough allusion to what might have been going on, or down, for the residents of Lake Side to fill in the blanks. Ashley heard as much at the grocer's a few weeks after the accident. Two of Ashley's mother's friends were talking casually about the affair in the checkout line. Ashley had heard the entire catty exchange from behind the nearest candy rack. The conversation culminated with her mom's former yoga instructor stating, "That's why I don't give head. I tell my husband all the time how dangerous it is."

Ashley ran. She hadn't yet mastered the art of confrontation. But the experience did ensure that Ashley would always be prepared in the future. Not only would she disallow any one to disparage her mother, she would control all of the dialogue on the matter henceforth. The main thrust of her new and managed talking point: It wasn't the mouth, it was the dick.

Ashley's militant protection of her mother's legacy did not bode well for Mark. She had already pulled away from him emotionally the day she learned of his father's betrayal. It took Ashley only until the funeral to realize that Mark had half of his father's dick down his own pants. It was simple genetics. Twenty-three of Mark's chromosomes were identical to his father's. By the law of averages, fifty percent of Mark's dick was in Ashley's mother's mouth the moment she died. This scientific fact could not be ignored.

Ashley supposed Kim scamming on Mark wasn't the worst thing in the world. It did nothing for his standing. If anything, with her extra weight and the gobs of make-up, Kim hanging on Mark served to sink him lower beneath the muck. Besides, now that she was dating Todd, the school's most popular and persuasive figure other than herself, Mark's fate had been sealed.

Chapter 15
The Other Pit

It appeared to Ashley that, at times, Todd took more of an interest in hating on Mark than she did. What he had planned for the school year seemed more personal and degrading than anything Ashley had considered. He'd opened the semester with a post on Instagram admonishing anyone in school who might take Mark on as a friend. It was a stern warning that lacked a specific consequence, but the underlying implications were real, and Todd could back them up.

Todd had a fight with Cogal last year. It took place at the pit. Cogal was a legit loner and the star of the wrestling team. He was big, six-foot-two, with cubed muscles stacked down his wooden frame, incredibly, like an upside-down pyramid. His face bred fear. His bulging eyes burrowed below a protruding brow topped with a proper Mohawk which he yolked with two eggs daily. Cogal refused to speak with anyone at school. He had no friends; he just went to class and earned his sixty-fives while wearing earbuds throughout each period. Every day after classes, without fail, he would hit the gym and train. Cogal had won the counties his junior year and had come second in the states. No one fucked with him.

Todd didn't care. He had just killed it in his first season as Lakeside's starting quarterback. Cogal was headed for the states again and didn't like all the attention Todd received during what was supposed to be his own championship run. The drama started when Cogal pulled his earbuds during shop class and spewed shit, like an open-aired stoma, towards anyone within earshot.

Word spread quickly, and before lunch Todd found Cogal in the hall by his locker. He told Cogal they should meet at the pit after school.

The pit was no joke. Lord of the Flies type shit. You fight in school and sure, you get suspended, but it was worth it for the security of the situation. Nothing went too far before three nearby teachers did their best to pull the combatants apart. A couple of punches, a few big words, and that was that. But at the pit it was mob rule. The beatings lasted longer, and by no means did they stop after one party hit the ground. It usually took a least three kicks to the face before one of the self-appointed moderators stepped in to end the carnage.

The fact that Todd suggested the pit meant something. The fact that Cogal responded that they should do this, "right here, right now," meant even more. Todd smiled as he walked away. He repeated, "the pit."

The pit was just that, a pit. It was a drainage ditch located a short mile behind an isolated industrial park. The pit adjoined the woods at the far end of the high school soccer field. It measured forty yards around and thirty feet deep, all sand. Atop, surrounding the entire perimeter, was a six-foot chain link fence that had long been rendered impotent by neighborhood kids with lock snips and idle hands. At any point between the fence and the drop there was roughly fifteen feet of graded landing. This shelf provided enough space to comfortably accommodate half the student body of Lake Side High.

This fight carried with it the gravity of a championship bout. It was essentially for the run of the school. There wasn't a student in the junior class who would go at Todd. Same could be said about the senior class and Cogal.

Before Cogal made his entrance the pit had neared capacity. Standing room remained sparse on the landing. As per uncodified protocols, only Todd had been allowed access to the sump's lower sanctum.

When Cogal emerged from the wooded path that connected the school grounds to the drainage ditch, the crowd screamed, riotous in celebration. The audience parted for Cogal as he ducked between a cut-out in the fence and stepped into the arena. When he arrived at the pit's precipice he looked down and saw Todd, shirtless, sitting Indian-style with a blank expression. It freaked him out a bit. Cogal had been in a few fights, and there was nothing more reassuring than a loud mouth puffing his chest in vain, wasting both energy and precious oxygen. Cool, calm, and collected was always more terrifying. Cogal didn't know what to make of Todd. He barely knew Todd existed before he went all cock-of-the-walk at quarterback the previous fall. He wondered why he agreed to fight Todd. Cogal had a rep and that should have been enough.

Cogal also knew better than to let his doubt become a distraction. Walk away from the fight and his aura was gone. He enjoyed both the silence and the personal space his reputation had afforded him. He reveled in the solitary world his headphones helped him to create.

Walking down the sump's shifting slope, watching the crowd cheer him on, or it on, Cogal began to focus. He had been part of this act in the past. He recognized, even embraced the fear, panic and excitement. Thanks to the wrestling mats, none of these feelings were foreign to him. When he reached the sandy bottom he sized up his opponent. Nothing he hadn't seen before. He dropped his bag and carefully pulled his shirt over his head, leaving his earbuds, which were threaded up his collar, in place. The music ended on the right beat. Cogal pulled his buds. The formerly muted sounds of the crowd hit him full force. He smiled.

Just as suddenly, the cheers turned to laughter. Cogal had been whisked out of his moment. He looked over to his opponent. Todd was in the process of licking a finger and alternately rubbing either nipple to get them to stand at attention. Cogal has seen enough. He lunged. Wrestling 101: shoot the leg. Just as quickly, Todd and his erect nipples sprang into action. A deft sidestep was followed by a crouching uppercut to Cogal's lowered head. It landed square. Cogal's nose erupted with pain, blood and bone. Todd's uppercut was followed by the reverse blow to the back of Cogal's neck. A flash clouded his mind as a nerve rattling bolt shot down both of his arms.

With tingling fingers and a clenched fist Cogal torqued his body toward his attacker and threw his first punch. It was too slow. Both the sand and his clouded mind sapped some of the pep out of what were normally Cogal's piston quick legs. The punched missed Todd's chin by the length of a cat's tail. This errant right cross left Cogal exposed. Todd, Lake Side's superstar quarterback, rushed to tackle his opponent. The wrestling champ renowned for tossing his opponents to the mat found himself flailing helplessly above the sand.

As he landed, a sliver of hope hit the ground with him. He wasn't the only person at the pit to sense a mistake in Todd's strategy. Todd had followed Cogal to the sand. He was all over him. Wrestlers were at ease on their backs with their opponents on top of them.

The instincts of both Cogal and everyone else who watched the fight proved mistaken. As Cogal positioned his left leg to twist up and around his attacker, he realized why his strategy had failed. Todd wasn't wrestling, he was kicking ass. That thought coincided with the impact of Todd's forehead parsing what was left of his nose. Cogal's mind spun.

A succession of blows to his head sent him tumbling into darkness. As Todd straddled Cogal, unloading on his face with a flurry of fists, his teammates were first to break down the hill. Todd got off five solid punches before he was sacked by his own linebacker. Cogal was out. Blood stained the sand. The mob had stopped cheering. The scene proved too violent for the masses.

Cogal still made the states his senior year but he lost his first match to a wrestler he wasn't supposed to lose to. Worse still, the day after the fight the faculty stripped away his ear bud privileges. His rep was gone. Even the teachers knew that much.

Incidentally, moments after the bout, Todd strutted out of the pit preceded by his newly engorged reputation. Ashley watched him intently as he passed her by. She was impressed. Quarterbacks weren't really her thing anymore. But that kind of pain was the exact sensation Ashley craved.

Chapter 16
Pant Cuffs

The bell indicating the start of second period had rung three minutes prior. Todd sat by himself on a donated stone bench located in Lake Side High's botanical courtyard. He had just hosted his first unofficial "I rule the school" meeting and it felt right. Todd didn't have to speak, and he was included in every conversation. It was effortless. Todd wondered how many big fish actually recognized that they ruled the pond. Todd had an advanced level of appreciation for the moment, a self-awareness that his peers outwardly lacked. For instance, no fewer than three of his friends asked him if he was "coming" after the bell rang, consecutively, within thirty seconds of each other.

"Todd, you coming?"

"Yo, Todd, you coming?"

"Hey, Todd, we going?"

It seemed gay to him in a way. Why should anyone care what he did or contemplate the motivations behind why he did it? He didn't give a shit about any of their actions. Yet to his friends, Todd's torpidity was as magnetic as his accomplishments. Senior year pond maintenance, Todd projected, would be less an endeavor than a facile exercise in nurturing the status quo. Todd decided to savor every succulent, algae-free drop that hydrated his personal oasis.

One instance concerning the impromptu get-together did bother Todd. Ashley left without as much as a glance his way. She stood by his side the entire time. She touched his arm, twice, and smiled at him in the middle of one of her cute, sixteen-year-old, hot chick stories. Ashley's anecdote began with her wearing striped wool socks, boxer shorts and a tank top, and it ended with her doing laundry or some such shit. Todd listened to the entire tale wearing a proud, goofy grin. Simply hearing her speak filled him with rapture. Everything Ashley did was exhilarating. If he were to savor anything at all this year, it would be Ashley.

When the bell rang Todd waited for, anticipated, and internally begged for her "good-bye." It never came. It drove him crazy. What did it mean? Did the missing gesture signify anything at all? Todd analyzed every interaction they had - sometimes, oftentimes, in the moment of the interaction. Was Ashley happy, nervous, or bored? Had he behaved coolly, idiotically, or insanely? Did he use the correct words and laugh at the right moments? Was he being funny? Had he made the proper eye contact?

Todd's checklist was endless. During each of his conversations with Ashley, at nearly every point and breath, Todd stressed over any combination of the above doubts. For Todd it was all one big mess.

Todd was persistently aware of the drama surrounding him, specifically how he and others were being perceived within any apparent moment. Most of the time this knowledge manifested as background noise, like his heartbeat or a hungry crow. But with Ashley he was living two realities: the one before him that he shared with her, and a second reality, the one in his mind, which he shared with his insecurities. Being with Ashley exhausted Todd, churned his mind, forcefully unknotted acculturated lobes and unwound strands of elemental membrane as he worked to recreate an identity of comfort and will. This was the reason he needed Ashley to say good-bye. Todd could not decide if he lived as either a founder or a fraud. He might succeed in continuing to fool the world concerning his big-fish status, they seemed willing enough to take the bait, but he harbored no certainty regarding his own future. Todd had agreed to attend UCLA after graduation. He wondered if he could even excel in such a large, open and competitive environment. But he realized he hit pay dirt with Ashley. He'd follow her off a cliff if she asked. She was the epitome of a big fish in the ocean; the illicit offspring of a blue whale and a great white.

Success and beauty were made with her, defined by her. She had already secured an agent. She had recently declined two separate roles on network television sitcoms. Ashley couldn't help but succeed. After she logged a few more years in between her situation and her mother's death, Ashley would be a star in whatever she pursued. And right now she loved Todd. And even more precisely, more "right now," the last thing that Ashley did was leave without saying good-bye.

One thing kept jawing at him. One person seemed to be the crux of all his misgivings regarding Ashley. Mark. Ashley seemed to hate Mark more than she loved him. Todd didn't know what that meant exactly. He understood her hate, cock in the mouth and all, but he knew there was too much of it. And it wasn't the right kind of hate. It was too personal and with too much regard.

Todd hated artichoke hearts, so he simply avoided eating them. He paid them no mind other than a grimace when they were served during dinner. Ashley, on the other hand, obsessed over Mark: who he spoke with, what he wore, and what he did. Every action Mark took inspired Ashley to hate him further. Todd presumed that hate for Mark was a positive sign in general, it was safer than love. But it had become a thing in Todd's restructured mind and it had to be dealt with.

Todd abandoned his tangled thoughts and looked down at his legs, which were extended and crossed at the ankles. He wore a stitch of dark, slim-fit, Diesel jeans and a black pair of Camper three-quarter cut boots. He liked looking at the junction where his pant cuff met the collar of his boot. It just looked right; the pant cuff hugging the neck of the scuff-less shoe, a slight fold of fabric in his tailor-fitted jeans just above the ankle. It was the form of style. Every other cuff/shoe combo existed as a flickering shadow on a grimy cave wall. Todd smirked to himself as he sat alone, absent valediction, in the center of Lake Side High's efflorescent square.

The second period of the first school day was well underway. Ashley had left without saying good-bye. As far as Todd was concerned there were only two other fish in his pond. There were only two fish that mattered. One had just left without acknowledging him, without soothing his insecurities. A little wave might have done it; maybe a slight turn his way and a sexy smile.

Todd wanted to be embraced. He craved both its ember and comfort. He realized this would never happen. Not as long as that other fish swam around his pond. Ashley despised Mark more than she loved... liked... no, *loved* her boyfriend. This was the problem. This was why she hadn't said good-bye. There was one solution, a single answer to Todd's lone dilemma. He and Mark had to fight. They had to be in the pit together. After he destroyed Mark, buried him in the sand, then Ashley would have to say good-bye.

Chapter 17
Interruption

The first half of the school day went as expected for Mark. He kept his head down, paid attention in class and dissolved into the background. The latter being no small feat considering his astonishing physical presence. Mark was six feet tall and sculpted of a finely polished and translucent alabaster. His mesmeric beauty attracted incredulous stares from the whole of his species. To behold Mark inspired at least one of only two possible sentiments: awe or envy, usually both. Mark noticed it all the time. Even today, moments ago, he had surreptitiously observed three freshmen girls creeping while he toiled on the lunch line. As he queued up near the tater tots, he heard one of them say, "You're hot!" and giggle sheepishly with her friends. Ashley wasn't around, so there would be no blowback. And regardless of whether or not they believed him to be gay, Mark was hot.

This reality helped Mark cope with the current state of his life, the non-permanence of it all. Even in a place where he'd been ostracized, where he wore a sign that read "do not touch," a banner crafted and branded by the powers that be, Mark created a buzz. Both his stature and good looks provided assurance that he could not be ignored forever. College would be his salvation.

For now, Mark would wear his badge of dishonor with quiet dignity. At times he'd revel in his vilipend assessment. He knew that in truth some of his female classmates actually desired him, and knowing exactly which ones, served to keep his rolodex of masturbatory fodder up to date. His size and muscle tone kept his male antagonists at arm's length. Even Todd, who seemed to wallow in Mark's misery, had never actually taken a swing at him. As long as Mark remained content in his role as martyr, so long as he refused to engage, these next three years would be an unremarkable testament to self-preservation on the road to reinvention.

Of course, Mark's mother would still be fat. When he left for college she would be alone and fat. Worse still, she would be alone, fat and surrounded by filth. But at what point would Mark be absolved from her imposition of being? Mark had three years to figure this out. He had maybe a year's worth of space left in the garage. With scant effort he could reorganize the basement and create a surplus of the precious cubic feet needed for his storage system.

Mark's property was large enough, and he had the money needed to requisition the construction of a shed in his back yard. Mark possessed both the room and fortitude required to keep the shit-storage machinery running through graduation. But could he leave her? Could Mark allow his burden to spill out onto the driveway, across the front lawn and into the community? Mark had witnessed in real time, during his bus ride to school, what an unchecked hoarder could do to a home and a neighborhood in just a few months.

The Parson property formed a sprawling and luxurious estate located in the Golden Hills, an exclusive Lake Side community whose residents were stewing in mostly old and tainted money. Inherited wealth from a fluid succession of ease and entitlement that spanned endless generations. Miss Parsons had lived there since forever. After she passed, the demesne was willed to her spinster niece. Mark couldn't be certain of what had happened to the new Miss Parsons, though he assumed she had been assaulted by a sanitation worker as a child, because as an adult she was incapable of carrying anything to the curb. He watched each day, beginning in fifth grade, as the once resplendent Parsons Manor transformed into a Salvation Army stock room. The windows quickly filled with both grime and tchotchke. The yard cluttered with, among other things, decorative posts and potted plants, neither of which would ever stake root in the ground. Nothing she brought back to her home served its intended purpose. It was all wistful yet unreasonable expectation on the part of the new Miss Parsons. In a little over a year, storage containers materialized in the driveway. The endless supply of other people's junk grew in tandem with the weeds and the now formless shrubbery. The new Miss Parsons had an antique business downtown, two of them, and they'd both failed. She couldn't discern between antique and old, treasure and trash. Her customers could. Instead of liquidating, she consolidated. Everything came home. Even the Parsons estate, a mansion that once comfortably ensconced the old Mr. Parsons' thirteen children, was powerless to contain the beast she had wrought on the neighborhood. As the structure rotted on the outside and oozed its insides across the yard, the neighbors organized: Petitions were signed, codes were enforced and senators were called. Still, the new Miss Parsons was unable to act on her own behalf. Nothing could be thrown away. Finally, her cousin, one of old Mrs. Parsons' very wealthy brood, paid Mark's father, ironically, to erect a retaining wall around the entirety of the estate. It was a glorious construct, faced with brick and capped with stone imported from a dilapidated castle in Ireland. It defied every code the town had in place, but no one dared to interrupt its construction. It solved the problem. The wall's beauty obstructed the blight. Everyone was happy. Presumably the new Miss Parsons was still decaying alongside her filth behind the embellished bulwark.

Mark's father was dead. Mark wondered if Ashley's dad would approve of and build a fortified moat around his mother's house after he left. It was just one of the thoughts that kept him up at night, one of the musings that twisted his stomach in knots.

Mark paid for his food and went to find a seat. The cafeteria was both oversized and empty. Most of the students went out for lunch to either of the two delis or the pizza place within walking distance. Provided it wasn't raining, seating was plentiful in the Lake Side mess hall. Without having to turn his head, Mark found an unoccupied table. He sat down, organized his tray and pulled out his history textbook. One of the hidden blessings in having no friends was ample, distraction-free study time.

"Hey, Mark."

Mark looked up from his book with a mouth full of green bean goo. The staff in the cafeteria overcooked everything. It would be laughable if it wasn't so disgusting. Kim took a seat across the table from him.

"I changed my schedule."

"Yeah. Why's that?"

Mark already knew the answer to his own question. He was the answer. It was a rude question. He didn't like himself for asking it. Mark noticed Kim blush. Not in the cheeks of course, too much icing on those cupcakes, but her neck was switching shades like a cuttlefish.

Mark wasn't sure why Kim imagined he would get with her. Could she not attest to the staggering dissimilarities in their genetic pedigrees? It annoyed him. And not as an embarrassing "I don't want to be seen with her" nuisance. He was above that. It was more a straight-up "how pathetic do you think I am?" irritation. Was Mark so hard up, so needy, that he would suit up for a team three leagues beneath his talents just to play ball?

He could go online and meet anyone, literally anyone, and she would be more attractive than Kim. He had a profile on Kindler, and fuck if his inbox wasn't full on a weekly basis. In fact, he was one red Iroc away from a lay a night. He had actually been on a couple of dates already. A few older chicks, good-looking chicks with their own cars, had picked him up for a night on the town. On one of the dates he had to shove an over-anxious female off his lap. He had been called a fag then, too. But Mark didn't want to sleep with anyone he met online. On each date he had planned to fuck. He was sixteen and a virgin, but there was something off-putting about the girls he had met. Mark realized that he didn't like them on a personal level.

Mark knew he liked Kim as a person. Besides her constantly trying to have sex with him, she was a smart, confident and caring individual. This past spring he had witnessed her donate money to a breast cancer charity. He had been behind her in line at CVS, purposely avoiding her eye when the option to donate one, three or five dollars appeared on the credit card display. Kim selected five. Mark knew this didn't make her Mother Teresa, but it was impactful. It meant something; there was a substance to the act, a corpus, thick and dense, like the human cankle.

Chapter 18
The Question

Lester arrived late to lunch. He had spent the first five minutes of the period on the phone with Mr. May. He was having a tough time of it. No one wanted anything to do with him. This was fine, normally, but Lester had been trying. He had attempted to make friends throughout the day while warily governing his desire to punch everyone in the face. His first semester at school was long and lonely, but he understood that he had to be patient. His summer had been just as long and equally as lonely. Had It not been for the forest and its endless acreage of exploration, he might have gone mad, gotten mad. Twice at the Hess Mart where Lester purchased his weekly can of Red Bull two separate jagoffs on the football team had mouthed off to him.

Each time Lester imagined the look on his opponent's face as a ferocious uppercut to the chin splintered his teeth and exploded his jaw shut. This intense pain to be compounded by a left hook, just below the eye and half on the nose, accompanied by the white light, the purity of impact, a quick reboot of the brain. Not like a weasel, but like a lion.

Each time Lester thought better of it and walked away without incident. The second insult at the end of August was tough to ignore. Victor – Lester later learned his name – stopped at the gas station on the way home from football practice. He still wore his jersey, his plumage indicating that he was a special kind of antagonizing prick. Lester had turned from the fridge, Red Bull in hand, when Victor snuck up behind him.

"Are you a nigger?"

Lester was surprised by the starkness of the question. It was bloodied and raw.

"What?"

"Are you a nig-ger?"

This second more deliberate slur Lester understood. With that comprehension an inkling of a roar tickled his weaselly throat. This roar was quickly muted by the little bird riding his shoulder. Mr. May chirped incessantly into Lester's ear. The Weasel kept his response both simple and civil.

"No."

"So why you wearing your hat like a nigger?"

Three days prior Lester had found a Marlins cap at the Salvation Army. It fit. It looked right. The weasel had tried on many hats in his fifteen years of life. The few that looked decent came with a thirty-five-dollar price tag from the fitted youth rack at Lids. The secondhand hats at the local thrift shops had the right price but invariably left Lester looking like a train conductor for the local sports team. The weasel, along with his pointed nose and beady eyes, had a pea-sized skull. It was difficult to find a cap that didn't poof out at the crown relative to the tight band fastened around his tiny mind. Lester never liked his head. People would constantly make fun of it. The clever types would serenade him with the Witch Doctor song – oo, ee, oo, ah, ah – It was horrible, and to Lester's dismay there wasn't a doctor around, neither modern nor witch, who could inflate a patient's skull. He had learned in health class that a small head could be a sign of fetal alcohol syndrome. Lester didn't like that syndrome. He didn't like those three words near to each other. He tasted copper in the back of his throat whenever he heard that phrase.

Lester messed up. The night before he met Victor, the Weasel noticed some douchebag on YouTube wearing his Mr. Beast cap with the brim slung to the side a bit. Lester thought it looked kind of cool. When the video ended Lester sprinted to the only mirror in his house, the cracked one over the bathroom sink, and experimented. It took nearly a half hour of looking at himself from every angle, with multiple facial expressions, but he decided that the tilted cap looked good. So the following morning, with many reservations, Lester tried it out in public.

Lester remembered something Mr. May had told him when they were discussing both how he looked and the economic realities that determined his wardrobe. Mr. May told him that style was perceived, not actual. Two people wearing the same exact outfit could look completely hot or not, depending on how they wore it. If one guy thought he looked strange or felt uncomfortable with the way he was dressed, that's what the world would see. If the other guy liked it, felt good about what he had going on, his peers would feel the same way. They wouldn't even think twice. He told Lester to buy what he liked at the thrift shop and rock it. That's what he said, "Rock it." Wear it like you own it.

Mr. May's advice had made sense to Lester. He had seen people that he thought looked stupid with the outfit they chose to wear, but they also looked good looking stupid in that same outfit. He supposed what Mr. May said and what he observed were two parts of the same conceptual whole.

Lester's insecurities must have won out at the Hess station, because he found himself at the mini-mart fridge being called the n-word by a high school football player named Victor Plaza.

Lester didn't mind niggers or chinks or spics or any other type of person, for that matter. After taking to Mr. May he stopped using those terms as flippantly as he had in the past. Mr. May told him it was unbecoming. He said they were the wrong words used by the wrong people for the wrong reasons.

Mr. May told Lester that those wrong words had the wrong people fighting and blaming the individuals to their left and their right, distracting from the real fight, up and down.

It wasn't a big deal for Lester to stop. Racial epithets would still slip out from time to time, but he didn't mind that much, either. He wasn't convinced by May's class war, per se. Lester just, after a while, took Mr. May's advice by rote, specifically because Mr. May was giving it. Besides, the spic/chink thing, it didn't mean anything to Lester. He wouldn't call a Mexican a spic out of disdain, but because it was easy, and apropos. A spic was a spic. It was neither negative nor positive. Or it was both. A spic could steal a TV from Best Buy or score the winning touchdown in the Super Bowl. It didn't matter much to Lester, just so long as he could identify who did what. It was similar to the way his father expressed himself. "The fuckin' ice cream gook ripped me off again." It was an easy way to distinguish one asshole from the next.

But there, at the mini-mart attached to the Hess station, Lester had been called the n-word and he did not like it at all. It seemed negative. Unpleasant. Nevertheless, the lion retracted its claws, turned its back on its kill and placed the Red Bull can back in its fabricated plastic slot. Lester quietly retreated down the aisle away from Victor. After making his turn around the Frito-Lay endcap he paused than took off his hat and threw it back over the shelves in Victor's direction. He waited, sensed nothing and exited the store. Lester was not exactly sure why he threw the hat. Poor angling aside, he did like how it fit his micro-head. He supposed that it was the lion's last effort at provocation. The fucked-up thing was that Victor, a week and a half later, wore Lester's hat on the first day of school. It was angled a bit to the side and he looked good. Victor had rocked it.

Lester stood by the water fountain, lunch tray in hand, and searched for a seat. No one noticed him. The cafeteria's population was well below its maximum occupancy, and he could have sat anywhere, but he had a mission from Mr. May. He needed a friend. He needed Mark.

Mark was attempting to pay attention to part two of Kim's summertime adventures. She was discussing the events of week three at her parents' bungalow. Mark wondered how many weeks her family had stayed in Delong and if anything even accidentally interesting had occurred. Soon after these musings he stopped paying attention to Kim's words altogether. He was utterly distracted by the ice cream sandwiches on Kim's lunch tray. There were two of them. Two. Fifty cents apiece; it was a good deal. Kim had bought two frozen desserts along with a heap of tater tots and a hot dog. Mark could not take his eyes off the ice cream. He didn't understand. Kim didn't deserve this food. She needed a salad and a rice cake. Or just a salad. Mark felt the look of derision on his face and quickly switched to a sly smile before Kim finished licking her fingers.

Lester sat down next to Mark. He sidled up in his Chuck Taylor's and plopped down four tray lengths to Mark's right. Mark's look of derision reappeared. Lester recognized that look. Mark had made that same disgusted face at his overweight lunch buddy just moments before Lester sat down. It was time for Lester to make a friend.

"So, who's the fat chick?"

Chapter 19
Inside

Kim's initial reaction combined, deep inside, both horror and humiliation. The feeling didn't last long. A quick sting, a drop of the stomach, and the worst of it dissipated, seeped back to its original realm: an allegorized world of relative worth and perceived affliction.

This wasn't the first time Kim had been called fat to her face. Ashley's minions were relentless. But the last such incident had occurred nearly six months ago in the early spring. Nothing all summer. Now, on the first day of school, the Weasel hit her right in the lumpy stomach. The Weasel.

Kim called Lester the Weasel because that's exactly what he looked like. It wasn't meant to be disparaging, just observational. She didn't realize that everyone else called him the Weasel until two days before school ended last June. Lester had caused a minor stir when a classmate "accidentally" tripped him down a flight of stairs, causing his face to plant itself on one of the wall-mounted fire extinguishers. His eyebrow split open, and according to everyone who witnessed the misstep it was hilarious. Other than discussing Lester's lacerated forehead, Kim didn't see much of him and he wasn't talked about often. Lester's only relevant attribute, his single significance as a being, was that he undoubtedly looked like a weasel.

Kim would never tell him this, nor call him a weasel out of spite. Even after Lester's insult, she wouldn't lower herself in that way. She was capable of it. She'd hit Ashley pretty hard last year, but even then she pulled her punches. Kim lacked the desire to spread pain. Not even to those who deserved it. That's why when Ashley called her a pig, she felt the sting, then bit her lip. Her first thought was to call her a cocksucker. "Whatever, cocksucker." Instead, Kim controlled her dialogue. The implication would have been horrendous. Ashley's mom had died sucking cock. It would have been an attempt to crush and mortify Ashley. Kim didn't have it in her. In fact, she couldn't understand why anyone would choose to hurt anyone else, ever.

Kim wasn't a prude. She could mix it up with her classmates, mess with their insecurities a bit. She was able to live and have fun. When her friends behaved foolishly, she called them on it. Never spitefully nor manically, but as a person should. If we couldn't laugh at ourselves, our brothers and sisters, why bother laughing at all? But Kim could never sink to that level, the abyss where pain resided. Nor could she relate to anyone else who could.

After her gut settled, she faced a new predicament. The Weasel had called her fat right in front of Mark, her shy, anxious squirrel. She had been feeding Mark sweet and crunchy nuts for over a year, hoping to get him back to her nest. She had served him daily; in fact, Kim had been baiting Mark in that exact moment, acorn in hand, only to witness a slimy weasel spook her timid prey.

Kim knew Mark thought she was overweight. She also knew that it disgusted him. Just seconds prior she had caught a glimpse of his repulsed face as he judged her stack of ice cream sandwiches. But she had already made up her mind. Fuck Mark. Not only fuck Mark, but to fuck Mark. The sentiments were not mutually exclusive. In truth, one was the reason for the other.

First, on fucking Mark. Kim thought he was gorgeous, and he was, but that didn't make him better than she. She wants to fuck. He wants to fuck. And you know what; no one else was scratching at his bedroom door. It wasn't Kim's fault that Mark's dad had screwed Ashley's mom. And it wasn't Kim's fault they both died while doing it. It just happened during the course of life in general. If this small occurrence somehow led Mark to squeeze between her thighs, so be it.

Secondly, Fuck Mark. Fuck Mark for thinking that she was taking advantage of his less-than-upstanding reputation. Fuck Mark for counting her ice cream sandwiches. Fuck Mark for thinking she was undeserving of his cock.

Kim wasn't the only person in the world to eat two ice cream bars at lunch, return home, then get fucked hard by some slick stud. And if it did happen, she wouldn't be the ugliest nor heaviest person for it to happen to. It was a numbers game. The planet begrudgingly stocked over seven billion human inhabitants. By the law of probability there had to be a heavier, uglier girl eating two fudgesicles at any given moment who would later be bounced by a guy as hot as Mark.

Kim didn't believe she deserved to be fucked by Mark. She did believe she had the right to try. Kim constantly wondered whether she needed or even wanted a man. Before she was forced to decide, just once in her life, preceding her inevitable affair with a "nice boy" sporting a hair lip and a comic book collection, she wanted to fuck the shit out of some banger. Mark's stock was low right now, so it might as well be him.

Kim felt no shame. She felt no guilt. Her parents had taught her well. They told her more than once that no one was better than she. They also relayed the flip side to that coin: She was better than no one. We as humans were simply a bunch of sentient atoms floating on an ungodly rock in the middle of a random galaxy inside of an incomprehensible universe. With this discursive understanding of the collective as her foundation, Kim was determined to have the glut of matter that defined her be ravaged by the network of atoms that encapsulated Mark.

When the pain completely subsided, Kim looked at Lester. He wore a weaselly little smile on his weaselly little face. He had been enjoying himself. Kim was about to call him a dipshit, when, to her astonishment, the previously diffident squirrel brandished its claws.

Chapter 20
Reverberations

Mark's heart refused to beat in his pitted chest. He now knew his earlier misgivings about the Weasel and his Chuck Taylor's had not been unfounded. Lester was attempting to make friends. The one bona fide piece of pure trash in the school, who happened to live in Mark's back yard, was looking for a pal. Fuck Lester, and fuck Kim. This was not going happen, with either of them.

Mark lunged for Lester's throat with his left hand. His movements were quick and powerful. In an instant, Lester was yanked from his bench and savagely thrown to the floor. Just a quickly Mark straddled his prey.

"If you ever…"

Mark stopped himself. He'd meant to say, "…talk to me again," but his conscience knew this was not supposed to be the reason for his aggression. Mark was supposed to be defending his portly friend's honor.

Before he could reframe his threat, the entire cafeteria had figured out what happened. They were standing and salivating. In the reflections cast by the mirrored eyes of his peers, Mark saw his own naked body - except, on his feet were a pair of black Chuck Taylors.

Mark let go of Lester's throat. Without looking at anyone, he strode out of the cafeteria. If throngs of people had been there to witness the altercation, they would have parted for him as he left.

Chapter 21
Comic relief

It had all happened so fast. Lester was surprised by Mark's ability to summon such ferocity from what appeared on its surface to be a relaxed state. The Weasel hadn't been blindsided in a fight since the last time his dad punched him in his sleep. Lester had hit the floor hard. He felt no pain, just the hush and scratch of the blessed white noise.

Lester had been in this position before. Throughout his unbearable childhood his father had ritualistically handled his son by the neck. It occurred to Lester growing up that his dad might have confused a loving paternal embrace with a drunken form of limited asphyxiation. Two hands on the throat and a knee in the chest, like daily catcalls from the grounds of a commercial construction site; it was endearing if only in its habituation. One time, around the age of seven, Lester actually lost consciousness. There was too much pressure on his chest and not enough oxygenated blood reaching his brain. He woke up three hours later in his bed next to an opened bag of peanut M&M's. Turned out the fucker was only half a monster half of the time. Either way, this was not an unfamiliar situation for Lester. He had seen it countless times in dozens of MMA fights. Lester knew what he had to do - a double hammer punch to both of Mark's ears would buy him the time needed to break free. Both fists had to be thrown within a second of his back hitting the over-waxed tile.

His palms never left the floor. Lester remained a new man. He took his lumps, stoically.

Lester was genuinely confused by Mark's reaction. Mark was obviously perturbed by his fat friend. Lester had assumed Mark would chuckle a bit before telling him not to be a dick. That's what friends did. They jibed each other. They didn't attack. Not unprovoked, anyway, with such intensity.

The moment passed before Lester could completely process his current predicament. Mark had made his move, voiced his half-threats, and promptly walked away.

Without looking around, Lester got up off his back and sat down at his lunch tray. He was knuckle deep in tater-tot crumbles when he heard a childish sniveling emanating from the fat chick section of his table.

"Why are you crying? I just got my shit tossed."

Kim snapped back at Lester as swiftly as Mark had lunged for his throat.

"Go fuck yourself, dipshit."

Kim stormed off, leaving her lunch tray behind. The ice cream was getting soft. Its ooze began to penetrate the machine-folded, waxy white wrapper. As she exited the cafeteria Kim threw one last barb at the wall. The room was empty and quiet. Her snide remark echoed all the way back to Lester's tiny rodent ears.

"Weaselly little shit!"

Chapter 22
Imperfection

Todd's notebook had been closed for five minutes. He couldn't take notes. He couldn't concentrate. It was Local Studies anyway. Who gave a shit, really?

Actually, at that moment, Todd cared for nothing at all except the following period, lunch. Ashley was in the classroom next door. After Local Studies, the instant the bell rang, Todd planned on taking her to Taco Bell. Taco Bell was a twenty-minute ride and their lunch period a mere forty-two minutes long. It would be a pleasant drive, just the two of them.

Todd wasn't certain, but he hoped Ashley would be without pants for most of the trip. The previous Saturday, in one of her rare modes of flirtation, she'd joked about a secret and strange love of eating soft, sloppy tacos in the nude. Ashley said, with a flirty grin, that if Todd brought her to the Bell for lunch she would take the ride wearing only her underwear. Todd questioned her sincerity. Nothing in their short history together suggested Ashley enjoyed anything either sloppy or naked. Nevertheless, he had been masturbating to the scene twice a day since she mentioned it. Everything about Ashley exhausted Todd.

Potential pleasures aside, the anticipation of just being next to Ashley for the better part of an hour was near maddening. What drove Todd insane was that even though both he and Ash had been an item for the entire summer, Todd had no clue what type of underwear Ashley wore. Shit, he was barely familiar with her bra.

For Todd there was only one certainty regarding Ashley and her panties: they had to be cute. He saw no way around that. Even grandma underwear would be hot on Ashley. Even his own grandma's underwear would be hot on Ashley, incontinence and all.

Todd envisioned seeing one random curly hair poking out of the elastic seam near her inner thigh. For Todd, it didn't matter what was there. Whatever Ashley possessed, Todd would kneel before it on command. During his twice-a-days Todd regularly imagined loose hairs or a slight discoloration, a darker hue to her entire area, possibly a mole. Todd's modest self prayed for something, anything, to stilt the perfection. This was neither out of jealousy nor a desire to mar her majesty. The opposite, actually. If Ashley offered Todd a blemish or a flaw, it would be their joined insufficiency. Only he and Ashley would share it. Ashley's fault, along with Todd's singular recognition of that failing, would bring him, them, to a place where no one else could be. Todd would revel in their flawed perfection.

Todd had accidentally discovered a comfort in imperfection with his previous girlfriend. Lauren was a senior last year and maybe the hottest girl at Lake Side besides Ashley. Top three, anyway. Todd caught Lauren's eye shortly after he was promoted to feature quarterback over The Hass. The Hass had been a starting varsity player since tenth grade. No small feat. Todd beat him outright for the spot before the season started during summer practice. Todd was three inches taller and he could throw rails. The Hass, even with two full seasons' experience, never stood a chance.

Lauren liked it. She began dating him three days after he had fought Cogal in the pit. Todd being an absolute badass sealed the deal. Their relationship didn't last long. Ashley was at that fight, too. Ashley knew she wanted Todd, but there was no urgency in her situation. Lauren had been accepted to her mother's alma mater, Yale, and Cogal had scraped together the grades needed to graduate. The entire senior class for that matter, they would all be gone, save a few plaques and pictures – their consequence negated by simple, inevitable absence. Sure, Todd was essentially HNIC after the fight, but that would be a certainty the next fall. Ashley decided that she would let Lauren have him until at least the last day of school.

Lauren had a lot of him. They would fuck all the time. Lauren's parents were divorced, and her mom worked long, lucrative hours at a brokerage firm downtown. Her newly renovated, three story colonial was always clean, welcoming, and with the exception of Lauren, empty. Todd slept there most weekends. Lauren's mom seemed to like him around, a man in the house. She would flirt with him all the time. Make it a point to buy him his favorite foods. She even bought Todd a PlayStation after one Friday night when he used its absence as an excuse to leave. It was a nice set-up. Todd might have loved Lauren. He didn't know. She was squishy over him. Lauren's friends stopped talking to her after she bailed on them three weekends in a row to be with Todd. Todd would go out and tell her to "hang tight" in case he got bored with his friends. Lauren never left the house.

One Friday night last April the police had raided the pit. The pit doubled as a hang out on random weekend nights. There was always a fire, frequently a keg, intermittently danger, but seldom was there genuine communion. Every now and then, regardless of the gathering's purpose and mostly at the end of any given month, the cops would disrupt the festivity and issue summonses. Some quota bullshit. After the authorities ruined the evening, Todd returned home to his woman in wait. Lauren's mother decided to spend the night with a work friend. In her absence she left the house warm and well stocked with both carnal and epicurean delights. Todd even enjoyed the smell; an understated yet sublime mixture of Ivory soap and frosted cherry Pop Tarts fresh from the toaster.

When she had the house to herself, Lauren liked to flop around in only her underwear and a tank top. Todd wanted to be with her seconds after he walked through the door, but he restrained himself. Time was ample. Instead, they sat on her couch in the family room and watched a movie. They selected a Netflix special, some torture-porn, slasher pic with no "real art" as far as Todd could tell. It was then, in a day-lit scene of a bloody and artless film, that Todd noticed a faint blond hair on Lauren's toe while her bare feet rested flat on her mom's glass coffee table. It was silhouetted by all seventy inches of the TV's warm and muted glow. One wispy hair on her big toe, a slight imperfection. Lauren wasn't hairy or anything; in fact, Todd had never before noticed a single stray whisker anywhere on her body. The hair, so fine and delicate, required a razor's touch, at best, twice a year. Todd imagined Lauren's smile, her mirth, maybe a giggle as she shaved this gossamer strand that last appeared when the earth was on the opposite side of the sun. After observing the hair, Todd looked at Lauren for the second time in his life. Lauren was both gorgeous and a fantastic fuck. This flaw humanized her. It made her real. More than a woman in wait. It made her perfect.

For a moment, after noticing the toe, Todd actually felt for Lauren. She loved him. She was devoted to him. And now she was flawed and perfect. Until then, Todd just ate food out of her refrigerator, played video games on her TV and fucked her on her mom's king-sized canopy bed. He had never thought about the love.

Todd's right hand involuntarily crossed the breadth of its owner's heart and chest to gently caress the nearest tit it could reach. Lauren looked at the hand as a spontaneous draw of breath sent tingles through her back and down to her toes. His rouge extremity decided to slide itself underneath her tank top as she grabbed for Todd over his grating jeans and kissed him full. They fucked for nearly two hours, there was a substance to the experience. Todd remembered leaving Lauren's house the next morning feeling satisfied.

Lauren had shaved her toe by the next time Todd saw her feet. He never saw the hair again. Two days before the earth's aphelion, Ashley had intervened.

The bell rang, and Local Studies ended for Todd along with everything else insufferable. Todd grabbed his packed bag and stood up from his desk. He had to adjust himself. He couldn't help the bulge, Ashley was just too close. It took all of his forbearance, but Todd waited patiently for his turn to exit the room as the luckier students who sat closer to the door funneled out in front of him. The teacher, Mrs. Worthington, attempted to give final instructions to the fleeing students. Todd wasn't listening. No one was listening. Todd stepped into the hall just in time to see Ashley walking the wrong way. He watched as she stormed off in the opposite direction, with Tammy. They were engrossed in conversation.

"Ash!"

Ashley turned toward her name. She was upset. She noticed Todd, threw up a little wave, no smile. Then Ashley turned and walked away, with Tammy.

Chapter 23
Villus

"Fuck."

Ashley was driving Todd insane. If they were to make the Bell, they would have to leave this instant. This left no time to talk to Tammy. No time for a little wave. Ashley knew this.

"Fuck."

Todd had a brick in his stomach. He wasn't an unreasonable person. If Ashley needed to cancel, then she could cancel. "Just tell me," he thought. "Don't walk away all pissed off and give me a little fucking wave."

"Fuck."

Again, Todd was confused as to the significance of his latest encounter with Ashley. Earlier today, in the courtyard, he had been turned halfway around himself because he wasn't offered a little wave. Now, after reluctantly adapting to this morning's contortions, he was flipped back the other way entirely because of the little wave he did receive.

Todd had no idea what to do next. He needed Ashley to reciprocate. He needed her to walk around in her underwear so they could bond over her imperfections.

Todd considered running after Ashley to remind her about Taco Bell. Something stopped him. The game. He was so out of control over her. He could not forget the game. She liked his strength. If he became needy or vulnerable, he had no chance. Todd would not sit home and wait for Ashley on the couch while she gallivanted around town with her friends. Actually, Todd would wait in the trunk of his car if she asked him to. But their relationship wasn't to that point, and Ashley didn't need to know about the trunk; not yet anyway, not until she did. Todd turned and walked the other way, putting needed distance between his angst and its cause. He found Steve in the hallway leaning against a bulletin board with a wagging tail, half a grin and a glisten in his eyes. Todd was hungry. He didn't want to see Steve in his underwear, he didn't want to think about those stray hairs, but Steve did make for fine company.

"You wanna' hit the Bell?"

Steve tried, but he couldn't contain his joy.

"Yeah, brotha. Any time!"

"Let's do it, Fuzz Ball."

Fuzz Ball. It was a dig. It was gentle and in good spirits, but a dig all the same. Steve had a coat of hair over his entire body. He couldn't take off his shirt in public. Not unless he wished the unwitting onlookers to chuckle over his bristly shoulders or retch at the patch of ass hair that crept up his lower back. Steve had a thick, black beard. He shaved it every day, and you could tell. Fibers sprouted up his cheeks almost to his eye sockets. But he didn't dare to trim those hedges. Steve had learned that when you shave hair anywhere on your body, it provoked the rooted remains to grow back thicker. Starting in tenth grade, he cream-bleached all the quills that grew above an arbitrary border of follicles demarcated as a normal beard line. His classmates made fun of him all the time behind his hairy back. Steve had too much going on for anyone but Todd to go straight at him concerning his evolutionary obsolete pelage. He was tough, both on the football field and in the pit, demonstrating a second savage link to his feral ancestors. But when Steve's back was turned, he was known as "Hairy Beave Steve." He had tried laser electrolysis in the eleventh grade to disastrous results. The electrode caused his face to break open and ooze for two weeks. Steve was forced to stay home from school and remain locked in his bedroom as cursed tendrils, angered at aborted rejection, forced their way through the plated scabs on his cheeks.

Todd had taken the dig at Steve on purpose. He needed to redirect his emotions as he sanitized his pond. Like any other unnatural ecosystem, its function depended wholly upon the suffering of its inhabitants.

"Where's Ash? She coming?"

Todd shut his eyes before responding.

"She's busy."

Steve smiled. He loved Todd. He liked being near Todd. He wanted to be Todd. It wasn't sexual, he simply enjoyed watching everyone fawn over Todd. Steve liked being Todd's best friend. He was good enough for Todd, and others had to notice.

Ash wasn't going to Taco Bell and Steve was. Just Todd and Steve. Steve enjoyed the intimate conversation that blossomed when only he and Todd were together. They talked about all the shit that true friends tend to talk about. As Todd engaged, Steve rose and flourished. Todd listened to Steve's opinions and his problems; took interest and offered solutions. Todd discussed both his own life and Ashley. They made plans for the weekend. Their time together sowed purpose.

Steve noticed, worried, that the walk to Todd's car in the student parking lot dragged behind its intention. They had yet to pass through senior locker banks. If they wanted to make the Bell, Todd would have to pick up the pace. Steve couldn't wait until they entered Todd's Jetta. It was going to be a lot of fun. Just Todd and Steve. Plus, he didn't need some sycophantic fool waylaying Todd in the hallway, some tool bag trying to get in on Todd's dick. Steve decided to corner Todd's attention.

"Did you hear what happened in the cafeteria?"

"What, they get rid of the old-people smell?"

"Ha, no. Mark got into a fight."

Todd stopped mid-stride. He turned to face Steve. Before saying anything, he took a peek over Steve's insulated shoulder to see if Ashely had returned. To see if by blessed chance she'd remembered.

Three boys from the football team and one guy whom Steve didn't recognize said some form of "what's up" while Todd and Steve were standing in the hallway together. Todd didn't bother to notice. Steve did. For an instant Steve felt their shame and the stain of having been similarly ignored by Todd in the past.

"With who?"

Todd's eyes lit up like a high-wattage bulb angled above a suspect in a room reserved for interrogation. Steve felt the bleached blond hair under his eyes begin to grow. He broke from Todd's gaze before continuing.

"The Weasel."

"Who?"

"I don't know his name, but everyone calls him the Weasel. I've seen him. He looks like a weasel."

"Shit. I don't know who that is. Did he win?"

"The weasel? Nah, he's like five-five. Scrawny. Wasn't much of a fight. Mark supposedly just threw him around."

"That's it?

"That's what I heard."

Todd took one more look down the hall. He witnessed a sea of faces, but none that he cared to see.

Steve grew restless. Taco Bell was twenty minutes away and there was no urgency in Todd's actions.

Steve regretted telling Todd about the fight before they buckled up in his Volkswagen.

Todd pulled his phone from his backpack. There was a string of unread texts, most of them related to Mark and the Weasel. After a quick scan, he dialed up someone who wasn't Steve. Todd had the phone to his ear when he left Steve near the boy's lavatory in the hallway without saying goodbye. The skin underneath the blond beard on The Beave's cheeks tingled a bit as blood rushed to his face and beads of sweat polinko'd their way through and down the errant hairs sprinkled around his sideburns. The bell indicating the start of seventh period rang crisply in Steve's villus, moss-coated ears.

Chapter 24
Damned

Mark laid low in the south gym locker room; his favorite spot on campus. The south gym used to be the main gym. This was back in the seventies, when both the town and the school carried less burden. Currently the south gym acted as both an echo chamber and a surplus storage space. The janitors dug out the arena once a year during the phys-ed department's deck hockey unit. The custodial staff, with what limited influence they retained, insisted on protecting the main gym's hardwood floors from the slaps and scuffs of poorly handled hockey sticks.

The south gym's locker room still functioned, but only after school. It's where the intramural sports teams both changed and locked up overnight. The rest of the south tier, the classrooms located on the floors above the locker room, corralled a sparse and sorted population. The entire wing was reserved for the self-contained special ed students, along with another special room used for in-school detention. Mark had been clued into the locker room and its promise of solitude by one of his father's employees. PJ graduated high school a little over four years before the accident. He navigated his teen years as a ne'er-do-well on Lake Side's wrestling team. PJ discovered the locker room's exclusivity when he used its scale to weigh in on meet days. If he came in below his listed weight of 138 pounds he was allowed to eat lunch. As an added benefit, especially on food-free days, PJ could smoke a cigarette in school without risking a referral. Few of Lake Side's faculty members ever ventured to the south wing. Even these enlightened authorities conveniently avoided the special ed's and their doleful inconvenience.

The locker room suited Mark. That first year of high school, when Ashley decided to blame him for her mother's death, Mark found the seclusion comforting. He was left alone to both grieve and sulk. It didn't take Mark long to recognize exactly how much privacy he had. Beginning three days after discovering the spot, whenever Ashley would wear a particularly hot outfit, or just whenever, Mark would slip into one of the shower stalls and show himself a good time. There was little chance of being caught. Even if someone were to enter the locker room, which never happened outside of wrestling season, it wouldn't matter. The maze that led to his private stall was a construct of Daedalus: walk down one dark corridor of showers and up and around the next. Mark could be fully buttoned moments after the first echo of a footstep. If a classmate decided to negotiate the labyrinth that led to his pleasure chamber, at its end they'd discover a pariah napping innocently near a lime-scaled drain. An admittedly strange scenario in which to be exposed but, for Mark, the risk was well worth the mid-day release.

Mark's den proved most depraved at the start of spring. Mark had noticed, as early as sixth grade, that the moment the snow melted, before the earth offered up its first budding crocus, a good chunk of his female classmates shed their protective layers. It was barely fifty degrees and any which way he turned Mark found a chick in a mini-skirt and slides. This fashion-forward choice provided a refreshing change of pace for Mark after a colorless winter of straining to imagine himself past the shapeless hoodies and clunky Uggs.

Mark had no desire to please himself in the present moment. He eschewed his debased shower stall for a bench seat in front of a head-to-toe mirror offering an incongruous view of prescription and reality. Mark looked himself over. Nothing made sense. He dressed well, cut a gorgeous figure and stood tall with master craft muscle tone. An image unmatched outside an underwear ad in GQ magazine or on the pampered movie set of a potential summer blockbuster. Yet on the first day of tenth grade in a random public high school, for Mark, everything sucked. Mark stayed sure that the cosmos had made an error. His life was never meant to be this complicated.

Mark recalled the first day of eighth grade. Both his father and Ashley's mother were alive. His mom was sane, hot and skinny. Mark, at close to six feet tall, had made it through his awkward stage without much awkwardness. Everyone in junior high loved him and he loved everyone. There were few fights and fewer cliques. Mark liked to think he had helped to mold this serene environment. He was the most popular kid around, and he befriended every one of his classmates. Mark treated each middle school interaction as an end unto itself. He set an example for others to follow. It wasn't difficult. Mark didn't need anything from anyone. He had Ashley. More importantly, Mark was comfortable with himself. He had loved Umed. They'd grown up together, and even though Umed refused to play organized sports, he and Mark managed to hang out daily. They had their video games, comic books, the forest and all the leisure time their wealthy parents could provide. They liked what they liked, and they were never judged. Life existed without obstacle. The gates in the corner of Mark's yard were wedged open. Each of them, Mark, Ashley and Umed, could enter one another's houses without a knock. It flowed like a river.

Just two short years later and the hinges on the gates were rusted stiff. Umed lived on the other side of the Earth. Ashley resided in hell. Mark's father lay beneath a well-crafted yet comfort-less headstone.

Mark's bedroom, his living space, served as a set piece in the center of a disaster movie. It was one big mess with an apparent absence of flow. A poisoned river left dammed with two dead bodies, a weasel and thousands of boxes guaranteed to reach their destination in forty-eight hours at no extra cost. Embarrassed and ashamed by what he could no longer see in his reflection, Mark shut his eyes and turned away his head.

Chapter 25
Control

Standing in the middle of the hallway, lacking both aim and motive, Ashley felt the crowns of her teeth dulling to the strain of her clenched jaw. The dentist had warned her against this behavior after her mother's passing. Dr. Lee constructed a mouth guard for her to wear while she slept, but Ashley could not get used to the feel of the form as it hugged her gums. Consequently, as Ashley dreamt of gnawing at charred flesh, her teeth dulled and fractured.

Her current state of distress had nothing to do with the death of her mother. Ashley's asperity and angst, the incisors chewing through her naked belly, engendered the body of a rodent.

Ashley knew the Weasel well. He was the greasy animal she shared a property line with. Only the corners of their yards tickled each other's fence posts, but that touch, to Ashley, felt like a short-eyed molestation. Her father had lobbied the town to declare the Weasel's property condemned. It was a laborious battle he had to wage alone, due to the secluded placement of Lester's nest. It wasn't so much a community blight as it was Ashley's blight, thanks to her bedroom window being one of only two views of the impoverished rat den. She assumed Mark's fat mom had varied concerns other than what her son could see out his bedroom window. Attempting to gorge herself towards rebirth appeared to be her full-time profession.

Ashley's current issue with her unwelcome neighbor was that this land encroaching, trash-eating, feral beast had given Mark credibility. Apparently, each of her classmates was compelled to either talk or text about the resounding thud that engulfed the cafeteria after Mark slammed Lester to the tile floor. Mark was considered threatening, a badass.

"The fucking weasel."

How could such a worthless non-entity mess up all of Ashley's meticulous plans on the first day of school? The entire situation was disorienting. She found herself confused about her plans.

"Control," she thought.

Somehow this concept made sense to her. Control. The word alone helped to unlock her jaw. Control.

Chapter 26
Out of Control

Kim felt her plans spiraling out of control. It turned out that Mark as a topic of conversation interested everyone. Thanks to Ashley, Mark's stock had been kept artificially low through his entire freshman year. He had been taboo. To Ashley, he wasn't supposed to be. To the school, he was supposed to be everything.

Most girls were wet and bothered just being near him. Even the guys couldn't help but be stunned by his physical presence. Everyone remembered his quarterback attack. Mark was a monster in the eighth grade, a legend. After his second game of the season he was called up by the head coach of the freshman squad. He was their starter two Saturdays later and he was a beast for them, as well. Mark could not be stopped.

Mark had dated Ashley, the Ashley, for as long as anyone could remember. He was supposed to be a topic in high school. The Weasel reminded everyone of that. Kim couldn't stand it. Every girl that approached her to discuss the fight was told to "get a life." Her little squirrel was receiving way too much attention. Her weasel was, too.

Chapter 27
Gap Specials

Lester had spent three months as a freshman at Lake Side High before the start of summer break. It was an unremarkable ninety-two days. Lester was essentially anonymous. If it wasn't for his uncanny resemblance to a weasel, his existence at the school could have been disputed on some philosophical level. He served no actual purpose. He had no friends and not a single girl spoke to him. He chose not to join a club, nor did he play a sport. There was the gas station incident and a few random attempts to otherwise mess with him, but it never went too far. He kept his cool. He kept his mouth shut and his hands in his pockets. He walked away. Lester couldn't be provoked, so he'd been left alone to his studies and his future. One bold play in the cafeteria on the first day of tenth grade changed everything. It wasn't supposed to go down like that. Kim was fat. She was always riding on Mark. It was supposed to be a light jab thrown at a common enemy to secure a friendship. Instead it made Lester.

"Yo, Weasel!"

Lester heard it at least ten times since the altercation at lunch. He knew everyone called him the Weasel. It had been that way since the second grade. It didn't bother him much anymore. He looked like a weasel. It made sense. Incidentally, the attention he received defied compression. Lester lost the fight. It was all rather anti-climactic. The entire episode lasted less than eight seconds from insult to thud. Still, everyone insisted on talking about the school yard tussle. More precisely, they needed to discuss Mark and his latent savagery. The student yarns spun in a centrifuge. Already the resonant thumping sound of the Weasel's back smacking the floor had amplified into a thunder clap that shook the surrounding tables.

Lester wondered if he should have thrown that double hammer punch after all. An offering to his peers of something living to dissect.

Lester had a study hall following lunch. He sat at his desk in the back of the classroom randomly flipping through his Earth Science textbook. Every couple of minutes one of his classmates would glance in his direction and throw him a smile.

After the fourth or fifth look his way Lester remembered that he didn't like the outfit he wore. His pants were the wrong color. Lester had his eye out for a pair of jeans he'd noticed Mark wearing right before summer vacation. They were slim fit and dark. They appeared to be black, but if you looked closely enough you could tell they were actually a sleek-looking dark blue, almost mechanical in presentation. Mark had them cuffed at the ankle. They looked good. The weekend before school began, Lester found a pair of knock-offs at Target that cost thirty dollars. They fit well, looked tight with his Chucks, but Lester didn't have the cash. Lester briefly considered stealing the jeans. Then he considered Mr. May. Instead of shoplifting, Lester employed a dual-pronged strategy that consisted of daily visits to the local Salvation Army and nightly prayers begging for the style to appear on the rack in his size. These invocations, like all the rest, went unanswered. The best that God could provide were some obviously dark blue Gap throwaways. They fit all right, but every time Lester looked down at his pants he would see the wrong color.

Lester wore the Gap specials along with a white Hanes t-shirt with yellow armpit stains. Together they made up his showcase, first-day-of-school ensemble. He could tell he was wearing them, both the incorrect jeans and an armpit-stained shirt. He worried that others could, too.

Lester was freed from his meditations on style when Todd slid into the classroom to chat with the study hall monitor, Mr. Karl. The entire room had their eyes on the exchange.

Lester didn't like Todd. He reminded Lester of everything wrong with both high school and humans in general. Lester had witnessed how Todd treated his classmates. He was demeaning and hurtful.

Lester was equally disgusted with how everyone treated Todd. And not just the students, they were idiots by default. The faculty also smiled at and fawned over Todd. The English teacher, Mr. Courtney, would say "Yo, Todd!" as they passed each other in the hallway. He went out of his way, if Todd was out of earshot, skipping after him like a momentarily lost child who'd spotted his mother at the supermarket. It wasn't right. Even the principal had given Todd a high-five this morning as he parted the lobby doors. Todd was being ushered into a life of reassurance and esteem by the same people who constantly antagonized Lester.

Lester didn't mind that Todd was taller or better looking than he was. That was the luck of the draw. The genetic lottery. Lester understood that his father was a weaselly little twerp, so Lester, in turn, was a weaselly little twerp. In theory, Lester could have been a stud, an Adonis, if only his dad had fucked some kind of Amazon woman the night he let his half of Lester loose. That didn't happen. From what Lester could recall of his mother, she wasn't from the Amazon. Shit, she was barely a woman. She was best described as a bridge dweller. Though she wasn't to be confused with the bearded, troll-type from the lore of children's tales, it was a literal description. If you met her and she happened to mention that she lived under a bridge, you just wouldn't be surprised.

Lester's mother was a fuck-ugly, chain-smoking, logo-t-shirt-wearing, scratch-off queen. But all of this, each wholesome detail, was mere speculation derived from both Lester's dream-like memories and his father's poorly preserved photographs. What Lester knew for certain about his mother was that when she died, if she wasn't dead already, her bowels would evacuate. Lester could practically smell the rot.

Todd had won the genetic lottery, fine. Let him have it. What aggravated Lester was the doubling down. Todd already had what he had, so now let him work it like the rest of us to see what else he could acquire. No high-fives from the principal on the first day of school just for blessing us with his presence. No football freebies on tests. No unwarranted interest and obsequious smiles amidst pedestrian anecdotes. Wasn't it enough that every kid in the school was up his ass and on his dick?

By observing how grown-ups acted around kids like Todd, Lester realized adults were idiots, too. It was obvious that they didn't know any better than the children they were supposed to be guiding. How could they, if they responded to the same social cues? Some may have known better. Some thought that they did. But for the most part adults were insipid, self-obsessed assholes. Lester told Mr. May as much during one of their nightly phone calls.

Mr. May knew a few things and was one of the actual grownups in Lester's life. With his adult mind,

Mr. May had contemplated his own existence and made the conscious choice to better himself for the sake of those around him. In doing so, he let Lester in on what he thought about his peers. Most of the adults Mr. May knew were an emotional mess. Their brains had matured physically, so they were risk averse, but for Mr. May this modulated behavior led to a battery of beer-bellied conservatives who were both ignorant and boring. Most grownups didn't know how to treat one another. They were petty and small, even selfish. They lied to themselves and they cheated others. They stole and got drunk. Many had drug problems. Even more were racist. And "My God, how they followed."

Lester was alternately pleased and troubled to have his suspicions confirmed. He liked the fact that he had something on the adults, but he hadn't realized the rocky depths reached in their communal lake of immaturity. Lester saw the bottom clearly when he had swum around with his dad, but he had wrongly assumed that his father was an exception, an outlier. When one was young, anyone with a car looked put together. And most every adult Lester had known owned a car. Never mind the seventeen-percent interest rate on the principal they could barely afford.

What disturbed Lester most was the revelation that they were all, every last one of them, the good and the bad, insecure. This was a disappointment. Lester didn't like being insecure, and he was relying on age to put it to rest for him. Mr. May informed him that insecurity needed to be recognized, nurtured and finally, marginalized in one's mind. It took a lot of self-actualization to get this done. And even then, doubt, being both unformed and eternal, creeped and clawed its way back inside.

Now Todd, an asshole through-and-through, was having his insecurities worked away for him. Every suck-ass that laughed at one of his corny jokes, every "what's up" uttered by people he didn't recognize, all of it massaged his ego into a relaxed state. His peers needed to have Todd included in their lives. His approval made them feel better about themselves. Todd was placed in a feedback loop of attention and validation, merely because he existed. This behavior allowed him to feel secure in both action and purpose. It would all end, for sure, probably when his youth and looks began to fade. "But damn," thought Lester. "It had to be a fun ride." Lester noticed Todd had been stealing intermittent looks his way since entering the room.

"Fuck Todd," thought Lester.

"Weasel?"

Mr. Karl's voice betrayed a hint of doubt as the "el" at the end of Lester's nickname inflected upwards.

Lester's body froze in estimation. Even his heart paused a beat to assess it's new audience. The entire class turned around to capture the Weasel as both Mr. Karl and Todd cornered their wild beast using only their eyes.

"The principal wants to see you."

Lester collected his school supplies and left them in a neat pile on his desk. Then, with his head slung low, he dragged his feet to the front of the room, where Todd took over the instruction.

"The big guy wants to talk."

Lester hated Todd's cocksure smile. The principal was letting him walk freely around the school. It was annoying. Lester brought his attention back to Mr. Karl.

"Um… Weasel, that's not my…"

Mr. Karl scanned his attendance sheet. A couple of the kids near the front of the class snickered.

"What was your name again?"

"It's Lester."

Todd had his weasel, and his weasel had a name.

"Let's do this, Lester. Time is money."

A few more students chuckled at Todd's cleverness. Apparently proper genetics could also make the tired and clichéd fresh and funny again.

Chapter 28
Give him an ear

Lester followed Todd into the hallway. He was eye-level with Todd's chicken wings. Todd would be tough for Lester to fight. He'd first have to account for Todd's athleticism, strength and speed. The real problem was the weight advantage. Lester could not let Todd get a hold of him. Lester would have to bite his way out if he did. He'd done it before. Lester figured, if it came down to it, he would give Todd back his own ear, literally. The external part of the ear was little more than cartilage fastened to the head by a skin sock. Once you got a grip it took only eight pounds of earthbound torque to detach an ear from its base. While Todd was wallowing in his advantages, Lester would grab his left ear, detach it, and offer it back to Todd. The best way to win a fight was to end it before it began. Holding one's own ear had a way of making anything other than that appendage in your hand seem trite and insignificant.

Lester stayed two steps behind Todd in the hallway. Todd never turned to confirm that Lester was in tow. They just walked in silence, paced by Todd's assured steps.

Adventitious conversation had never been Lester's strong suit. A conversation with Todd, Lester imagined, would be torture. And not because of football, girls or PlayStation; Lester knew nothing about any of these topics, though he assumed Todd was a master in all three. The issue was that Lester had no idea how to talk to Todd. He didn't even know what words to use. It was as if they'd both been taught the same language but the dictionaries they were handed to define each term came with separate definitions. Todd's dialogue rang true to anyone listening. He stated what he meant, and his expressions held significance. Todd was given the benefit of the doubt. Whereas each syllable uttered by Lester was dipped in insecurity and smothered with ambivalence. It was impossible for Lester to articulate an internally valid opinion. To those on the outside, Lester's voice lacked precision precisely because it was Lester who spoke.

Talking to Todd in this instance would have Lester evaluating everything that both he and Todd said. "Am I being a dork?" "Is he being hostile or playful?" Lester couldn't function like that. It was excruciating to second guess each phrase, wondering about its meaning, its subtext and what kind of person would say the things that Lester said. Lester's humor was stunted. It was hard to be off-the-cuff funny when you are worried about how your actual shirt cuffs looked. Confidence was everything. The first step toward others' believing your worth was to believe it yourself. The latter didn't ensure the former, but if you failed to embrace the former you negated any possibility of the latter. Lester knew he didn't have the moxie to go quip-for-quip with Todd. He didn't have enough inside to explain to Todd what he had for breakfast. Lester felt his devaluation in the empty space between them.

What confused Lester was that his lack of confidence wasn't uniformly dispersed. Sometimes he could converse with anyone. It depended on his mood and who he was interacting with. For instance, Lester was not worried about how he would be perceived by Mark, this afternoon notwithstanding. This was one of the reasons he'd chosen to befriend Mark. He felt comfortable enough to talk to him. They had a few conversations when Lester first moved in, over the fence and on the corner of Lester's cross street. Their frequency lessened as Lester's yard increasingly filled with shit, eventually ceasing altogether. But there had been a comfort level. Lester felt he could be himself.

In the end, none of it mattered. Lester was right where he belonged, walking behind a complete ass hat on his way to meet the principal over a fight in which he never participated. Lester was certain he'd be suspended. The Weasel was always to blame, even when it wasn't.

Chapter 29
Empathy

Ashley was trapped in the back seat of Vanessa's black Lexus RX, sitting bitch between Laurie and Caitlin. Matt sat shotgun. They were all seniors except for Ashley, and they were all attractive. The five of them made up what was essentially the cool-chick-clique at Lake Side High. Ashley could have been friends with anyone. Everyone wanted her so Ashley selected the tier with the most advantages.

Mark and Umed used to be her best friends. Back then it wasn't about tiers, nor advantages. Ashley, Mark and by default Umed, were the most popular kids in junior high, but they weren't a clique, they were neighbors.

"All I'm sayin' is, who knew he had it in him?"

Matt spoke with an effeminate affect. Matt was gay. He was a bit of a diva, but everyone liked him. Ashley questioned whether he'd been born with that sassy timbre or had just picked it up and put it on one day. Not that either possibility bothered her. Ashley sometimes wondered about the lavender linguistics some gay men threw around. More specifically, who took them on first? She imagined a hot and popular gay guy in a seedy New York bar, pre gay rights, just talking like a bitch. Then all his sycophant friends thinking it cool and taking it mainstream. Again, it didn't matter; she was just curious. What mattered to Ashley was what Matt was saying, not how he said it.

"Hot and capable."

The three girls in Ashley's periphery giggled at Matt's evaluation of Mark. Ashley was disgusted. They were discussing Mark, and they were having a good time of it. Mark was supposed to be untouchable in the bad Indian kind of way. It was Ashley's doing, and it was a work of art. She had painted the first brush stroke of her masterpiece back at the beginning of ninth grade. Mark put up little resistance, and by Christmas his portrait was despised by everyone of consequence.

Ashley knew enough about shit-talking at lunch not to give Matt the high-sign. He was having too much fun. The only reason her plan worked as well as it had was because others wanted to please her. But if she came off as a bitch about it, insisting that others bend to her will, the entire affair could backfire in her face. As beloved as she was, Ashley could not stop juicy teenage gossip from whirling around the school. She had to let it run its course and then handle the damage control as it petered out.

"Fuck Matt," she thought with an audible groan.

Matt stole a glance at Ashley. He saw her pout. He knew she was pissed. He liked it.

"Fuck Ashley," thought Matt.

Out of the corner of her eye Ashley noticed Matt's snarky smile. Or maybe she could just imagine it. Either way, it was apparent he was enjoying himself. She assumed the other passengers in the car, her girlfriends, were just having fun discussing a hot topic. She hoped, anyway. What the hell did she know? Ashley was new to this crew. She'd only joined recently, after hooking up with Todd. Ashley had been around Matt long enough to know with some confidence that he was being a prick. She wanted to punch him in the gay face. Ashley couldn't. Todd could.

Ashley remembered, Todd could.

Ashley was conflicted about the entire situation with Todd. She didn't love him. She didn't even know if she liked him. She was attracted to him. Everyone was. It was impossible not to be. Deep blue eyes, long and wavy brown hair, negative body fat and a monster in the weight room. He was both gorgeous and a total badass. Physically Todd was the complete package. But Ashley didn't love him. Her dad didn't like him at all. He had told her as much, and it wasn't the senior/sophomore sex thing either. She was sure that was part of it, but Ashley's parents had been progressive enough to openly disregard the virtues of abstinence.

When she was in fifth grade Ashley overheard her dad conversing with Mark's father. The Brunson's had been invited over for dinner and drinks, a regular occurrence before the accident. Mark was sleeping at Umed's. Ashley had acting class early in the morning, so she was stuck at home in her own bed. She couldn't sleep. It bothered her that she missed the slumber party. Around midnight, driven by a mixture of both boredom and spite, Ashley crawled quietly from her room to the top of the stairs to eavesdrop on the adults. The four of them were pretty drunk by then and the conversation flowed with spirits. They were discussing Mark, Ashley and the sleepover, and how Ashley was upset about having to stay home. Her father wondered if it all had to stop soon anyway due to the impending onset of puberty. Mark's dad jokingly responded, "What, my Mark is not good enough for your daughter?" Ashley's father laughed and said, "Of course he is."

Mark's dad went on to suggest to Ashley's dad that his daughter would be having sex eventually. Not that he should send his cherished offspring off to be double teamed by Mark and Umed, but that, at some point, he would need to come to terms with it.

This is the part of the conversation that Ashley could not forget. Her father said that he and his wife had come to terms with it years ago. Not only that, they wanted her to have sex and a lot of it. Not in a slutty way, although he questioned the validity of that term, but in a life-is-short and sex-is-great kind of way. They wanted Ashley to enjoy her existence, to be happy and well-adjusted through all of it. As avant-garde as Ashley's father had been with his daughter's chastity, he did harbor some reservations. Although he had no issue with her having sex in general, he was concerned with whom she did it with. And whatever, she didn't need to set up an ethics advisory board and a credit check for every one-night stand, but "God damn," he hoped the person she went to dinner with at least held the restaurant door open for her, and kept it open for the elderly couple bringing up the rear. Someone with character and empathy.

Ashley remembered scrambling back to her room to look up that word, empathy. She was not sure that Todd had a whole bunch of it. Her father didn't think he had any. But he would not stop his daughter from seeing Todd. He trusted her. For her part, Ashley did not want to hurt her father so she questioned why she was with Todd at all. The answer always came back to Mark.

Ashley was concerned at times by how much of her life was devoted to making Mark's life miserable. She had other interests, other thoughts. She had her favorite cousin in Virginia, her father, her mother, college and acting. Did Mark's existence consume her? It was not like every waking moment of Ashley's was dedicated to Mark's misery. She thought it was comparable to playing an instrument. In her free time, when she wasn't acting or at the movies with her dad, or doing her homework, she would practice her flute. She wasn't attempting to become a pro flautist, but she did expect competency. Something for her transcripts. Ashley likened Mark to another instrument of hers. When time permitted, she was playing him towards the misery he deserved. Todd was her mouthpiece. He was the best mouthpiece money could buy, and Ashley had a lot of currency with men. She felt badly about this, but she didn't see a choice. She knew Todd was all twisted up about her. He wanted to fuck her from every which way. But they hadn't yet. They made out and he had played with her titties and what not, but that was it. She purposely kept their dates short and sporadic. They had been seeing each other the entire summer, yet they'd only hung out ten times. Todd was losing his mind over her.

They were supposed to be at Taco Bell right now. Ashley had planned on going before she heard about the fight in the cafeteria. She was even prepared to strip down to her underwear and jerk Todd off in the parking lot. Ashley was interested to see what Todd's dick looked like anyway. She wanted to know how big it was.

Ashley also had to determine if she could lose her virginity to Todd. Ashley wasn't against casual sex, but this was different. They were dating, and she wasn't sure if Todd was man enough to hold open the door for her. Not that he wouldn't, Christ, Todd would eat a door for Ashley if she were to ask. It was just that the door should be held open because Ashley was a person walking toward a closed door, not because Ashley was a girl who Todd wanted to fuck after the door was closed.

Ashley would have to figure it all out later. First, she needed to locate her expensive mouthpiece.

Chapter 30
The South Gym

Todd's felt his phone vibrating in his pocket. He knew it was Ashley before he looked at the screen. Life seemed to work that way for Todd. It never got too dark between each sunrise. The text read:

sorry about the bell :(where are you now?

Todd smiled and put his phone away. He knew how to play the game. It was challenging, but he had to stick to the rules. For now, anyway, while he still had a chance to win. Besides, Todd wasn't done with Lester, and he wanted to share his plans with Ashley when they were completed.

Lester was still a solid length of dog's leash behind Todd. They hadn't spoken. Specifically, Todd hadn't said anything to Lester. For Lester's part, it just wasn't possible for him to start a conversation with Todd. He could not imagine a single utterance that would hold any sway in Todd's reality. Lester noticed that they had passed the corridors that led to the principal's office a few stairwells back. He didn't say anything. How could he?

They made their way down to the old wing, and without much thought Lester followed Todd into south gym. Thirty years ago the south gym served as both a gymnasium and an auditorium. By the mid-nineties both the physical education and the theater departments had their own dedicated buildings. The south gym was left to atrophy like an exsanguinated appendage. With his first steps onto the lusterless hardwood floor, Lester perked up. The gym was empty, an arena without an audience. Lester's insecurities made way for his fight instincts. He briefly thought about fleeing, but his urge to hand Todd his own ear kept him from making the dash. Once Lester recognized there was more to this stroll than a mere peasant touring the kingdom with its illustrious prince, his confidence level took a boost. This unexpected detour had the potential for lowborn abuse and inescapable violence. Lester was comfortable with both. Maybe Mr. May had backed the wrong horse after all.

As he approached mid-court Lester noticed the grand enormity of the stage curtains. He was stunned that this formerly majestic tapestry was left to rot on its tracks as it hung heavy and rank with the odor of moth wings and exfoliated skin cells. It seemed wasteful like a lone woman masturbating in the bathroom of a strip club. The curtains were drawn except for a slight part at their center. Through the seam Lester saw a row of defunct vending machines and the discarded scenery from a 1992 performance of The Little Shop of Horrors. Lester also noticed a black steel pipe that was threaded at both ends and about the length of his forearm. It lay in front of the curtain at the fore of the stage, readily accessible. Maybe Lester wouldn't have to take an ear to get out of this situation. Five pounds of galvanized steel could easily leverage his handicap in the weight department. A mechanical advantage.

Todd continued toward the stage. In stride, and with a twist, he hopped up and sat on the apron. It was impressive. He was impressive. Lester wasn't worried. Todd's confidence would be his undoing. Todd had no idea what Lester was, what he could be. Lester felt good in the south gym. He had to remember to return on his own time. The space was large, old and useless. The stage was dirty and banal. Lester felt at home. He imagined spending his nights on the fatigued and dust-coated platform. He would wrap himself in the once resplendent curtain and breathe in its dandruff and gloom. It would be his cocoon.

The last of Lester's insecurities expelled with his breath. It was a wispy exhale, almost a hiss. He knew exactly what to say.

"Where the fuck's the principal?"

Lester was released. This was no longer a toddle through the halls two steps behind his better. This was an empty, out-of-the-way room intended for both theater and sport.

The unexpected expletive had no effect on Todd. He was secure in his place.

"Don't know. Don't care."

Lester took a step toward the pipe. There was no need for tact. Todd had no idea what lay ahead.

"What's up with Mark?"

Lester stopped. He had forgotten about Mark. In the beginning he had assumed that all of this was about Mark. Lester being blamed for another fight he had nothing to do with. But once they'd entered the gym he had thought only about this fight – the now fight with the ear and the steel pipe.

"Mark?"

"Yeah, Mark. Last period?"

Lester's chest deflated. They were conversing. Todd was comfortable on his stage. He looked like he owned it. But it wouldn't be a home for Todd. He wouldn't hide beneath its curtains late at night. Maybe Todd would piss in one of its corners after finishing an IPA at lunch.

Lester searched himself for the right words, any words that a human being would say. Casual, unannotated words for basic intra-species communication.

"Yeah, no. It was nothing."

Todd's phone vibrated in his pocket. Its hum and rumble were muffled by his tight-fitting Diesel jeans. Lester noticed that they were the right color. Lester looked at Todd's pocket. Todd paid the gadget no mind he just stared at his new friend with a lopsided smile. Lester was the focus of Todd's attention, and Todd wasn't finished playing with his pet weasel.

"What was nothing?"

Lester wondered if the curtains would pull from their moors if he wrapped himself up too tightly.

"He just slammed me down on the floor is all."

"Did it hurt?"

Lester was embarrassed. He should have fought back. "Fuck, Mark," he thought.

"Yeah, a little I guess."

That was a lie. Lester had felt nothing. Nothing compared to now. It was painful to stretch for the answers that would satisfy Todd. Lester's brain swelled from all its machinations.

"Why'd he do it?"

Lester could not sustain eye contact with Todd. Quick glances, like trying to get a peek at the sun, were all he could muster. He felt the onset of tears as his vision blurred and the blood rushed to his face. Lester closed his eyes and bowed his head.

"I called... I asked him who the fat chick was."

Todd didn't respond. He just furrowed his brow. With his head down, Lester stole a nostalgic peek at the steel pipe. He wondered if it was warm to the touch. Metal could be warm sometimes. He hoped it was warm.

Todd laughed. He fell back laughing. His bellows filled the gym. Lester looked around to see if anyone was near enough to catch the echoes. They were alone. He took the moment to wipe his eyes dry. Todd sat back up using only his sculpted core.

"Haaaaa. Aaahhh. Kim? Was he with Kim?"

Lester smiled. He liked it when Todd laughed.

"Yeah, I think that's her."

Another lie. Lester knew exactly who Kim was. He always had.

"Ha. Yeah. Kim's the fat chick. That's classic."

"Yeah I was... I saw she was fat 'n all and I was like…"

Lester's enthusiasm abated with the leveling of Todd's smile. The words weren't there anymore. Lester was betrayed by his own insignificance.

"She's fat."

It was barely audible, but that was all that Lester had left inside.

Todd dropped off the stage and skipped past his little weasel. He didn't talk to or look at Lester. When he reached the top of the key, he spoke without turning around.

"I'm gonna' fuck him up for you, Weasel. I'm gonna' fuck him up... for you."

Chapter 31
A Chance Encounter

The bench Mark chose to lie down on was narrow, only half as wide as his back. Mark had no fear of falling off, thanks to the fresh coat of lacquer gabbing at his clothes and adhering their threads to the pine. The custodial staff refinished the locker room benches each summer to fill in the anatomically indifferent cocks and pussies hewn into their surfaces over the course of the school year. This treatment worked fine for the light scratches, but if a student was tenacious enough to carve down into the meat of the wood, the fresh coat of lacquer immortalized the profanity creating, over time, a gallery of lowbrow etchings.

Mark, lost in an endless line of interconnected thoughts searching for a cohesive score, had closed his eyes for a brief moment when his sentience had slipped away. His mind began to play, to tinker with his subconscious. Mark wasn't sleeping deeply enough to ignite a real dream. What he experienced was closer to a black consciousness with a story reel. Within the narrative of this daydream Mark's mom was dead and two police officers were discussing their options for her removal from his house. Mark enjoyed the offering. He thought that both officers were kind and that he might want to be a cop after he finished college.

Mark awoke suddenly and with contentment. After briefly collecting his thoughts, he checked his phone. It was ten to one. The period was nearly over, and Mark needed to show face in shop class before the bell rang. On the first day of school, with the proper excuse, there was a decent chance he could avoid a cut slip.

Mark exited the locker room and turned right down the hall towards Lake Side High's proper wing. As he passed the entrance to the south gym, he stopped. A mobile mass had caught his eye. Mark's legs locked as he looked to his left. Todd stood proud in the narrow corridor that bridged the hallway and the south gym. It was an odd sight. Mark rarely saw anyone near the gym. What made it surreal was that behind Todd, across the basketball court, standing by the stage, was Lester. It didn't make any sense.

"What's up, faggot?"

Todd had to control himself. He was aching to act. He wanted to pummel Mark with every ounce of his tingling flesh. Todd envisioned repeatedly bashing Mark's face against the blue-toned cinder block wall that cased the hallway. Todd realized at that moment he wanted to disfigure Mark. He knew Mark was attractive, but there in the lower level of the south wing it occurred to Todd that he was actually stunning: almost a male version of Ashley. Todd wondered why he had failed to notice Mark's sublime looks in the past. He wondered if Mark's insignificance at school had somehow masked his naked beauty.

Ashley used to be with Mark. She had told Todd as much. They had been boyfriend and girlfriend since sixth grade, when prepubescent desire transitioned into awkward inclination. They never fucked or anything, but Mark did feel her up one afternoon in the forest behind her house. Ashley told Todd all of this. Why? He didn't remember asking or even caring. But now, with all of Mark's beauty before him, Todd cared.

"Hey."

Mark didn't understand why he had said that, "Hey." Todd wasn't being playful when he asked, "What's up." He certainly meant the "faggot" part. But Mark had said "hey" anyway. Maybe because it was easier just to be friends. Friends with Todd, with Kim and with Lester. Friends with Ashley. "Hey, guys. What's up?" It was terribly easy. It would be easy, too, if Mark's mom wasn't a fat packrat. That would be simple. "Hey, Mom, I like that we can use the kitchen without starting a fire." Or "Hey, Mom, I love that when I hug you I can clasp my hands around your back." It was supposed to be carefree, all of it.

"Hey yourself, homo."

Todd descended the four stairs that led down from the gym and into the hallway. He stopped and stood at Mark's toes. Mark was beautiful and big, maybe only an inch or so shorter than Todd. And he had felt Ashley's tits. Todd wanted to break all his fingers. The air surrounding the two of them was electric, ready to pop. Both Todd and Mark could hear a fresh buzzing in their ears until, instantaneously, Lester released all of the tension.

"You butt humpers gonna' kiss, or what?"

While engaged in a spirited session of gesticular masturbation, Lester skipped by both of his antagonists and up the stairs leading back to the main building. Both Todd and Mark were momentarily stunned. Who knew Lester had it in him? Together they were four times his size. Todd regained his composure with a wink and a smile.

"Nah, we ain't gonna' kiss, are we, Mark?"

Lester had left. There was no one around to impress. Todd's threats were for Mark's pleasure alone. Mark had no idea what to do. Thankfully, Todd had it all worked out for both of them. With fluidity and vigor, Todd grabbed Mark by the face and mushed him towards the cinder blocks. Mark was caught off guard, but he reacted quickly. He was able to get his back foot out before he hit the wall.

"Nice foot work, homo. We could use you on the field."

That was it. Todd turned and walked back up the stairs toward the main wing of the building.

Mark was confused. He had been waiting for this confrontation since Todd and Ashley began dating. He agonized over this exact moment while dreading its inevitability, yet it passed with a smattering of words and a face mush. The entire incident ended so quickly that Mark never found any time to be afraid.

Chapter 32
Yarboled

Jason hated the Special Ed wing. He detested walking down the halls with the ree-rees and the ass-burgers. He wasn't intellectually disabled, nor was he on the spectrum. Jason was deaf, and not even fully so. He used a hearing aid and he could read the lips on a fly from across the room. Jason could readily communicate with anyone willing to look him in the eye. His speech was a bit yarboled, but he rarely had to repeat himself. Nevertheless, Jason's guidance counselor insisted that he attend a resource room once a day to go over his notes. Since Mrs. MacCarin's skills were most useful with the A-bergs, Jason was forced to spend seventh period in the south wing. Even today, the first day of school, he had to make the disparaging trip. Jason would slip into Mrs. Mac's classroom late and slide out early to avoid the crowded halls in-between periods. Jason had been called a ree-ree on more than one occasion, and if being deaf hindered his chance at getting laid, being considered a retard guaranteed years of silent, lonely masturbation.

As per his arrangement with Mrs. Mac, Jason left a few minutes before the end of seventh period. Even though Mrs. MacCarin's class was located on the third floor of the old wing, Jason liked to walk the back way down the stairs to the lowest level that led to the lockers and the south gym. From there he spanned the hall, then took the stairs up into the main, normal corridors of the school. This way if anyone spotted him, at first glance they would associate his presence with the gym or the lockers instead of the Special-Eds. Jason noticed random students on the wrestling team ascend from the south tier's lower level five times a day during their winter weight watch. Not one of them appeared to be special.

Jason spotted a full pack of Bazooka Joe gum lying in the stairwell between the second and third floors. He left it there. On any other staircase he would have considered it a score; a small treasure in a life full of empty chests. But not in this stairwell, not even for his favorite gum.

Jason was sure it was some short busser's and that they had gummed it up with their "tard-o" hands. He watched them, all of them, pick their noses all day, every day. Not a minute went by without one of them having a finger knuckle deep in nostril hair.

Even Mrs. Mac took steps to protect herself from all of the booger baiters. She kept a dedicated closet replete with tissues, wet wipes and hand sanitizer. Nothing freaked Jason out more than boogers, with the lone exception of retarded boogers. Jason had already considered the facts. If a man held a gun to his head and told him he had to eat a snot sandwich or take a bullet to the brain, he'd undoubtedly pull the trigger himself.

It was decided. Jason would leave the pack of Bazooka Joe gum exactly where it lay, unmolested, for a man of less discriminating taste to discover.

Jason had nearly descended the final staircase leading to the south gym corridor when he was stopped cold. At the other end of the hallway Jason beheld a genuine south tier anomaly. Todd was there, Mark was there, and that little rat faced kid was saying something to the both of them. Jason couldn't make it out, but both Mark and Todd looked somewhat surprised by the comment. Moments after the Weasel left, Jason watched as Todd got right up into Mark's shit, said something, again Jay had no idea what. Then Todd violently mashed Mark in the face.

Jason was shocked. He glanced up and around to see if anyone else had witnessed the event. The halls were empty. Jason had the only seats available for the fight of the year.

Todd was a monster. Jason had not been at the pit when Todd fought Cogal, but he watched the fight on YouTube thirty-three times. And Mark was the toughest kid Jason knew. Jason had never actually seen nor heard about a fight with Mark, but everyone was scared of him. Jason wasn't scared of him. Not that he could take Mark in a fight or anything. He couldn't. Jason wasn't afraid because Mark was always so kind to him.

Starting in sixth grade and lasting until the accident, once every couple of days, Mark would invite Jason to sit with him, Ashley and Umed during lunch. They would talk, and Jay would listen with his eyes and what God had left him for ears. Every few minutes Mark would ask Jason a direct question, always taking care to locate the pupils of his deaf guest before he spoke. Jason loved every second of his lunch with Mark. There was no set day for the invitation. It happened around once each week depending on Mark's mood. Jason could hardly stand still on the lunch line while he anticipated the potential offer. He wondered each day if *this* would be the day. The day Mark, in front of the entire cafeteria, said to him, "Yo, Jay! Sit with us." Jason always waited for the invite. He thought maybe he could sit there every day without being asked, as a friend or what not, but he wasn't sure. Mark had never said so, and as much as he wanted it, Jay would not risk his one glorious day a week by being presumptuous. Jason was enamored with Mark. Not in a gay way, but certainly in some way that involved the love of one man for another. Sometimes after they ate, one of Jason's less popular friends would ask him about the lunch and what they discussed. But they never asked about Mark – it was always about Ashley, what she said and what she ate. Jason never had a good answer for them. Ashley was there and she was polite, and yes, pretty, but Mark was the reason he sat with them and Mark received all of his attention. No one ever asked him about the Indian kid. Jason barely looked at him.

Jason hopped up a few steps to the landing and crouched down behind the newel post for a better view. He couldn't wait. Todd would probably kill Mark, but it would be a great fight and an even better story. Just as Jason got into position, it ended. Todd had walked away. Mark stood there for a moment, watched Todd leave, and when Jason supposed Mark thought Todd was far enough away, Mark left, too. Jason was disappointed. Another empty chest.

Jason sat on the top step for a minute and huffed. The bell was still four minutes away. Without realizing it, he had his finger crammed up his snout. He was going for a big one. Jason pulled the snot ball out of his nose and prepped it for analysis. It was, all at once, brown, red, green and translucent. It trailed back to his nostril connected by a long and oozy stream. Jason had dug out a lot of boogers like the one presently glommed to his index finger. Especially in the winter, when his father insisted on heating the house with a wood burning stove. Jason stood up, and without looking around he deliberately wiped the booger on the banister, making sure to let its mire trail down the surface and sort itself into the grain of the oak.

Chapter 33
Plate Glass Lunch

Ashley skipped the restaurant. She sat in the rear seat of Vanessa's Lexus while her friends ate Chinese food and laughed. They looked her way every few bites and smiled through the large plate of glass that kept all the Chinese inside yet visible. The glass was crafted to be perfectly transparent, but it possessed a slight opaqueness, like someone smeared the pane with a thin layer of Vaseline. Ashley was happy she didn't have to cook Chinese food for a living. The whole place just seemed cramped and greasy. She noticed one of her classmates, Hon, behind the glass. Hon should have been in class. It was her first day of tenth grade, too. Instead, she was taking Matt's order and serving Caitlin her tofu. Someone had to work the register. Not Ashley.

Ashley's father had a lot of money. She was pretty sure her dad had installed the glass window through which she was watching Hon serve her friends. In fact, Ashley's father, along with Mark's dad, had overseen the construction of the entire complex that housed How May Kitchen and several other small shops. They made a lot of money that year. More than they needed. More than Hon needed, too.

Todd hadn't responded to any of Ashley's texts. He did that sometimes. Todd needed to be in control. It was annoying, but Ashley understood. At least she thought she understood. It was some sort of game. He had to make the right moves so that she would respect him. But what Todd didn't understand was that Ashley was not playing with him. She didn't want his respect. That was not true. She wanted his respect, but she didn't need it. If he didn't respect her, she would just leave. For Ashley, there weren't any rules or any moves to be made, only simple decisions.

Ashley had watched her friends stress out over guys before, and not just her ugly friends. Ashley understood how attractive she was. She understood its advantages. But Ashley wasn't the only pretty girl in town. She witnessed Kendal, a girl who could be a model, or at least some random chick in a commercial, lose her shit over some dimwit named Greg. Greg hadn't texted her in three days and Kendal didn't understand what it all meant. Fuck Greg. It was all so perfectly simple.

Caitlin was first to finish eating and join Ashley in the car. She handed Ashley a takeout tin with the remains of her garlic tofu and rice before buckling her seat belt.

"I couldn't finish."

"Thanks."

Ashley didn't want Caitlin's tofu, but she also didn't want to be impolite. She opened the container and took a few bites. It wasn't so bad. Hon's family consistently made respectable meals.

Matt got in next, followed by Vanessa and Laurie.

"Did he text back?"

Matt really was a dick. Ashley knew for certain that was not an affect. Before she even thought to tell Matt that he needed to die, Ashley's phone buzzed in her lap. She held her cell up with her left hand and gave Matt the middle finger with her right.

"Eeww, she is feisty this afternoon, ladies."

Todd apologized. Of course he apologized. Ashley wasn't even sure Todd comprehended the rules of the game he was supposed to be playing. He also wrote that he needed to see her. That worked out well because she needed to see him, too. Ashley didn't know exactly what she intended to say to Todd, but he had to squelch all this gossip about Mark. For Ashley it was imperative that Mark be returned to his status as a non-entity. Ashley wondered if she wanted Mark to hurt, to bleed, the way Cogal did at the pit.

"Why are you with that brute, anyway? I mean he's hot 'n all, but he's such a dude."

Ashley ignored Matt's question. She was being feisty. At that moment she was scrolling through the contacts on her phone. It was a long list. Ashley's thumb liked to hover over Mark's name. Ashley had never erased his old number, nor the photo attached to it. The picture was from two years ago. Mark was cute then, too. Skinny, a little dorky, but cute.

Vanessa started her car. Ashley shut her phone off and dropped the container holding the remainder of Caitlin's tofu out of the car window. Hon, through the greasy plate of glass, watched as her family's livelihood splattered in the parking lot. Ashley leaned out of the Lexus just a bit and pointed at Hon. Then she pointed at the tofu and garlic sauce scattered on the pavement before sliding back in the car and buckling up her seat belt.

Matt didn't say anything. None one did. Ashley was being feisty.

Chapter 34
A Thing at Camp

Mark arrived at shop class two minutes before the bell rang. He informed Mr. Garrison that regrettably, during lunch, he had left his backpack and phone at Utter Delight Deli and noticed them missing only after returning to school. He also relayed that he was unable to find a friend with a car and was left with no other choice but to walk all the way back to the deli and retrieve his belongings. Mr. Garrison remained unmoved by Mark's tale of misfortune. He responded that he didn't care for any excuse other than grave injury or death and that Mark could take up the matter with the AP's office.

Without arguing Mark took his seat for the last sixty seconds of the period and waited for the bell. He had to think. Maybe he could head back to the south gym lockers. He was already written up, why not double down and give himself time to figure things out? He would either avoid punishment for both cuts or get written up for skipping class. Since he was present for more than half the school day, cutting out on one period or bailing on the remainder of the afternoon held the same consequence, an extended detention; two-and-a-half hours in the pink room after school.

The pink room was in the same wing as the south gym. It was one floor above the locker room where Mark had just laid low. The room was located smack in the middle of the Special-Ed department and it served as a de facto prison for all of Lake Side High's unsavory inhabitants. Mark never actually had detention, but he had caught a glimpse of the pseudo-cell on one of his many strolls through the old building. Apparently, the walls were pink due to an article published in a scientific journal that a former student read way back in the 90s. The study examined the soothing tone of flesh-colored space. With documentation in hand, she finagled a small stipend for the supplies and painted the room herself. It was a genuine gesture on the behalf of her classmates, but it left the walls looking like the inside of a Pepto-Bismol bottle. If the color was soothing, Mark did not care to find out. Then again, two hours of free study sounded a hell of a lot better than "not kissing" Todd.

Todd had always antagonized Mark, even before he hooked up with Ashley, but never physically. Todd was happy to rail on the one kid in school who could possibly challenge his title as hotshot quarterback. When Mark started on the freshman squad, Todd would give him shit from the JV side of the locker room. Nothing too real, but he made sure Mark's promotion was more uncomfortable than it needed to be.

But why was Todd with Lester in the south gym? Why had it suddenly come to a face mush in the hall? It undoubtedly had to do with Mark's outburst in the cafeteria. Everyone was talking about it. Pat Berkley had just called Mark a "killer" in the hallway as they passed each other on Mark's way to class. Mark caused a minor stir as he entered the shop room comprised of stares, glares, giggles and whispers. Word had spread. Mark was a badass. It was gospel.

Mark did not understand why everyone cared so much. All of it over a scuffle with Lester at lunch. The fuckin' Weasel. If that kid didn't look exactly like an anthropomorphic rat, no one would have a frame of reference as to who he even was. He was a nobody. Not even a pariah like Mark. He existed as nothing other than a face (granted a face with character) in the background. Mark was certain Lester hadn't even spoken with anyone since he moved to town. Lester sat by himself in every class, ate lunch alone, and just failed to engage. The only reason Mark knew he lived and breathed was the whole neighbor thing. That and the god-damned Converse.

This wasn't about Lester at all. It couldn't be. It was about Mark. As the bell rang, Mark realized just how effective Ashley had been at marginalizing him. Mark was supposed a thing. His classmates wanted to talk to him, talk about him. People wanted to be around him. Ashley stopped all that. And Mark had allowed it to happen.

Mark recalled summer camp in between the sixth and seventh grades. It was sold to him as a two-week sleep away experience. Mark's mother and father had planned a vacation to Paris and they didn't want Mark tagging along. It was supposed to be their romantic getaway. Looking back, Mark was sure the trip had been purposed to rekindle the spark in their dimming relationship. Mark didn't want to go to camp. He wanted to stay home with either Ashley or Umed, but Mark's father felt it was too long of an imposition. Besides, Mark's dad was excited about the summer camp. He had attended Camp Edey when he was Mark's age. He had slept there and made a couple of great friends in the process. Mark's father thought he could recreate the experience for his son. Mark wanted nothing to do with it, but he didn't have a say on the subject.

When he arrived at camp Mark decided to protest his lack of agency by refusing to participate for the entire two weeks. For three days Mark spoke to no one. He sat brooding on the sidelines during each event and insisted on eating lunch by himself. A faraway gaze or a stink eye met any attempt at an overture from the counselors. His plan worked just fine until Ally, one of the cute blonds from the girl's side of camp, slipped him a note at the picnic bench he designated as his central protest station. Ally giggled as she dropped the artistically folded slip of paper on the table in front of him before skipping away with a screech. Mark opened up the note. It read: you're cute! There were hearts everywhere and it was signed by seven different girls. Mark looked back over his shoulder. There were a dozen girls standing by the rec-room, giggling and swooning in his general direction.

Nick, a random boy at camp, noticed the entire set-up, from note drop to swoon. He asked Mark what the letter said. Mark handed it over with a proud smile. Nick was impressed. He called over his buddy Seth to examine the heart-lined sheet of paper. Before the afternoon was up, the entire camp knew about the love letter. Mark couldn't brood alone at his picnic bench anymore. No one would let him. Seth, Nick and the rest of the boys begged Mark to participate during each event. The fact that he dominated in every way only helped to grow his legend. After a game of pick-up football, Mark was decreed a camp god. All the boys wanted Mark to set up dates with him and the other girls. Double dates and triple dates. He was forced to lead a brigade of randy, tween boys to the girl's side of camp after lights out. The clandestine operation culminated in a massive game of spin the bottle and a half-hearted reprimand from the counselors when they were caught. It was fun, but Mark had no choice in the matter. He was a thing at camp.

Seth told Mark two days before they left that he overheard the two hot counselors, Charlotte and Mandy, talking about how cute Mark had been. They agreed that they should look him up in a couple of years when he was of a less creepy age. That incident actually pushed Nick over the edge. Every boy in camp drooled over both Charlotte and Mandy. For the final two days Nick was hostile to Mark, either putting him down or ignoring him altogether. Despite the slow start and the rocky finish, Mark wound up having a great time at Camp Edey. He made no lasting friends, but the experience worked wonders for his ego.

Mark's Mother and father weren't as successful in Paris. They came home in the midst of a nasty fight. Mark's Dad actually slept at Ashley's house for the first two nights after their return. It eventually worked itself out, but their marriage was never put back on the right track.

Mark's inevitability as a thing did not bode well for him. Ashley wouldn't stand for it. The next few days promised to be dangerous for Mark. He surmised that the locker room wouldn't provide enough protection. For the first time in almost two years Mark wanted to go home.

Chapter 35
Wedding Bells

The moment the bell rang Mark broke for his locker. He thought about skipping out right there and then, but he had left his phone in the front pocket of his backpack. You weren't allowed to carry a cell during school hours. No one listened. Students texted and played games throughout the day. Most teachers did their best to ignore a random text or two, but if a student insisted on burying their face in their phone, eschewing all other worldly input, they would be asked to put their phone away. In rare circumstances certain teachers would sever and then confiscate the digital appendage until the end of the period. Mr. Bowns liked to collect any scofflaw's cell and keep it locked in his desk for the remainder of the week. Consequently, from Monday through Thursday he had the pleasure of supervising a colony of Luddites. No one dared to power up their screens in his classroom. Mark had little reason to be anything but compliant. He wasn't much for cell games and the Internet genuinely distracted him from his studies. He supposed if he had any friends he would need his phone for communication, but currently this was a non-issue. Mark thought he could do without his phone for the night, but he was not entirely certain when he would return to Lake Side High. He already decided that he was going to be sick Thursday and probably Friday. He would miss the final three periods of the first day of school and the following two full days leading into the weekend. In this way Mark killed two birds with one stone. His absence allowed for the Todd situation to decompress and, at the same time, ghosting both the second and third day of school framed a plausible excuse for not attending shop class. He would instruct his disgusting mom to call the office and inform them that Mark had fallen ill during lunch and would be absent until early next week. She owed him too much to refuse his request.

The halls were buzzing. Mark heard his name being mentioned with each step he took. Through the commotion of the crowd he discerned the impromptu monikers, "weasel killer" and "the exterminator." Mark never slowed his stride. He had devised a solid plan: locker, then home. Mark's sure-footed determination to escape without incident faltered when, through the din of the hallway muster, he heard a classmate calling after him. The echo of his name floating through the corridor had a familiar tone and a comforting acoustic. For an instant Mark was whisked back to junior high when his hallways were carpeted red and the entire school vied for his attention.

Mark was certain it was his name hanging in the air, but there was a phlegmy 'en' sound in the middle of it. He stopped to check it out. He shouldn't have, but at that instant he was curious and maybe a little nostalgic. Mark regretted his fond memories the moment he turned around. It was Jason. Mark had not spoken to Jason in two years, not since the beginning of eighth grade, not since before the accident. He liked it that way. One of the few benefits of being universally despised was the lack of onus that accompanied the hate. Jason was a muted but still onerous responsibility from Mark's past.

Mark anxiously awaited the seven or so ticks for Jason to catch up to him. Around second three he considering bailing before Jen, a cute sophomore wearing slides and denim cutoffs, gave him a long look and a smile. Jen was hot. Mark liked it. Then Jay caught up.

"Sorry, bro. I saw what happened."

"Yeah, it was no big deal. He was being rude to Kim. But listen…"

"Kim? What did Todd do to Kim?"

Mark's irritation morphed into interest.

"Todd? Nothing, why? What are you talking about?"

"In the hall, by the south gym."

"You were there?"

Of course Jason was there, hanging out with the Spec-Eds. Mark thought Jason kind of smelled like the Special-Ed wing. There was something crusty about Jason, like he had a thin blond film in all his crevices that crunched around when he moved.

"Well, yeah, sort of. I was on the stairs."

"Did you tell anyone?"

Jason was discomfited by the stern expression riveted on Mark's face. It was the same mien that Jason's mother wore if she had to repeat herself more than once while conversing with her only child in public. Mark never broke eye contact with Jason when they spoke. It was one of the traits Jason had admired in Mark. He felt engaged and important. Presently, Jason had to avert his eyes as Mark questioned him. He felt threatened and insignificant.

"Oh, no. I wouldn't…"

"Listen, do me a favor, this is no joke. Just keep what you saw to yourself. I can't… I don't want…"

Mark's eyes had softened, he seemed to be pleading. Jason exhaled with a smile.

"Yeah, bro, no problem. We're old lunch buddies. Whatever you need."

Of course this entire back-and-forth between two old friends was punctuated by Jason's gamey, barely comprehensible speech. Mark got it all for the most part. He wasn't sure about the "lunch bunnies." But whatever, right? So long as he kept quiet.

"Look Jay, I got to go. Let's get lunch tomorrow."

"Yeah, sure. Sounds good… I just wanted you to know that I had your back."

Mark was skipping backward and away from Jason as he spoke. The absurdity of what Mark heard forced him to stop.

"What?"

Jason was compelled to look at the ground while he addressed Mark.

"Your back. If Todd did anything, I would have helped you out."

Mark smirked at the sentiment.

"Thanks, Jay."

Jason found encouragement in Mark's charismatic smile.

"Yeah, no problem. You were always really nice."

"Cool, Jay. I gotta' go."

Mark didn't wait for Jason's throaty goodbye. He was practically running down the hall towards his locker. It was great-and-all that Jay had his back. And that he thought Mark was "nice," but what did it matter? The kid was deaf. Who gave a fuck, really?

Running at full speed Mark turned the last corner that led to his locker bank, avoiding any and all collisions that might have occurred. His arm got him the starting quarterback position, but it was his footwork that made him an all-star. Kim waited by his locker.

"Fuck."

It was under his breath, but he meant it. Mark didn't have time to practice the art of accommodation. He sprinted to his stall with his head down and started in on the combo.

"Mark?"

"Hey."

Hey. It was such a breezy and carefree expression. No one seemed to understand this.

"Mark?"

"What?"

That "what" came with an attitude. Mark missed the second number in his combination. He was forced to begin again.

"Mark!"

He stopped fiddling with the dial to look at his most recent impediment. Kim had been crying and her makeup was out of place. Foundation caked her cheeks, while the remainder of her bundt face was frosted with dollops of smudge. It looked horrible. The worst part was that it was old, both the tears and the blotches. They had dried into something hideous. The ledges created by the scrapes and splotches were thick enough to cast shadows. Mark was repulsed.

"You need to fix your shit, Kim."

She was jolted all the way through.

"Wh… what?"

Kim had purposely kept her makeup mussed up to garner sympathy from Mark. She couldn't find him right after lunch, so she waited him out in the girl's lavatory.

"Mar..."

Kim began to cry. Mark went back to his combo. Kim turned and left without saying anything. Mark felt bad, maybe. She should have fixed her face.

Mark opened his locker and grabbed his bag. As he turned to leave, both his feet and his heart were frozen in place. Ashley stood before him. Steve 'The Beave' was beside her. Todd was there, too, and he had taken off his shirt. At that moment Mark wanted Kim and Jason to get married. It was what they deserved. She would put on a lot of makeup and be fat. Jason would constantly complain about the cosmetics and the obesity, but his words would ooze out unintelligibly so Kim wouldn't get upset. They could fall asleep together attempting to discuss how much they loved eating lunch with Mark. It would be beautiful.

"So, we're going to the pit after school. I think you should come."

There was a crowd. Todd with his shirt off was spectacle enough. Todd challenging Mark to the pit, and you could charge admission.

"Thanks for thinking of me, Todd, but I'm busy this afternoon."

Mark was surprised at his composure. He wondered why he had been in such a hurry. Then Ashley spoke.

"What? Your fat, disgusting mom needs a bath?"

Ashley wore a smile on her face, a grin, both crooked and sadistic. It was the simper of a woman asking a man with no arms to caress her naked breasts.

All the color left Mark's face. His eyes were locked into hers. Mark hadn't stared at Ashley for nearly two years. Not from this close. Not with this much intimacy. Of course, she knew his mother was fat. The Domino's dispatch alone was confirmation enough. Also, Mark's mom did go outside a few times each season. Their paths must cross. Ashley was both beautiful and cruel, not blind. All his neighbors must know: The delivery trucks, the fast food, it. Mark thought of the koi pond. It was nearly completed. Maybe he could purchase the koi next weekend. It would be beautiful.

"What's with the strip show, Todd? You hustling up a date for the prom?"

Principal Dunn had arrived and he knew exactly what was happening. He used to pull the same no-shirt, douchebag move when he was the king prick senior of his own high school. Todd didn't respond right away. Mark and Ashley were locked in a gaze of preternatural contempt. The emotion between them was both gooey and unrefined. Todd couldn't stand a second of it. He thought his hate for Mark was abject in the south gym hallway when his beauty had fully metastasized. When Todd realized that Mark's gorgeous hand had touched a twelve-year-old Ashley's tit. Todd's tit. But there had been more hate available. Watching Ashley clench in agony over being near Mark was unbearable for Todd. That was the emotion he wanted from her, that passion. Todd wanted Ashley to agonize over his existence.

"The prom's not for a while, Chief. I'm looking to dance at the pit."

The bell rang. Mark used the distraction to break eye contact with Ashley and slink his way through an incredulous crowd. Principal Dunn addressed the audience.

"Okay, ladies, we are all officially late to class."

Ashley walked away without offering Todd a smile. There was no little wave, either. Todd slipped back into his shirt. He imagined following Ashley to the first bathroom they passed, yanking her through the door and fucking her from behind over a shit stained toilet, the way she deserved. If she didn't want to, even better, then maybe Ashley would despise him, too. The idea alone was warm and intoxicating down to Todd's core. Part of it felt real to Todd, as if it had already happened.

"Todd, if you want to talk the Principal's Office is always open."

"Thanks, Chief. But everything is going to be just fine."

Chapter 36
Both

The school district failed to designate an early afternoon bus for humiliated students; a rather myopic decision on behalf of the administration. Mark was convinced that the transport would reach its capacity by lunch time.

Mark's forlorn trek home left him with little else but time to brood. Mark was torn. He wanted to fuck Ashley more than ever. Just being near her inspired a mess of impure thoughts and desires. Ashley's beauty was astounding. He felt badly for her and was saddened at the thought of her dead mother. If only Mark could fuck her and make her feel better. That's what Mark wanted to do, he wanted to fuck Ashley well. He also wanted to punch Ashley stupid. Mark wanted to meet Ashley in the pit. Just the two of them without an audience. He would throw lefts until the bloody pulp of her face was indistinguishable from the clumpy, red-clotted sand surrounding it.

Up until now Mark was able to bask in the security of his solitude. No friends? That was easy for Mark. This left no one to entertain in his cesspool of a home. There were no disabled kids for him to reassure in the cafeteria during lunch. There were no cliques for Mark to detangle from their incestuous affirmation. Mark embraced the seclusion he shared with his grief over his lost father and his lost life.

Ashley threatened to expose him, to make even his reclusion unbearable. Up until this point Ashley had kept her attacks at school, leaving his home life at his garbage-filled house. It seemed kind of her. She must have known all along. He must have known that she did. Yet Mark spent all his free time fixing up his yard, working on the exterior while the interior melted and then fused. Ashley was evil.

During their shared childhood, Mark had been privy to cantlets of Ashley's impiety. Specifically, in how she treated Umed. It wasn't often but Ashley mocked Umed on a personal level. She called him "purple foot" when they went swimming in her pool. Mark supposed Umed's feet did take on a purplish hue if he stayed in the cold water too long. But was it necessary to point it out? Ashley liked to mimic his mother's Bengali accent when she called her son home for lunch. With Ashley's theater-driven speech, voice and diction lessons the impersonation was spot on. It hurt. Mark could tell it hurt. Ashley could tell It hurt. Yet it persisted.

Ashley smoothed everything over by being her other self the rest of the time: flirtatious, kind, engaging and beautiful. Ashley gently scratched Umed's head or tickled his forearm with her manicured nails when they sat on the couch to watch a movie. She bought the both of them, Mark and Umed, personalized gifts when Ashley's mother took her to the mall. She laughed uncontrollably at Umed's jokes and took interest in what Umed found interesting.

Ashley was both thoughtful and beautiful.

Then she called Umed Apu and asked him when the Kwik-E-Mart opened.

Ashley was both hurtful and beautiful.

Mark never said anything because it was easier not to. Plus, the ridicule never lasted long. And Ashley was beautiful.

Ashley's ascendency was assured with each passing day. When she reached the twelfth grade her power would manifest absolute. Until that time, like an arranged marriage between imperial families, she dated a silver-backed senior to ensure capitulation. Her friends were upperclassmen and they fawned over her. Everyone did. One minor incident involving a weasel, and Ashley had lost control over Mark's narrative. Consequently, she intended to enforce her authority and write a new story with a plot that had the ability to make Mark's life unbearable. And for what? Because he had stood up for Kim's honor? For assaulting Lester? Lester, the white trash, Converse-wearing rodent. The outward manifestation of the insides Mark worked so hard to conceal.

It was nearly a half of an hour into Mark's journey home when his salvation took focus. He would have to deal with Lester. If Mark planned to salvage anything from his remaining time at high school, it would be at Lester's expense. Mark was not the only one in town with a fat parent. No one had actually seen the inside of his house. Ashley was in a position of power, but she did not retain the exclusive rights to Mark's biography, not without his complete submission. Mark decided to fight for his current status. He would draw a line in the sand and protect his solitude. The path forward wasn't entirely mapped out, but a plan was formulating in his mind. What Mark knew for certain was that if he had any chance at retention it would involve Lester remaining in his own yard and wearing his own shoes.

Mark wasn't asking for much, only stasis. He needed things to remain as they were just long enough for him to both prepare for and implement his escape.

First, Mark had to escort the Weasel back to its cage.

Chapter 37
Mookie Fuckin' Wilson

Lester had heard about the scene at Mark's locker. It was all anyone at Lake Side could talk about. No one could have predicted the amount of drama packed into only seven periods on the first day of school. Needless to say, the student body as a whole was ecstatic about the prospect of two, possibly three people hurting each other badly.

Lester had art eighth period. Mr. Gibbs tasked his students with the freestyle design of a works folder to be used for project storage and submissions. It wasn't a graded assignment so one could expend as little or as much effort as they saw fit on its presentation.

Some of Lester's classmates were already digging in. Three minutes into the period Krissy McGerald was halfway through the first panel of an original sequential comic strip. Krissy had decided she would be getting an 'A' in art. A few other students, those that were either too smart or too insignificant to care about Lake Side drama, were also focused on the design of their folders. The rest of the class, around ten boys and girls, were consumed with Lester. Six students had jammed themselves in at his table, which was designed to comfortably fit four. Three other students actually slid their station closer to Lester's and stopped the madness only after Mr. Gibbs asked them, "What the hell are you doing?" They were endlessly quizzing Lester about his relation to both Mark and Todd.

They wanted to know what he did to Mark and why Todd had his back. They asked Lester if Kim hooked up with Mark and if Ashley was mad at Kim. Megan, a sophomore with a missing index finger and a nose ring, asked Lester if he and Kim were with each other.

Lester didn't know how to answer any of their questions. That wasn't entirely true. He knew that the rooted response to each one of their queries was simply, "Fuck off!" but he understood enough about both civility and decorum to bite his lip. What Lester could not explain was the need of his classmates to question him in the first place. It was preposterous. Lester could not figure out why anyone cared in the slightest. To Lester a fight was an end unto itself. It was what happened. Why it happened was of little concern to him especially since, for the most part, there was never a good reason. A fight happened when it happened for the sole purpose of fighting. That's what humans did.

Lester knew what he said about Kim but even with his best peg he had Mark's response valued no greater than an apathetic "Fuck you." But what exactly did Lester know? Lester had no friends and few interactions other than confrontation.

Lester left Lake Side High at the end of eighth period. He couldn't stomach another ulcerated second of the tenth grade. He knew he would get a cut slip, his first one, but a couple of hours in the pink room sounded like a vacation compared to another forty-two minutes of insipid questions concerning shit he cared little about and understood even less.

During his walk home Lester realized that he would have to give Mr. May a call to discuss the day's events. He ached for Mr. May's guidance, but this enthusiasm was tempered by the lump in his throat. Lester had already connaturalized Mr. May's inevitable disappointment. He wasn't going to like Lester's "fat chick" comment at all.

Lester's mouth began to dry. His stomach sank a bit. He was both embarrassed and ashamed. He began to chant just under his breath.

"Mookie. Mookie. Moo, moo, moo, moo, Mooo-kie."

Mookie referred to Mookie Wilson of the '86 world champion Mets. Lester's dad was a big fan of the team. With absurd frequency, he watched an aging collection of VHS tapes that documented their championship run. Instead of investing in a DVD or a Blu-Ray player, Lester's father instructed his son to bid over fifty dollars buying up extra copies of the video on eBay and then he spent another hundred or so on a second VCR, head cleaners, and two dozen blank cassettes. These low-tech steps were taken to stave off the inescapable degradation of the video's quality. Lester heard this type of behavior described as being "old school." But he knew better. His father was both ignorant and scared. He didn't want to change up his media because doing so represented an investment in the future, or at least the present; two things Lester's dad had long ago forsaken. Instead of embracing and utilizing the spoils of contemporary industrial science, Lester's father mocked and derided its accomplishments. He laughed at all the children and their inferior institutions. There was one way to live as a human being, technologically or otherwise, and it peaked, coincidentally, at the same moment Lester's father lost his ability to effortlessly adapt. He was like a fifty-nine-year-old born again, gleefully awaiting the rapture. If Lester's father couldn't help to mold or at least appreciate the future, he didn't want anyone else to, either.

Discounting the still life of his father, Lester did enjoy watching those Mets tapes. It was one of his earliest and most pleasant memories. Lester sat with his dad on the couch as he broke down every meaningful playoff at bat. He'd listen as his dad extolled the pitching staff, with their ace Doc Gooden, as the best ever assembled. They screamed together in rapture at Darryl Strawberry's mammoth home runs. There was Ray Knight, Keith Hernandez, Gary "The Kid" Carter, the Teufel Shuffle, Nails, and the list went on. Each player had his back story and each was a character, a real person in his father's life.

What made the experience surreal for Lester was that his dad attended the second game of the '86 Series. The opening innings featured the fireworks of gunslingers Dwight Gooden and Roger Clemens. Hometown legend Billy Joel sung the national anthem. The Amazings lost by six runs but if you paused tape two, exactly thirty-two minutes into the action, you'd catch a close up of Lester's father in the crowd with a puss on his face.

Beyond everything and everyone, the man that gave Lester's father a purpose, his absolute favorite was Mookie Wilson. It was Mookie in game six who hit the grounder between Buckner's legs. Mookie played every inning with heart and passion. Most importantly, Mookie bought a beer for Lester's father at a dive bar in downtown Brooklyn. Mookie fuckin' Wilson, a real stand-up guy. "Mookie" was the second word Lester had learned to say. The first was "shit" thanks to a concerted effort by Lester's parents to impress the regulars at Sam's Royal Lounge. Mookie meant everything to Lester's father. Just mention Mookie's name and his eyes ignited. He included his son in his passion and Lester loved their shared emotion. It was one of the few moments in his life, watching those tapes, that Lester witnessed his father as he was, without weight or distress. Nothing from the outside could agitate or contort him. He allowed himself to be happy. For Lester this was peace.

So when Lester recalled a horrible event in his own life, an awkward or foolish moment that he was responsible for, Lester chanted Mookie's name repeatedly. In his mind he wouldn't envision Mookie Wilson, not for long; instead he would we see his father – full of pith, sitting on the couch, sipping at a Bud Light, and above all, content. He was satisfied and with purpose. This visual relaxed Lester and allowed his stomach to untangle and his mistakes to pull back behind the focus of the ritual.

After settling his anxiety with the help of Mookie Wilson, Lester decided to examine the cafeteria and the fight with Mark. Lester wasn't embarrassed by his role as victim in that fight. He was not ashamed of his passivity. Lester knew that not fighting was both the evolved and non-white trash response and more importantly that if he did reciprocate Mark would have immediately regretted his role as aggressor.

After finding satisfaction in his behavior with Mark, Lester allowed small bits of his words, what he said in front of Kim, to seep into his analysis. With the teachings of Mr. May scaffolding his mind, Lester acknowledged his mistake. He had been using Kim, treating her as a means to an end by discarding her feelings for his own gratification. Lester understood this now and maybe he even understood it then. Lester decided that he never desired to hurt Kim but at the time causing her pain seemed, paradoxically, both inconsequential and expedient; an obvious way to bond with Mark over a mutual enemy. Lester knew Mark disliked talking to Kim; he was annoyed that she was always hanging around. His body language was explicit. Mark avoided any eye contact and his face twisted and gnarled as she spoke at him. Of course Kim must have been aware of her own conduct. This didn't excuse Lester's bearing, but he was being honest, observational. "Who was this fat chick and why was Mark putting up with her?"

Lester would put up with her. In fact, he jerked off to Kim often. She was the only girl in school to which he could masturbate. For Lester it had to be believable in order for it to work. He wasn't one to beat off to movie stars or models. He simply could not imagine a scenario in which a beautiful girl would willingly get with him. Lester couldn't even check himself to hot, real chicks in school nor at the mall. Not without ever having spoken to them. And even then they were good for maybe one or two tugs. No, the scenario had to be plausible, at least remotely, for his mind to allow ejaculate to exit his body. His reproductive system wouldn't allow Lester to waste his seed on an impossibility.

The most likely situation that Lester could scrub together was befriending Mark, and in turn hooking up with Kim, taking her off Mark's hands. That was it. That was all he had. It was a fabrication based on proximity and future aspirations. Kim was the only actionable entry in his masturbatory contacts list.

Lester was annoyed at himself for not considering his nighttime proclivities when he chose to use Kim to befriend Mark. Now, after calling her fat, before he could use her in his mind, he was going to have to imagine a situation, a side story, where it all worked out in the end. New layers of fancy and prevarication in order to sculpt a plausible reality in which Lester could live out his only fantasy. Maybe, he devised, his new story would begin with a heart-melting, sympathetic apology. An act of humility to set the stage for the eventual depravity. Lester smiled at the thought. He felt the uncomfortable nettle of his off-color jeans as the blood left his brain for more urgent matters.

It was during the synthesis of both the fantasy and the reality of his current predicament that everything coalesced for Lester. He knew how to make things right with Kim and more importantly Mr. May. Lester realized he would actually, in the real world, have to apologize.

Mr. May would force him to, anyway. Maybe even freeze him out until he did. Mr. May did that sometimes. Withheld his love until Lester conformed to his notion of humanity. It was a tough love that consistently yielded results. Mr. May's love was the only love he possessed, and Lester couldn't bear to be without it.

Lester could always choose not to tell Mr. May what happened, but that was harder than it sounded. He was obligated to respect the man, the only man, who respected him. Honesty was the foundation of their relationship and Lester was not willing to chip away at the only structure in his life.

Lester decided there and then that he would apologize first, before consulting with Mr. May, so he could inform his mentor that he had already known that he was both horrible and wrong. He could show Mr. May that he was learning and growing.

Lester would call Kim, and she would tell him to "fuck off" and hang up before he could apologize. Maybe after that he could text her and be done with it. When it was over, he could imagine a texted response, one with pictures attached. It was a solid plan of action, and Lester was happy with its implications. It was the key to satisfaction in both his real life and his fantasies.

Lester's enthusiasm dimmed the instant he saw his father's ice cream truck in the driveway. Lester had forgotten that his dad's hours changed once school started. You can't sell ice cream to kids who aren't there. Lester's father was going to be drunk. He couldn't drive the truck while inebriated, so he would lose the afternoon, too. Then he would wake up the next day pissed about the lost wages and drink some more, ensuring another day of lost wages. This destructive pattern would continue until at least Saturday morning. It was going to be bad, all of it.

The first week of school was habitually bad for Lester in every way. The only silver lining was that school started on a Wednesday this year. The blistering hell that routinely accompanied one of his father's benders would be condensed to three days. Graciously, his dad's drinking ritual included sleeping - blackout drunk - through the entire afternoon. Any trouble Lester might face would be apportioned in the morning. Lester knew that he wouldn't be going to school on Thursday nor Friday. Mr. May had even instructed him to stay home on bad days. It was better to miss a day of classes than to be suspended for a week. And Lester, even with all his growth in these past few months, could feel the slip knot tightening at the end of his rope. He had few cheeks left to turn. The concentrated attention he received after the fight only exacerbated his frustrations. In recognizing his own deficiency Lester had matured. Lester thought it was ironic that his strength - his ability to maul another human being - was actually his weakness.

Lester walked past his home, straight into the forest. At the foot of a well worn path he dropped his school bag and took off his shirt. The afternoon lay outside of time, staid, warm and blue. Lester had planned to catch a deer before the first snow. His prey had been gorging itself for the impending winter dearth. It's belly was swollen, it's reflexes were dulled. Lester was not hunting for a fawn, nor was he searching for a doe. He sought after a buck with a full ten points.

Chapter 38
Release

Ashley could not get comfortable. She was only a few hours into her sophomore year and everything with Mark had come to a head. Ashley supposed that she expected him to break at some point. Maybe fight back, maybe go away. Whatever the outcome, it was firmly embedded in a matrix of hate; a block of animus so true that it extended both forward and backward in perpetuity without taper. Truthfully, Ashley had no idea what she intended to accomplish by hurting Mark. She had never thought it through. Ashley lived in the present with Mark. She wontedly considered how much she hated him and how miserable he was and what she could do the following day to make his suffering incrementally greater. There was always another tomorrow that held the promise of fresh and decorous amusement. She never actually envisioned an end game. It began, without predication, the moment she discovered that

Mark's father had his penis in her mother's mouth. This convoluted mess of angst, rancor and malice, it had its own momentum and, Ashley believed, its own ending sometime in the near-distant future. But this, what was happening on the first day of tenth grade, it felt wrong, unmoored. It wasn't part of the game.

Mark had become a name, an entity, someone to speculate about. Maybe after the pit he would be done, total humiliation. Todd needed to get him there. Ashley needed to take control of whatever this was and bring it to a manageable conclusion. It was daunting to think about. She didn't want to end things with Mark. She didn't want to force his hand. She desired nothing more than stasis comprised of sempiternal and monolithic hatred. Ashley needed to think, to clear her mind. She needed to find a solution.

There was a way. Ashley felt her hand on the inside of her leg. She was aware of its movement, it's tingly warmth. Moments prior it had been a reflexive slide of the thumb, back and forth, near the crevice of her thigh. Now her entire palm was moving slowly in and around that same cleft.

Ashley sat in the back of a darkened room. Ninth period was her biology lab, and the class was watching a movie about frogs. It was their first lab of the year, and Mr. Slavinski had had enough. He was old and drunk and done. Behind his lectern at the front of the room stood a door made of stained oak with a glossy black jamb that led to a smaller room of science. Officially, the space was used to store laboratory equipment, including: beakers, Bunsen burners and unbalanced scales. It also housed a cushion-less chair, a surface-less desk and the promise of isolation. Over the course of a day, any day, Mr. Slav liked to slip into his private chamber and lock the door. This illicit act could occur during class, between classes, in the morning or the afternoon. You always knew when it was time, when Mr. Slavinski intended to leave his students without a charge. There was a sign, an involuntary tick that served as a tell. After his armpit sweat stains grew so prominent that even with his arms at his side the rings were visible, only then would he sneak into his personal parlor and take a nip from his special beaker. Sometimes the door would be locked for a minute, other times for an entire period. It depended on how much isolation he needed.

Mr. Slavinski had put on the frog movie and entered the back room seconds after the bell rang. Eight periods on day one was all that it took. Perspiration permeated the pits of his white t-shirt and saturated his baby-blue cotton/polyester button down.

Everyone in class was on their phone either texting or playing games. They knew to keep quiet with their fun. The students were smart enough, after a few semesters of adaptation, to avoid bringing outside attention to their freedom. Everyone wanted Slav for science lab, which was like winning the lottery. A full semester of little more than edutainment

DVD's and fill-in-the-blank/word pool worksheets. If you completed the dittos you were guaranteed to pass. Slav didn't check the answers. It was a mutually beneficial arrangement.

Ashley sat alone in the back row at a counter-length, black laminated lab table. She had few real friends in tenth grade, and no one there was brave enough to test her current level of approachability. Nearest to her was Neal. Neal was in the same back row, but he was across the aisle at the other end of his table. Together they bookended an empty space filled with teenage insecurity and imagined hierarchy. Neal was sleeping. It had been a long day.

Ashley furtively opened the button to her black, skin-tight Lucky jeans and let the zipper unlock itself. After a sly lick of their tips, she slipped her fingers beneath her underwear. Instantly, her tensed body relaxed. She felt her knotted mind untangle. Ashley thought that if any one of the boys, and fuck, half the girls, knew what she was doing they would go crazy, out of their minds. That thought made her crazy, out of her mind. Sex was its own aphrodisiac.

Ashley moved her two fingers side to side as briskly as she could without attracting attention. There was a gentle sound, barely audible, of two frictionless fabrics rubbing together. It sounded right. It felt right.

Ashley had been helping herself using this technique for the last year or so, after life had become too much. Sometimes in her room when she couldn't exhale because the jumble in her stomach pressed up into her lungs she would relax herself this way. After the release there was a release. Most of the time, during it, she didn't even think of anyone. Ashley would simply concentrate on what she felt in the moment. Her ninth period science lab session was different. She had just seen Todd with his shirt off. She hadn't seen that since the pit. It was exciting. Ashley imagined that she might not be the only Lake Side student searching for a release at the end of the day. There had to be at least fifty girls in the hallway watching Todd and Mark, the two hottest guys in school, puffing their chest, being men. She thought of Mark. How confident he had been when Todd challenged him. It disgusted her. Ashley couldn't stop herself, the vision of Mark standing tall, even for that moment, against a shirtless Todd. She had to stop. This had to stop. It did stop, abruptly, when she recalled the look on Mark's face after she mentioned his gross mother. She slid her hand from her Luckys and took a deep breath. She didn't need to finish. Ashley had found her release.

She looked to her left and saw Neal quickly and tightly pull his eyes shut, like a found child up past his bedtime, pretending and hoping. He had been watching. He would tell others. Ashley smiled. For an inscrutable instant, in the tenebrous aft of a suicidal man's asylum, Ashley's normally crooked world leveled off with clarity and peace.

Chapter 39
Tensile

Mark came home to the recurrent spectacle of a Domino's delivery man leaving his back yard. Mark cut diagonally across his front lawn as the nineteen-year-old pizza pilot schlepped down the driveway. Mark dropped his head before any eye contact was made. He pulled his phone and stared intently at the lock-screen to garnish the illusion of inaccessibility.

"Hey man, if you want, I can get you some fish when you're done."

Mark was put off by the engagement. He liked to avoid all contact with the delivery men. Someone came essentially every day, usually twice daily, and a few of the guys had been dispatched to the Brunson residence regularly for over a year. Anyone who worked for one of Mark's Mom's favorite eateries was behooved to make the trip whenever it was available. Mark arranged it so that each driver got at least a ten-dollar tip. More if the order topped twenty-five dollars. Mark didn't want to know any of them. He didn't want to see them or be seen by them. Most were only a few years older than Mark and he didn't care to know what they thought of the daily back door drops of baked cheese and fatted meat. Mark hung the phone by his hip and offered the Dominoes guy the side of his eye.

"Excuse me?"

"For your pond. Some koi. I actually raise them."

The delivery boy was proud of his accomplishments. He didn't just sling pizza. He created and groomed aquatic life into a marketable commodity. He was just like you, respectable and of value.

"Oh. That's cool. Yeah, thanks."

Mark pulled his phone again.

"I'm kinda just starting out but I sold a few already. No complaints, ya know?"

Mark kept at his lock screen. He wasn't actively trying to be rude. He just didn't want to have this conversation or any other conversation in the future with the Domino's boy.

"Sounds good, I'll let you know."

With his phone up and his head down Mark lurched toward his front door. He was compelled to remove himself from the discussion with the novice koi farmer. It was a near imperative. He was only allowed three strides before he was forced to be cordial again.

"It's nice."

"What's that?"

"The pond. You do good work."

"Yeah, thanks."

Mark opened the front door to his house just enough to slide himself in sideways before slamming the door shut. It annoyed him that the delivery boy knew what he had built. He was even more annoyed by the compliment. "Fuck Domino's."

Once inside, Mark closed his eyes and collected his loosed emotions. He understood that it wasn't necessarily the pizza guy's fault. The Domino's employee just did what all humans do: he made an observation. People notice things, a lot of things, all the time. For instance, Mark had observed this delivery boy, several times, on his front lawn holding a stack of pizza boxes. He observed him as an upperclassman named James Hollis at Lake Side High. Finally, Mark had observed James as a person, as a member of the community, gallivanting about town. What stuck out most in Mark's mind, his greatest observation, was the NHL plumage that James peacocked around the neighborhood. He routinely sported either a hat or a jersey, James had even rocked a pair of hockey sweatpants while waiting on the computer automated checkout line at Lowe's. They were New York Islanders sweats. The tensile pants were blue and orange with elastic cuffs and the word Islanders was silk screened down one of the legs. Why was James an Islanders fan anyway? Who the fuck enjoyed hockey enough to invest in a team logo?

In particular what irked Mark about this pizza hack was an incident he'd witnessed this past winter. Mark had ridden his bike downtown in an attempt to be normal. There he spotted James hanging with whom Mark presumed to be his girlfriend at the local Subway shop. She wore a hockey jersey, Islanders of course, with a cut of stony, blue/white mom jeans and a pair of thick-tongued, bleach-white, K-Mart crawlers. Mark couldn't look away. It was probably the worst outfit he had ever seen a woman wear. A guy in a hockey jersey was bad enough. Fuck hockey. Fuck sport jerseys in general. But a girl in a hockey jersey was unforgivable. Maybe it was okay on some hot chick trying to support a new boyfriend in one of his immature endeavors. But that was only if she was being dragged to an actual game.

The sight of this style anomaly made such an impression on Mark that he took the time to research on his phone if the Islanders were in town. That would at least provide a modicum of justification for their peculiar behavior. They weren't in town and wouldn't be for a while. There wasn't even an Islander game on TV that night. They were scheduled for Pittsburgh two days later. Mark spent the next twenty minutes nibbling his sandwich and watching the hockey fans eat and exist. It was confounding on every level. He conjectured about what they could be discussing and whether their discourse could have any general relevance or necessity. He wondered if their existence was either a prank or a social experiment. He even gave the restaurant a neck bending inspection in search of a hidden camera kiosk.

Now this guy, this Dominos delivery boy with a hockey fetish, wanted to sell Mark fish for his unfinished pond. It was weird, Mark, on his walk home, had just determined he was going to both complete the pond and fill it with koi as soon as possible. He had not yet decided where to purchase his carp and he was positive this upstart, half fish breeder - half pizza puck, would give him the right price. But he was also certain that he couldn't buy anything from a man who dated a woman who randomly wore a hockey jersey. It was a matter of common sense. How could an individual that dated a girl who enjoyed hockey also know what to do with the PH level in a koi hatchery? How could a person like this understand the intricacies of breeding a separate life form if they didn't understand the customary social attire for themselves or for their love interest? For Mark these forms of knowledge were not exclusive, and he had every right to discriminate.

"Mark? Is that you?"

He could hear the gamey, partially digested and processed cheese clinging to her throat as she called to him.

"Yes, it's me."

"Why are you home so early? Is everything okay?"

"No, everything is not okay. You are an obese, trash-eating, pack rat and you're ruining my life."

He didn't say it, but it was on the tip of his tongue. Not because of the scene with Ashley and Todd at his locker, nor was it due to the astute, puck-loving Domino's guy. It was on the tip of his tongue because it was always on the tip of his tongue. It was tattooed there with an alchemist's mixture of blood, stomach bile and the bitter nectar of indignation.

"Actually, I'm not feeling well. I need you to call in for me tomorrow."

"Okay, sweetie. Just get me the number in the morning."

Mark's mom was eating, and she didn't want to get into it. She didn't ask Mark what was wrong because she knew that nothing was. Mark had not had so much as a cold since grade school. She knew that sometimes he just needed to be home. He needed to both grieve and adjust. Mark's mother understood this completely. She was mildly concerned that it was the first day of school, but she was certain that whatever the bother he would bounce back from it fully. Mark performed exceptionally in all of his classes. He could afford to miss a day every now and then. She was so proud of him. At least once a week during the school year Mark's mom logged on to his Lake Side DEC account to comb over his scores. The comments section updated every month or so, and the grades every two months. She couldn't get enough of seeing the A's accompanied by written adulations. He was such a good boy.

After the second bite of the second slice, Mark's mom put down her pizza. She felt a warm drop of liquid running down her jowl and under her chins. She grabbed a napkin and dabbed at her neck. She had assumed the drop was an oily discharge of baked mozzarella cheese; fat forced from the curds during their 550-degree trip through an impinger. When she looked at the crumpled paper rag, there was no sign of the orange, clot-filled grease. The wet spot on the napkin was pristine, like spring water.

With the twice-bitten slice of pizza placed back in the box that was carefully stacked on top of the pillow beside her ham hock of a leg, Mark's mother felt a second crystalline drop stream down her cheek.

Chapter 40
Virtual horror

Both Thursday and Friday were exhausting in their monotony. Mark holed up in his room only leaving to eat and use the bathroom. He said good morning to his mom and helped to get her laptop back online. Other than that, they didn't speak. It was a bit out of sorts for Mark's mother. Usually, when Mark was home, she would engage him on a regular basis until she sensed his growing irritation before finally letting him be. Besides the laptop issue there was none of that. For Mark it was both pleasant and unsettling.

Mark was struck by another abnormal incident when he entered her room to fix the computer. There was a full garbage bag beside her bed stuffed to the point of stress marks in the plastic. Its streaked and textured bulge reminded Mark of the backside of a bloated tick. In the cleared space, the former deposit of the garbage now in the bag, lay a yoga mat. Mark was left astonished after he spied a newly opened Blu-Ray case to a Denise Austin's workout video. Mark's mom used to exercise to Denise regularly before her husband died. While back on his spurs, Mark decided against reading any type of renewal into the situation. His mom had attempted to clean and to a lesser extent to exercise in the past. He didn't dare to hope, but Mark had been uncharacteristically kind to his mother the entire time he serviced her MacBook. No cracking wise. Zero attitude. It felt nice for them both.

That was it for Mark. He didn't allow any optimism over the occurrence to permeate his mind. He had walked that path too often, only to find a pile of mayonnaise-stained hamburger wrappers at the end of it.

Mark split the remainder of his time between both work and play. He had emailed his teachers asking for the rest of the week's school work. Being the first few days, there wasn't much work available. After he finished their initial assignments, Mark emailed his teachers a second time requesting extra work, projects due later in the month. Only Mrs. Haskey, Mark's ELA teacher, obliged. A three-page paper would be assigned the following Tuesday on Shirley Jackson's "The Lottery."

Mark had read the short story on his own over the summer so after a quick scan of the text he dove right into the essay. In it he discussed conformity and the dangers of binding tradition. He got in his say about the modern church and its anachronistic tendencies. He even mentioned the often vile and hidden subconscious of man. He discussed how we as humans arbitrarily decide who we should stone, maybe not with rocks, but with verbal jabs and snide mimicry. How there was always an open alter waiting for the next sacrifice to the gods of culture and ideology. How anything less than a prescribed beauty and an amenable attitude was burned and banished even in our modern, seemingly progressive times. The paper turned out to be seven pages in length. After Mark typed the last word, he saved it in his designated English assignments folder to be emailed to Mrs. Haskey Tuesday night. Mark had a habit of not revising his work. He enjoyed the economy of a first draft.

With nothing important left to accomplish Mark took to the virtual world. Hours were spent as third person mercenary for a special ops unit. Pixelated bullets were fired with precision at sculpted avatars living for their less functional more biological counterparts. As school let out Mark's digital landscape was frustrated. Eleven-year-olds without parents, Mark imagined, took to his terrain with fearless skill developed during ten-thousand hours of forfeited time. The battlegrounds grew fierce as high-pitched expletives were flung from the mouths of children who lacked both the security and presence needed to properly command their own insults. The only discourse less availing was that of the adults who engaged these boys on their terms with practiced vulgarities from an extended childhood. Besides distinguishing octaves Mark found it difficult to differentiate the maturity level of each person he encountered over his headset. The similarity of each avatar solidified for Mark the fiction of a homogenous world of tween minds in apathetic bodies of varying size and impurity. After finishing no better than fourth in twelve straight rounds of Crucible, Mark had to disconnect.

Mark's evenings were spent in another virtual community of facilitating avatars. His name was all over social media tethered to either of the words "fag" or "pussy." Intermittently a female classmate would pop in with an offer to suck him off. In some threads conversation would vacillate between how "hot" he was and what a "pussy" he was with each post. Some less brave, more anonymous types took their shots at Todd, calling him a tool and hoping that Mark would kick his ass. Another anon told the school of a brush between both Mark and Todd in the south gym hallway. They mentioned that Lester was there while Todd punched Mark in the face. This started a thread of conjecture about why Todd was sticking up for Lester. One person wrote that they were cousins and even though Todd was ashamed of him he was doing right by his family. Another guessed that The Weasel was Ashley's cousin and that her father had put him up in a shed behind Ashley's house. An unknown user confident in their anonymity wrote that Lester and Todd were both gay fags that liked to blow each other.

Others speculated on the fight between Mark and Lester. Most of that discussion centered on Kim fucking Lester to make Mark jealous. Many tangents just made fun of Kim, her makeup and her weight. The relationship between the three of them was described as a love triangle that was obviously obtuse. One anonymous comedian verified Kim's obesity via mathematical prof: if one adds the angle designated K to the angles representing both L and M the sum of all angles in the love triangle KLM > 180 degrees.

It was all horrible. What concerned Mark most was a post on how he beat up Lester because The Weasel wore the same sneakers as Mark. It was an off-hand comment made without context that failed to trigger a single response, but it pissed Mark off to no end. Mark knew who said it. It was Sofía from his home room, she had logged on as herself. Sofía was Hispanic, one of the few Latinos to attend Lake Side High.

Marks response was anonymous, automatic, without contemplation, almost binary in execution. First he told her to shave her mustache with her dad's weed whacker and then to fuck herself in the ass with a Dos Equis bottle. It was hurtful and it started a torrent of relentless spic bashing. It wasn't difficult to induce a chain of virtual horror. Many of the barbs were thrown by students who had logged on as themselves. They didn't bother to hide their bigotry behind a digital veil. Mark wondered how people could behave so cruelly so quickly and without provocation. He was both disgusted and confused. Mark didn't understand how anyone could be that way. Sofía did not deserve their kind of savagery. It was all one big mess.

Shortly after Sofía logged off in hysterics, Mark signed himself out and went to bed. He tucked himself in while contemplating the disgusting side of humanity. Mark's day had been both physically and emotionally draining and he had little trouble falling asleep.

Chapter 41
The Facade of Purpose

Mark's digital surrogacy lasted for two days. Forty-eight hours of little more than feeding and shitting in his two realities. By Friday night Mark recognized that he had to leave his home. There was a football game scheduled for Saturday morning, Lake Side's first of the season, against Forrest Side. It was a big deal. Both districts were projected to finish first or second depending on the racist leanings of the analyst making the prediction.

Mark decided to attend. He hoped to find Lester, though Mark doubted he'd be there. Mark hadn't seen Lester for the last two days, even though he had been actively monitoring Lester's yard from his dormer. Every so often Mark would catch the older rodent out back on Umed's rock, drinking a beer amidst his piles of shit. It was sad and gross and Mark didn't like seeing it, but he had to deal with the Weasel.

Mark didn't know how or what, but something had to be done. Lester had to stay away from him. If Mark was going to salvage his old new life, a life of fending off Kim's advances and hiding his mother in between Ashley's insults, Lester needed to be dealt with.

That was the bad news. The good news was that anyone who would bother to mess with Mark at the game would be on the football field, Todd included. There might be a few of Todd's sycophants in the stands who would consider going at him, but Mark couldn't think of one that he was worried about. Besides, Mark knew this was personal for Todd. That much he had figured out. Todd needed to beat the shit out of Mark. That was why he'd involved himself with Lester. Lester was a pretense; Todd was "sticking up for the little guy." The facade of purpose.

The real reason had to be Ashley. Either Ashley asked for it directly or Todd instinctively understood what he had to do for her. Regardless, Mark would be safe at the game. Plus, it could potentially make Monday less of a deal if Mark were to show some face at a school function. It would serve to cut some of the tension out of an otherwise inscrutable four-day abscond.

Mark was determined to avoid the pit on his way to becoming a nobody again. Whatever Ashley said about his fat mom would just have to be weathered. Ashley could have an inkling about the internal state of his home, but she could not have any idea of the scope. If he was able to keep Lester away, in his own yard, in his own shoes, with the space left in his garage, and a rearrangement of the basement, Mark imagined a possible release. With the right plan, properly executed, Mark could still escape his current life on his way to college and beyond.

Mark was eager to return to his status as a pariah. Mark was fine carrying that cross; he had grown used to its girth and weight. If he could just get through these next few days, find a way to set things as they were, maybe he could avoid being nailed to it.

Chapter 42
Rivalry

Mark heard the roar of the crowd before he stepped onto the school grounds. It was both raucous and exhilarating. It used to be for him. Not on the same scale, but the parents at a junior high football game could really get into it. Mark's passes were clean and bullet quick. He ran like a jaguar zeroing in on it's kill. The audience appreciated it. Mark's team was undefeated in every game he played. There was no championship in junior high, but the crowd valued each of his victories and Mark's roll in securing them.

Mark missed it all: the football, the fans, his father, Ashley. It was all hard and it all hurt.

As he approached the field, Mark noticed the screams emanated from the visitor's section. It was late in the first quarter and Forrest Side was up fourteen to nothing. The away team's bleachers were packed. The guest bleachers were smaller than the

Lake Side stands, but there were just as many fans. Cheering moms and folding chairs cluttered the sideline. Forrest Side was the next town over. The two towns, Lake Side and Forrest Side, were close and tangled. Their school districts were combined until about thirty years ago when the area's population had reached a critical mass.

The border between the two townships consisted of a string of lakes that ran both perpendicular to and underneath Main Street. The lakes originated in the mountains and let out into the bay. The forest surrounding the lakes played host to both parties and fights for the local high school talent. There was even a homegrown spook that haunted the woods. The kids at Lake Side called him Diaper Dan, while Forrest Side, with less imagination, referred to him as Diaper Man. He supposedly lived in the woods because along with his sanity he had trouble controlling his sphincter. Dan had an overgrown and nappy beard and he wore nothing but adult diapers. Every other asshole you asked believed he actually lived in the forest.

The rivalry crossed both the lake and the economy. Forrest Side was the wealthy side of the lake. Considering the affluence of Lake Side, it seemed foolish to compare, but for every number one there was always a one-A.

Economics was not the deciding factor in their competition. Bragging rights were based neither on tax brackets nor on majority shares. The score was always settled on the gridiron.

The rivalry was fierce, partisan, illogical. Even the adults in town, the parents and bar hounds, would get into fistfights in the week leading up to the game. On the night before kickoff, students from either side just didn't cross the lake. It wasn't the old west or anything. You weren't taking your own life in your hands by heading into a town filled with the sons and daughters of America's white and privileged elite. After all, the security of wealthy white children had always been the pretext for any western civilization. Near to game time It was just wise for everyone to stay away from any haunts of bored and drunk teenagers.

It was an irrational hatred expressed in an irrational way. Individual accomplishments on the field were fine. State championships were great. Winning both games against your opponent on the other side of the lake was sublime. It didn't happen often, maybe once a decade, as there was too much at stake. The home team usually found a way to win.

Last season it happened, Lake Side had won both games, and it was all because of Todd. He ran for two-hundred yards and three scores between the two games. He threw for another four-fifty and a dozen more points. Everyone in Lake Side was in love with him. In their final meeting last season, with three minutes left, Todd ran thirty-two yards for the go-ahead score on Forrest Side's home turf. He broke three tackles along the way. The residents of Lake Side were in bliss. There had been a decisive answer to the question of which town was truly superior.

Lake Side's euphoria wore off shortly after the school year ended. It was replaced with a low-key hostility driven by fear. It was all anyone could talk about. Larry T. had grown up.

Chapter 43
Larry T

Mark avoided the stands. He hung out alone near the perimeter fence, between the scoreboard and the parking lot. He wasn't sure if anyone had noticed him, nor did he care. What he witnessed on the football field was too unbelievable. On Todd's first play from scrimmage he fumbled the snap, recovered the ball and optioned to the short field. Three fearful steps into the flats and he was eating dirt. Larry T. was all over him. Todd was terrified and helpless. Mark was ecstatic.

Larry T. was six-foot-five and two hundred and fifty pounds. His movements were amazingly quick. His technique was flawless. His strength was scary. Larry T. was black.

On a field of nearly one hundred kids he was one of three African Americans. His presence was felt on every down, whether he was involved in the play or not. For at least two reasons it was hard for the Lake Side fans to watch him compete.

Larry was the son of John Thomas. John Thomas had been an all-star linebacker for the St. Louis Rams. Ten years of sacks and interceptions made him a legend. He retired a few years early with three herniated disks and a fused spinal column, but his hall of fame credentials had already been codified. Now those same credentials were being passed forward, ten yards at a time, to his only son.

Larry T. was on the Forrest Side squad last fall but he was nowhere near the physical presence then that he was now. Last year Larry was around 6'3" but he was skinny, barely two-hundred pounds. His coordination wasn't all there either. Larry was still a force last season but it was mostly at tight end. His size made him a natural target and his hands were coming along. An asset for sure but not a game changer. Two inches taller and fifty-five pounds heavier Larry was now going both ways. There were five large student athletes anchoring Lake Side's offensive line. They had an average weight of 195 pounds but they could not contain the beast that was Larry T. The best they could do with consistent help from the full back was slow him down every other play or so. No one could cover him on offense. Mark arrived late to the game, but he was sure that both touchdowns were Larry's.

After his most recent sack, Larry was pulled to the sidelines. His father wanted him to play, encouraged it, but he was having the coach save his son the constant contact. It wasn't that anyone on the Lake

Side squad could actually hurt Larry; it was just a fact that unforeseen accidents were stitched into the game of football. For instance, a linemen could roll over his ankle or he could receive a low block to the side of his knee. It was difficult to control the entropy in between the hash marks. Larry would play early, build a comfortable lead, and only return to the field if Forrest Side needed to score or maybe for a key stop on defense.

Everyone in Lake Side knew this was coming, but watching it in real time was both disheartening and astonishing. The word spread concerning Larry's new body during finals last year. By the time summer practice rolled around, the corporeality of Larry T. compressed into a singularity towards which all of Lake Side's communal banter flowed. Most of this conversation addressed concerns with the unforgivable sin of losing both games to Forrest Side. The remaining discourse focused on melanin.

Mark had never heard the n-word as much in his life as he did this past summer. #BigNig was a hashtag whenever anyone texted about Forrest Side football and it wasn't used solely by the students. Mark was glad Lake Side was getting smacked around for more than just personal reasons. Racism infuriated Mark. Mark's father had taught him well.

Mr. Brunson had discussed racism with Mark at a young age. Who and what he was going to encounter as he grew up and experienced the world. How where he lived was in no way indicative of the rest of the planet's demography. How horrible people were in general, especially the privileged.

Mark learned just how serious his father had been the summer before he died. Mark's dad ran a large business that used a ton of manual labor. The work was tough and the days were long. Turnover was a regular part of the job. Early on he hooked up with the parole department and took on ex-cons that needed a break. He was glad to do it and the situation worked out well for everyone involved. Not all the former prisoners were black, but enough of them were that you noticed. Not all were good workers and not all were bad. His lead Foreman, Jon Hutch, who now was second in command under Ashley's father, was a black guy from Quentin. Mark's dad said more than once that Mr. Hutch was the best man he had ever known. But these were ex-cons nonetheless. In every group of people, regardless of who they were or where they came from, there were always a couple of assholes. Some of them stole, some lied, some fought and some were just belligerent dicks. Six months before Mark's dad died, a black guy who had all of the above qualities was caught pulling a spool of copper from a commercial job site. Mark learned of the incident while his father and Ashley's father were embroiled in an argument over whether or not they were going to press charges.

Around that time Mark asked his dad, "Why do you keep on hiring all these black people if they were just stealing from us?" It was the first and only time Mark's father ever hit his son. He quickly realized his mistake and pulled his boy in close for a hug and apology. He went on to explain that some black men steal from him some of the time but no more than the whites or Hispanics. Some people were just that way. It had nothing to do with race. It was mostly economics and that was the issue Mark's dad was attempting to resolve. He offered a solid day's pay to anyone who was willing to work for it. Paroled convicts needed a second chance and he was glad to give them one. Over the years they made him a lot of money. More than he could spend. Mark's father made lasting friends and commanded a small army of employees that would die for him if the opportunity arose. He told Mark never to conflate race with motive. The two were never a corollary. He finished by saying that if Mark ever did it again he could expect to get smacked harder because now he knew better.

There were only four black families that resided in Lake Side. Mark specifically recalled the Sterlings, who lived around the corner from him. They were both well off and well liked. Mr. Sterling owned a temporary employment agency, Sterling Personnel, which had locations in three states. Mark remembered hearing a lot of unsolicited compliments on how polite the Sterling family was and how well Mr. Sterling and his sons had dressed.

Besides the Sterlings there was a section-eight apartment complex near the train station, maybe ten units, and two of the families that rented there were black. Mark recalled it was a good spot to pick up some smoke. But for the most part Lake Side was a small town with little ethnic diversity. Even the surrounding towns, while not as lily, had scant minority representation. It just wasn't a thing. Mark's only other uncomfortable memory concerning race involved Umed.

Chapter 44
Broken

When Mark was in sixth grade both his family and Umed's family took a vacation together. They went skiing, and the nearest resort with fresh powder was a two-hundred-mile drive up the interstate. Umed rode with Mark so the two boys could to keep each other company.

Halfway into the trip Mark's parents decided to stop for gas and food at a crowded service station. It was Christmas break, and it seemed as if everyone in the state was traveling at the same time. Mark and Umed chose to eat at McDonald's, a rare treat for Umed, whose parents would never have allowed it had they made the same roadside stop. The boys sat in silence as they ate and people watched. It was refreshing just to be out of the car. During the incident Mark's parents were waiting on a never-ending line at a Starbucks Express.

As Mark and his friend scarfed down supersized French fries, a family of four approached their booth while scouring the complex to find a table of their own. The family was textbook nuclear: mom, dad and two teenage boys, all were black. Both of the boys were wearing Beatz and they were cued into their cell phones. They weren't able to hear their parents.

"What do you guys want? Guys?"

Their father turned around to see why his children hadn't responded. The older of the two boys didn't notice his folks stop and walked right into his mother. His father was annoyed. He pulled his son's earphones off his head.

"Think about what you do. Always."

As he passed by, the younger of the teenage boys watched as Umed, unwittingly yet reflexively, glared at his family with disdain. In return he menacingly mouthed the word "bitch" and walked away.

Only after Umed's antagonist was out of earshot did he drop his French fries and let out an audible huff.

"Why are they like that?"

Mark had no idea what Umed was talking about.

"Who?"

Umed motioned to the African American family now six table lengths away.

"Them."

"Like what?"

"Cursing and starting fights."

"I don't know."

They both went back to eating. Mark took out his phone. People watching was boring him. Umed had something to say.

"I can't help it. Whenever I see them the first word I think of is... nigger."

Umed said this last word softly. If one could call it a word. To Mark it was lightning: explosive, jarring and brilliantly white.

Mark looked around. He needed the coast to be clear. He had never heard Umed utter that more-than-a-word before and he wasn't comfortable with it at all.

"What are you talking about?"

"Black people."

Umed seemed fine with it. He was quiet and aware, but he was firm in his suppositions. Marked looked over to his parents. They were both on their phones. The coffee line hadn't moved. Mark thought it looked a little longer.

"You think they're nig-"

Mark couldn't even finish. He looked down at his food.

"No, not at all. It's just when I see them."

"I don't think that's right."

Umed was embarrassed. He peered out of the nearest window and into the chaos that was supposed to be a parking lot. He ate another fry. Mark slid what was left of his Big Mac to the side and went back to his phone, hoping the conversation had ended.

"I'm not saying they are that. It's just that's the first word that pops into my head when I see one."

Mark kept his eyes on his phone.

"I don't think that's right is all I'm saying. You should stop. Black people are hard workers. Mr. Hutch is black. And he's the best."

Umed was not happy that Mark disagreed with him. It annoyed Umed to no end that Mark backed his alternate position with facts. Mark was smart but Umed was smarter.

"What? You don't think that when you see them?"

Mark raised his eyes and looked at his parents. Mark witnessed his father in his own world toying with his screen. Mark located the African American family sitting at a booth in the corner. They were all on their phones. They were all black.

"No. I don't."

"So you don't notice that they're black?"

"No."

"Now you're lying."

Umed was getting loud. He was smart, smarter than Mark. People needed to know this.

"Hold it down. My dad's right there."

"Whatever. At least I'm honest."

Mark didn't like to be called a liar.

"I'm honest. I don't think that word whenever I see them."

"That's not what I asked. I asked if you noticed they were that way."

Mark knew what Umed was doing. Even at the age of twelve, both of them knew what was happening. Umed was creating a corollary between words and ideas. They both noticed them, but Umed had a different way of noticing. What was the difference if they were both placing people in categories? Mark felt trapped. It angered him that a Starbucks Express was incapable of providing speedier service.

"So, what? I noticed…"

Umed was ready.

"It's the same thing."

"I knew you were going to do that. It's not the same thing."

"We both notice first."

"I didn't say first."

"So you're lying again."

Mark never lied.

"Whatever. It's like noticing if a girl is pretty."

Umed replied quickly. He always had an answer for Mark.

"Or Chinese."

Mark needed this to end. All of it.

"Or Indian."

Umed clammed up. His face flushed, and his eyes welled a bit. Mark failed to observe Umed's tears only because, at that moment, he could not look his best friend in the eye. Umed was one of a handful of Indians in the entire school district. It was mildly uncomfortable for him. There were over a billion Indians on the planet, but not many of them settled in Lake Side. Umed's mom said they were going back to India at some point. It terrified him mostly, but something primordial inside Umed really wanted to be there.

Mark went back to his phone. The discussion had ended. Mark wasn't happy with exactly how, but he didn't want to think about it anymore.

A few minutes passed. Some angry birds killed some pigs. Mark's parents waited for their drinks at the counter on the other side of the register. They had finally placed their order.

Umed was sulking. Mark wanted to apologize but he didn't know for what exactly. It was just a statement floating in the ether. Mark looked over to his father. He was showing something from his phone to Mark's mother with a smile. She smiled, too. Mark smiled before surprising both Umed and himself with what he said next.

"Are you a racist?"

Umed was licking the salt off his finger after pressing it into the leftover remnants on his wrapper.

"No. I don't hate anyone."

"So why do you call them that?"

"I don't call them that. I said I think it when I see them."

"Why?"

Umed turned around to steal a peek at the family. They were all eating. No one was talking. He turned back to Mark.

"I'm not a racist. I can't be."

"That's not what I asked. I asked why you think that way?"

Umed didn't like that, Mark using Umed's own words against him. He was angry. Umed needed this conversation to end. It had to stop, and he had to finish it with as much of his dignity intact as possible.

"Because it seems like everything they touch gets broken."

Chapter 45
Almost Alive

Lester decided to call Kim Thursday night. She answered on the third ring. Lester hung up as soon as they connected. Kim called back immediately. Lester's voicemail was a computer recording that stated only his number, so he wasn't compelled to answer. Lester's phone number existed in a vacuum. It was just digits. It referred to nothing. No one in school, no one anywhere, with the exception of Mr. May, had Lester in their list of contacts.

Lester was amazed that he even had a phone. His father had gotten it for him two Christmases ago, and once a month he handed Lester a phone card with five hundred fresh minutes on it. What ever happened the day before, a cursing match, a drunken assault, it didn't matter. On the first of the month Lester's dad performed for his son a cellular revivification. A gift that was nothing less than a dash of modern thaumaturgy to facilitate Lester's inviolable lifeline to Mr. May.

Lester considered texting Kim after the first aborted call, a quick apology, but he knew in his gut that wouldn't be enough. Kim called him a second time Friday afternoon. Lester didn't answer and she did not leave a message. Late Friday night, right before bed, Lester dialed her number again. Kim answered quickly, leaving Lester no time to succumb to his anxiety.

"Who the hell is this?"

Lester almost hung up. He had his finger on the end button.

"Eat shit and die!"

Even with his phone held out the length of his arm, he sensed Kim's disgust through the receiver. He placed the phone to his ear, nothing. Lester wondered if she had hung up. He looked at his cell. They were still connected, Lester's commoditized seconds irrevocably ticking away. Lester broke the silence.

"Hello?"

"Who is this?"

Kim was still on the line. She seemed kind for a moment, curious not angry. Hopeful.

"It's Lester."

"Who?"

Lester didn't respond. There was still time to end the call. Lester took a moment to reconsider the virtue of a texted apology. He looked at his phone. It continued to time their conversation.

"Is this the Weasel?"

Lester put the phone back to his ear.

"Yes."

"Fuck you, Weasel! What do you have to say now? Fuck you!"

Kim's voice trembled. Her throat attempted to regurgitate itself. But she didn't hang up. She didn't run.

"You wanna' call me fat again? You couldn't wait 'till Monday? Is that what…"

"I'm sorry."

Lester mumbled a bit, but he did it. He got it out.

"What?"

Even through the network of towers and orbiting satellites connecting their phones, Lester could sense the exasperation in Kim's one-word reply.

"I wanted to say that I'm sorry."

More silence. Almost thirty seconds had passed. Lester considered hanging up again. Sweat beaded in the hairless corners of his widow's peak. Lester was an instant from ending the call when he heard Kim gasp and sniffle.

"Why? Why'd you do it?"

Lester wanted to say, I don't know. It would have been easy and believable. But he didn't. Instead he thought of Mr. May and how the world was. How everyone was judgmental. How everything was wrong. He remembered how Mr. May spoke to him and how he always told Lester the truth no matter how hurtful that truth was to either of them.

"I wanted to impress him."

Kim could not find her breath. When she finally spoke her voice cracked, tempered vibrations lacking a medium. She was barely audible.

"Who?"

Kim knew who Lester meant. She knew exactly who Lester wanted to impress. She was ashamed that she knew. She was ashamed that she asked Lester to speak his name. Lester was also ashamed. He was telling Kim the truth. It was front facing, naked and open. Despite everything, he continued.

"Mark. I wanted him to like me, and I thought…"

He didn't need to say any more. She knew and he knew. Lester thought by making fun of the fat hanger-on Mark would get a laugh. It didn't need to be said. Not even euphemistically.

"Okay."

Lester was confused.

"Okay?"

"Yes, okay. I accept your apology."

Kim wasn't crying anymore. Lester didn't know what to say, so he said nothing. Kim filled the void.

"I'm gonna go now."

Kim's demeanor had shifted. Lester was grateful for her newfound composure.

"Oh, okay."

Lester looked at the face of his phone again. It was demarcating his father's gift. He put it back to his ear.

"Kim?"

She didn't say anything at first. Then finally, to Lester's relief, Kim spoke.

"Yes?"

There was no hint of her former tears. She was stoical and she had stayed on the phone, with Lester.

"Thank you."

Another brief pause. Lester heart stopped beating in anticipation of her response.

"I'll see you on Monday, Lester."

He pulled the phone away from his ear and stole one last look at its face. The call had ended with each of its seconds frozen in efficacy. The value of each tick that passed held no measure. She had called him Lester.

Lester put down his cell and unbuttoned his pants. He looked at himself. All nine inches were throbbing. Almost alive. Lester barely had to move his hand before his chest was covered in one big mess.

Chapter 46
Blinds

Ashley slouched low in her chair with her legs extended towards the window. Her bare feet, with the exception of their athletically formed arches, were flat against the wall and spaced evenly on either side of the sill. She needed to be in that position to peer out of a slit that she left at the bottom of her mostly drawn shade.

From her bedroom window there was an unobstructed view of Mark's bedroom window. His TV was on and tuned to Fortnite's title screen. She could see Mark moving about when he passed between his television and a mislaid slat in his own drawn blinds. It was hard for Ashley to comprehend how much she hated Mark. Just looking at his house made her heart beat faster. She could feel her jaw clench and the flesh of her arms and legs tingled with each pass he made in front of the television. Ashley's cheeks were aching and her eyelids were sore from the countenance of a permanent scowl. There was so much emotion that it was near thrilling for Ashley to see Mark's body, even just its shadow, move past the triangular aperture fixed in his window treatment. With each of Mark's steps Ashley would hold her breath, involuntarily, until the monitor's pixels reappeared. Ashley finally closed her slit when she noticed that Mark had been blocking the TV's radiance through a long and needed exhale. "Fuck Mark."

After the shade was down Ashley turned on her desk lamp. She was supposed to be writing a seven-page paper on To Kill A Mocking Bird. All of Mr. Guidi's honor students were tasked to read the Harper Lee classic over the summer. Ashley had read it last year. It bored her. She thought Boo was a freak.

Instead, Ashley recalled an uncomfortable incident that occurred three summers prior. It was the last summer her mother was alive. On a lark she and Mark had both chipped in on a discounted pair of Lighting McQueen walkie-talkies they found in the sale bin at Target. Ashley thought it would be fun if they each took one of the receivers and snuck in a conversation before they went to bed. Ashley was excited. She imagined the experience might be like sleeping in the same room. It wasn't fun and the entire affair met none of her expectations.

They both sat at their windows and stared at each other. The idea itself was foolish because they were close enough to whisper to one another through the still summer night. Not to mention the fact that they both had cell phones. It turned out that they had nothing to talk about over their walkie-talkies. It was the only instance in Ashley's life that she could remember feeling awkward in Mark's presence and she didn't enjoy a single second of their planned time together.

Ashley didn't like Mark showing up at the football game earlier in the day either. She thought she had won. Todd had challenged him to the pit and he declined. That along with her thorough dig at his mother led Ashley to believe that she had sealed the deal. Mark had skipped the following two days of classes. Ashley had assumed he was signing up for a private school. God knew he had the money to pay for it. Ashley's wide eyes had seen the size of the checks her father cut to Mark's mother each month.

Ashley had lost. Mark showed up at the field and for the moment it was all anyone could discuss. His presence provided a needed distraction from the abject embarrassment of a football game the crowd was supposed to be enjoying.

Todd was humiliated. What's worse was that he was scared. Everyone could see it. He was terrified of Larry. Lake Side lost by twenty-six points. It would have been more, but Larry didn't play the entire second half. He didn't need to. Lake Side never scored. Ashley wasn't sure, but she thought Todd took a few hits that normally wouldn't have phased him and rode them to the turf. She noticed that he overthrew a couple of passes that he regularly iced without effort. If the offense made the red zone, Larry T. would be back on the field. Todd knew this. Everyone knew this. And there was still the away game to look forward to.

Todd's cowardice during the game didn't upset her. Ashley cared little about football and even less about a childish rivalry. What she witnessed that annoyed her most was Mark's smile. Even over the distance of the football field and through the hundreds of people that separated them, Ashley noticed Mark's face light up with each pulverizing hit Todd's body received. What pushed Ashley over the edge were the three freshman girls that went out of their way to stroll by Mark and say, "Hi." They giggled as they walked the full perimeter of the field, through enemy territory, and back to their seats. Ashley watched them the entire time. Liz was the leader of the group. She was pretty, fun and well liked. Ashley overheard the senior boys on more the one occasion talk about banging her. Ashley would have to put a stop to that, eventually. Right now she needed to gain control of her own life.

Mark left after only one quarter of football. Ashley guessed that he saw all that he needed to see. More than half of the Lake Side fans bailed at halftime. Everything was hard to watch. Ashley stayed the entire game. After Mark left she could delight in watching Todd struggle. Ashley knew that she should have felt badly for him. It wasn't his fault that Larry had become a man over the summer. Ashley liked having Todd around. But Mark had shown up irrespective of Todd's threats.

Ashley left the moment the game ended. It was easy to navigate the near-empty stands. She didn't search for Todd and he didn't look for her. Not even a text was exchanged between them. Ashley wondered if he was broken. Caitlin had stuck around until the end of the game to watch Steve play. She offered Ashley a ride home, but Ashley politely declined. She felt like walking.

Ashley followed the fence around the field to where Mark had been standing. She even found the divot where she noticed Mark had been toeing the ground in between snaps. Ashley realized that from where Mark had stood there was a fantastic view of both the game and the bleachers.

Ashley turned and followed in what she imagined would be his footsteps home. She thought about her mother on the way. Ashley missed her, dearly.

Chapter 47
Bacon

Lester woke up later than intended on Saturday morning. He rocked the same jeans he had worn the night before, only they were splayed open at the zipper. His phone lay beside his head. There was no time to for Lester to lounge underneath the sheets. No moment for his dilated eyes to painlessly contract. It was possible that his father could crawl back on the wagon and hawk Fun Dip for the afternoon. But if he woke up drunk, a likely occurrence, he could just as easily crack open a fresh Bud Light while he sprayed his morning shit around the rim of the toilet bowl. Lester's dad had no problem riding a bender all the way down. Lester managed to avoid his father so far by getting out of the house early and staying away until late in the afternoon. Even his dad, a professional grade alcoholic, couldn't keep awake much past dusk after a true session of pre-noon drinking.

Lester didn't want to see his father whether he was drunk or not. Things were rolling for The Weasel. He had settled everything with Kim and spoken to Mr. May. Mr. May was proud, prouder than he had ever been, in fact. Lester could practically feel the head rub through the phone. For the first time since he moved to Lake Side Lester felt good about himself.

Lester scrambled out of bed, grabbed his shirt and shoes from the floor and ran out of the house. It was an unusually warm September morning. No humidity. He heard his neighbors buzzing with their yard work, fancy automobiles and soccer-mom-approved play. The kind of play where it was impossible for the children to get hurt, but the trade off was a lifetime of co-dependency. He wanted nothing to do with any of it. Lester threw on his shirt, tied his shoes and sprinted into the woods.

Lester had learned to track game by reading articles in Outdoor Life and watching tutorials on YouTube. It was difficult at first to pick up a trail, but by mid-morning he had discovered a fresh print in a patch of moss that ran as ground cover up and around a cluster of red oaks. From there he found any number of signs that more than one deer had been through the area. He followed the herd for hours, losing them at times only to slide over their scat or a tuft of freshly turned earth. By mid-afternoon the movements of the deer grew conspicuous in Lester's assimilated mind and he walked a beaten path blazed by his prey.

When the sun set it left the sky a hazy blue with scattered wisps of pink clouds. Lester tracked the herd of deer, seven strong, to an open field of bramble and tall grass. Two of the deer were lying down across the way from his approach. The other five were intermittently eating from the mulberry trees that lined the far side of the meadow. One of the deer was a buck with at least ten points. Lester knew this wouldn't last. The mulberries were seasonal. Three weeks to be exact. He remembered from his old neighborhood how for twenty-one days the uncollected fruit stained the roads and sidewalks beneath their branches with a purplish pulp. He also recalled climbing to the tops of those trees and grabbing at the plump berries that no one else bothered to pick. Lester could only imagine what a fresh currant must taste like to the members of his herd. After eating little more than bark and roughage all year, they would be pleasantly distracted.

Without making a sound Lester took off all his clothes at the edge of the woods. He thought about removing his underwear, but he didn't like the idea of his junk dragging on the ground as he crawled. He'd just have to hope that his tightie-whities didn't smell as badly as they should. Next, as quietly as he could, Lester rubbed handfuls of dirt all over his near-naked body. He spent extra time grinding the earth into his crotch and armpits before coating his feet with what were essentially socks made of mud. After holding a wet finger to the breeze one last time, Lester began to creep beneath the grass toward his prize.

Lester inched his way across the field one elbow after the next. It took him a half of an hour to cross the forty-five yards to the herd's side of the meadow. He kept low and slow, only popping up an eye every few minutes to make sure he was still on the proper track. Two of the does were near. He could hear them periodically rolling around as they fluffed their straw beds. The does didn't matter to Lester. It was the buck that he wanted, with all of its magnificent points. The stag vacillated between eating the mulberries and lying in the grass. Its desires were conflicted. It wanted to eat from the trees forever, but it also had the urge to lie in the bedded grama and never rise up again.

There was less than the length of a school bus between Lester and his points when he, once more, dragged himself forward with his extended left elbow, careful to make no noise. He was about to take another peek when he spotted a patch of grass that seemed unnaturally matted by contrast with the swirls and strings he had been crawling through. He slowly prodded his fingers from his right hand forward to investigate. At that instant, the weeds he sought to inspect animated before his eyes. A fawn was lying an extended arm away from the weasel's snout. Lester must have missed it in his scouting. She was barely the height of the inflorescence and not yet smart enough to endlessly fill up on the berries. The fawn maneuvered its neck all the way around to get a look at what it was sensing. For a brief moment both the deer and the weasel locked eyes.

Fine-tuned by fifteen years of survival, Lester's instincts were sharper than the fawn's. Before the three-month-old could react, Lester sprung to his feet and leapt over her. The fawn's mother and one of its older cousins were lying just a gallop or two ahead of their pup. By the time they realized it wasn't their baby gamboling on through, Lester had scrambled between them.

His buck was in sight, maybe a car's length away, craning its neck to partake of what was left of the ripe morsels that were within tongue's reach. The remaining deer, heeding the amiss, scattered. Lester was only three steps out when the majestic stag realized his sanctuary had been invaded. It made its move. Lester smiled when it broke for the field. In the woods, between the branches and the undergrowth, Lester wouldn't have held a chance. Before the buck could straighten its body to stride Lester had a hold of his prize. His left hand had caught one of the buck's ten points. Lester was able to pull the deer's head toward his chest, but he underestimated the strength of the fleeing animal. The terrified deer went with the pull, turned its entire body inside of itself, and with a whip of its neck flung Lester to the ground.

The buck had overestimated the size of its predator, because it too was thrown through the turn and had to stop itself from falling by planting its front hooves and taking pause. Before it had time to regain its momentum, the weasel was in the air. Lester never remained on his back long. Too much could happen down there. He knew what it felt like to be stepped on, to be trampled.

With the buck's first stride Lester had both hands locked on either side of its antlers. Lester was even with the beast's shoulders, attempting to weigh the massive animal to the ground. The buck would have none of it. The life-starved deer kicked its legs violently as it thrashed and struggled to break free of its human yoke. Lester was being tossed around, and with each thrust he risked losing his hold. The next time the stag turned down and into Lester, Lester went limp with it. He crouched on the ground, still clasping his points. As the deer yanked its rack away from Lester's clutch, the weasel shot up from the mud, utilizing the buck's own force to coax its neck past where it was supposed to be. The ten-pointer had no choice but to go with the twist or risk damaging its spine. They both tumbled to the ground, where the scratch and whip of the tall grass entangled them.

The buck struggled to get back on its hooves, but Lester still had his grip and with it the leverage. He was holding the deer to the ground by its rack. The buck couldn't move unless it wanted to leave its skull behind. "The body must go where the head goes." A lesson Lester learned while fighting a guido with a gold chain and a ponytail at the mall two years prior.

The animal continued to flail until Lester had whisked around its head and planted a knee on its neck.

The buck ceased its thrashing. Lester let go of its points. He felt the weight of his knee on the buck's windpipe. It felt right. With caution and purpose he slid his left hand over the stag's throat. He grabbed hold just underneath the hinge of its jaw bone. Lester applied pressure with his thumb and forefinger as he lifted his knee. He never broke eye contact with his prey. It was strange for Lester to see this animal up close, with its antlers in the mud and its tongue half hanging out of its mouth. The experience seemed detached from Lester, as if he was watching a movie about a dirty boy and his wild buck. Lester smiled at the fear in its eyes. He laughed at the creature's absurdity.

"Fight for it," he thought aloud.

It didn't fight. Instead the deer waited to die.

Lester loosened his grip. The buck did nothing. It just stared at its master with its now vacuous black eyes. Lester broke their gaze for the first time. He glanced to the edge of the woods where he had entered the meadow. Lester could barely make out the rest of the herd through the approaching twilight. They were standing stone-still, watching and waiting for their stud to succumb.

"You're all fucking idiots"

Collectively the leaderless herd tensed up at the sound of his voice, but they didn't flee.

Lester looked back at his catch. He scanned the length of its body. The pointed buck was frozen in contortion. All of it was pathetic. He was just a weasel. It had no idea. He reinitiated eye contact before leaning his face into the buck's neck. Lester was only a hair away from its throat when he parted his lips, just a bit, revealing his plaque ridden incisors. Lester inhaled deeply as the broken animal waited without revolt. Lester shut his eyes as he kissed the stag under its berry-stained jaw before releasing his grip.

"Don't eat my fucking berries."

Lester leaned up, waived his arms and yelled, "boo!" The deer sprung to life and sprinted away without turning back. The rest of the herd broke for the safety of forest. Lester stood up, laughing uncontrollably. With his high-pitched staccato bursts he sounded exactly how one would expect a human weasel to laugh. After Lester collected himself, he noticed the rows of berry trees lining the meadow. Within the release of his addled mind he spit in their direction.

In the little light the sunken sun had left to offer, Lester found his clothes and dressed himself. On his journey back through the woods he briefly stopped at a stream and quenched his thirst with one small sip of its flows. Finding his way home was easy. Even in the dim light of the veiled moon each tree in the forest looked different from the next. He didn't walk or run. He floated back to his house. His sense of direction never faltered.

Lester stepped out of the forest thinking only about his phone. He had to call Mr. May. His benefactor wouldn't understand, but at least he would listen. He casually opened the front door to his house like it was his home. The light was on in the kitchen. He was greeted with the unmistakable, irresistible sound and smell of sizzling bacon. He loved bacon. He could not imagine a greater meal with which to fill his empty belly. Lester thought that this might be the best weekend of his life.

Lester took a seat at the dining room table and said hello to his dad, who was sitting at the table's head. Lester stuck out his hand and grabbed one slice of bacon from a Styrofoam plate lined with three sheets of single-ply Bounty Basics. As Lester savored his first taste of transcendence, his father stumbled up from his chair, spit on the filthy floor beside his filthier bare feet and cocked his left arm.

Part Three

Chapter 48
Presumed Sanctuary

Mark sat back in his dormer overlooking Lester's disgraceful back yard. The ebbing moon illuminated every useless heap strewn about his property. There was a permanence about the landscape that Mark had failed to notice in the past. Mark had trouble remembering how Lester's yard used to look when Umed was around. He had difficulty envisioning a reality in which Umed was present at all. He certainly could not imagine Lester's yard being in any state other than its current state, even if Lester were to leave, assuming Lester was even able to leave. The big mess that was The Weasel's back yard seemed daunting in its victory. Part of Mark found solace in accepting life's infallible materiality. It was as it should be because it was as it is. This part of Mark, the acquiesced, flowed with peace and warmth. The other part of Mark, the agnostic, it was getting lit.

He didn't drink often, but on special occasions Mark visited the refrigerator located in what was left of the usable space in his garage. The fridge was loaded with craft beer. Mark's father had liked the look of an icebox full of libations. He wasn't a heavy drinker, but he did take pride in his diversified stock. The refrigerator was at capacity the day he died. After the funeral a multitude of guests, in their mourning, emptied the top shelf and most of the door. That left three full shelves, a blond to black mosaic of pilsners, loggers, stouts and IPAs. Mark cracked and downed his first ale the following summer. Including the beer in his hand, he had drunk only about a case in total. It was difficult for Mark to cut his drinking teeth on a supply of strictly artisan brew.

Crouched in his alcove, Mark was two beers deep within an hour. He had a good reason to force down the fermented hops and barley. Mark was going to the mall in the morning. Tubby McCrap-Save was going with him. Hallmark had decided to sell its annual Country Cousin's limited edition figurines, or whatever the fuck, and they were available for purchase only in store. Mark pleaded with his mom, begged her to let him go and pick up the creepy porcelain children in her stead. She retorted that there were five different cousin set-ups and that she did not know which ones she wanted to buy. Mark knew that was a bullshit excuse and that his mom would undoubtedly purchase one of each. He told her as much. Mark said he would buy the five of them gift wrapped with extra tissue paper that she could throw all over the room.

Hoardy McFour-Shits wouldn't budge. Maybe she couldn't budge. She wanted to go. Mark's mother didn't venture outdoors often, and he supposed for her this was as good a reason as any to leave the house. She did compromise to a degree. Mark's mom wanted to shop at the Hallmark downtown. She knew Peggy, the owner, and she wanted to say hi. Mark demanded that they instead run up to Forrest Side Mall just off the highway outside of town. Mark's mom threw a shit-fit. With a beet-red face and projectile phlegm she called Mark a control freak and insisted that she was the parent in their relationship. She hadn't seen Peggy since the funeral and he could not stop her from seeing Peggy now. Mark changed her mind after calmly offering to drop a match in the middle of her crap pile and locking all the doors to her room. He wasn't proud of his method, but in the end it did convince his mother of the benefits in visiting Forrest Side Mall. After she composed herself, Mark's mom smiled and said she couldn't wait for their drive tomorrow.

Mark went straight from his mother's room to the garage. After launching a tire iron into the meticulously crafted wall of trash threatening to envelop his prognosticated I-Roc, Mark grabbed a six pack of Hoptical Illusion out of the fridge. Mark was three sips into his third bottle when Lester finally made an appearance in his back yard.

"Fuck you, you crazy fuck!"

Lester stood on Umed's rock. His shirt was off. His arms were spread wide.

"You want some more, Fag-a-fuck? I'll give you everything I got."

Lester's dad stammered out of the back door with a wooden baseball bat in his hands. His nose had been split open. Blood cascaded down his chin and stained the front of his white Hanes tee shirt black and red.

He swung his bat at the garbage pails sitting near the back door as he spoke.

"I'll fucking kill you!"

Mark stood up.

Before Lester's dad could recoil the bat in his sodden arms, Lester was on top of him. He was quick, superhero speed-lines quick. In stride, Lester gave his dad a right cross to the temple. Lester's father dropped the bat on impact. He chased it down to the ground after a carom off the door-less jamb. Lester followed his father's bounce on the cement walkway with three swift kicks to the ribs.

"You're getting old, fuck rat. I'm done running and hiding."

Lester kicked his father in the face. Lester's dad was forced to swallow two of his own teeth.

Without a thought, Mark made his way downstairs. He bumped over a shit stack as he sped through the hall. Drunken navigation through the pig-trails of a binge collector was an exclusively amateur sport.

"Mark! What's going on?"

"Go back to bed, Ma!"

Mark fumbled with the lock at the back door. He was distracted by the stack of boxes that had been bordering the path near the rear exit until he had clumsily knocked them over. The boxes and their contents were now sullying his breakfast nook. He glanced at the pile littered about his only functioning dining space. It stung a little, like the boxes had landed on him. Mark was brought back to the situation at hand by a victorious cackle emanating from Lester's back yard. He pulled open the door and broke for the fence. After stumbling to a stop, he grabbed a picket and peeked over to the other side. Lester stood on his rock and laughed at his father as he crawled back into the house.

"Lester? Lester?"

Lester snapped his head around his body, his hands held fists, his intractable frame tensed as he readied for battle. It took him a moment to locate his audience, but he inevitably discovered Mark's near-perfect visage glowing in the moonlight.

"What the fuck do you want?"

With the moon at Lester's back, Mark could not see Lester's face or his sardonic smile.

Boom!

The garbage pail lying on its side in front of the doorway exploded. Lester dropped behind his rock, Mark ducked behind the pickets. He learned of the brand new floodlights installed in Ashley's backyard when his shadow joined him at the fence. Mark heard one of the neighborhood dogs bark at the disquiet. Unsure of what to do next, his eyes were drawn to the corner of his yard and the distressed bungee cord securing the gates.

Lester peeked out from behind the rock. The fuck rat had his shotgun. He could barely see with his bloodied and swollen face. He could hardly breathe with his busted ribs. But he could wield his unmarred shotgun with fluidity, precision and grace.

"Who's the rat fuck now?"

Lester quickly weighed his options. He could scale Mark's fence, only a few steps away, but the cross board was on Mark's side. He knew he could do it, but he'd hate to misplant his foot and give his dad a shot. He was deftly aware of his father's proficiency with a shotgun. Shooting with skill was the only thing that Lester's father was proud of about himself, and rightfully so.

Lester could also break for the front of the house. But he wasn't sure he could outpace his dad even with his father in an inebriated state. There were at least ten strides of open yard between Lester's rock and the corner of his garage. At best Lester gave himself a fifty-fifty chance of outrunning the spread of the buck shot. Considering Lester's father was stumbling gleefully closer to his son those odds grew bleaker for Lester with each of his racing heart beats.

Lester turned around and faced the corner of his yard. He could belly crawl and keep behind the rock. He could stay low until he breached the shadows under the oak tree before he sprung up to catch the corner of the fence that adjoined Ashley's yard. There was still no cross beam, but the ability to plant his feet on the two corner fence sections combined with the cover of the large, low-bowed oak tree made it his best option. Lester immediately stopped thinking and started crawling.

Lester had crossed half the distance to the fence when his father let loose another slug behind the rock. He hadn't even looked. Lester's progenitor just hung the gun over the backside of the boulder where he assumed Lester would be and fired.

"How's that bacon taste, son?"

Lester scrambled to his feet and made his break for the shadows of the oak while his father cocked the gun.

The corner of the fence and Lester's presumed sanctuary approached quickly.

"The rat is out of its hole."

Lester's father was enjoying himself. He was truly happy in his present moment. Life seemed without consequence, with neither a future nor a past. It just was. Lester's father was both filled and fulfilled with the sole purpose of shooting his son in the back.

Lester was an instant from leaping into the corner when the gate, and coincidentally his footing, popped open. He quickly cut into the passageway. Once Lester was through, Mark pulled on the bungee to slam the gate shut.

"What the fuck, man?"

"He's drunk and an asshole!"

Lester's father had sauntered his way under the oak tree. He looked up into its canopy. It was dense and dark, pierced by strands of dapple light emanating from his haughty neighbor's back yard. The oak was full and lush, it stood tall and straight, its brush seemed impenetrable. He knew he could never climb the oak. He knew Lester would be safe within its grasp.

"Where are ya, ya little fucker?"

Mark put a foot against the fence and held tight to the bungee.

"I called the cops."

Lester's father was surprised by the strange voice. It was both deep and assured when compared to his rodent son's squeal.

Mark felt a pluck on the fence. Lester's father didn't pull hard or try to yank the gate open. It was more of an exploratory tug. Mark was emotionless when he heard the gun cock. He assumed he would see the picket gate explode as a mortal cavity was bored into his stomach. Mark imagined himself soaring toward his house with his viscera trailing in the air.

Mark held fast to his bungee. He waited for the loud noise. The bang that should accompany all death. The alarm to the fact that your worthless life would soon be over. It never came. Once time began again, Mark stepped on a cross beam and lifted himself up for a peek over the fence. Lester's father was gone. As Mark stepped down to level ground, he looked at Lester for the first time. Lester's face and bare chest appeared both gleaming white and diffuse with points of darkness. He stood out distinctly in an otherwise flat and insignificant reality. Lester leaned his shoulder against the fence, like a frat boy working the room at a freshman mixer.

"Did you call the cops?"

"No."

Lester straightened himself up and casually put his hand near the hinge of the gate to support his weight.

"Cool."

They heard the ice-cream truck start and Lester's father tare out of the driveway. The instrumental version of Mulberry Bush crackled and popped as it blared over the truck's corroded PA. Mark wondered how many kids were going to be in the back of the SUV Lester's father plowed into at eighty five miles-per-hour.

"You got anything to eat?"

Mark looked back to his house. The koi pond cut a pleasant cast in the moonlight. He thought that he should finish it tomorrow after the mall.

"Yeah, I don't…"

Mark was interrupted by the sound of sirens in the distance. Lester looked toward the alarms. For the first time ever in front of Mark, Lester appeared anxious. Mark shoved aside the strange urge to put an arm around his neighbor.

"Yeah, let's get something to eat."

Chapter 49
Some Kind of Chicken

Mark stood at his back door and stared at the brass knob. It was buzzing a little. He was buzzing a little. There was some lingering adrenaline coursing through his body. Mark found himself confused and conflicted. He didn't want to go inside. Not with The Weasel. Not with his mom. Not with it. Mark fumbled some with the knob before turning to face Lester.

"You wanna go to the diner or something? My treat."

They could both hear the sirens growing louder. There were at least two neighbors making man noises and being pretend tough in Mark's front yard. Lester held out his arms and inspected his bare chest.

"Yeah, I don't know if now is the right time for a Greek omelet."

"I know. It's just... Fuck it!"

Mark twisted the knob and kicked at the bottom of the door. It was a mistake. The beveled slab of cedar swung open and knocked over a mountain of precariously stacked magazines, causing an avalanche of glossy print to line what was left of the pig trail leading to the back door.

Lester's eyes bulged.

"Ho, shit! You read any good magazines lately?"

Mark twisted his body towards Lester's with a snarl and a scowl. He didn't know how he would react to an outsider taking a jab at him in his own home. His first instinct was a visceral one. He summoned the same anger that had surfaced a few days prior in the cafeteria. Before Mark could lift an arm in defense of his honor, Lester's innocent and amazed face had pacified him. Lester inhaled the strange atmosphere like a child who just took their first steps past the proletariat checkpoint at Disneyland. Mark was calmed enough by Lester's mien to retort with his own witty response.

"Yeah, last month's issue of Doll Reader was a real page turner."

Mark reached down with one hand and grabbed a random glut of magazines.

"Here it is."

He pitched the whole lot against the dining room wall. After the resounding thud and splatter, the magazines, in foolhardy obedience to gravity, attempted to sleuth through the stacks of shit in a futile effort to reach the floor. When they settled nothing had changed. The room was as it had been. Mark and Lester laughed at the absurdity, together.

"Mark! Is that you? Mark! What was that noise?"

"Nothing, mom. I'll be right there."

Mark turned to face his neighbor. With both squinted eyes and a grin Lester attempted to read a magazine using only the moonlight.

"Listen, follow the trail upstairs. My room is the only one you can get to on the right. I'll bring up something to eat."

"Mark?"

"I'm coming, Ma!"

Lester dropped his copy of Better Homes and Gardens and smiled through the insanity.

"This is great. It's like a fun house."

Lester followed the trail, stopping to inspect different piles of it along the way. He was amused. Mark's house was like being in the forest for Lester. He could get lost, hunt and explore.

Mark entered his mother's room, trying his hardest to abide without breathing. It didn't take long to explain what had happened and to inform her that Lester was staying the night. Mark failed to mention that Lester's father technically had tried to kill his son. Mark instead told his mom that he fired two shots in the air to scare him a bit. He said, "It was a hillbilly thing. Nothing too real." She was a little worried, guns freaked her out, but Mrs. Brunson for the most part took it all in stride. Mark asked his mother not to answer the door if either the police or the neighbors rang the bell. Not that she could squeeze her fat ass through the boxes that lined the hallways. It was more of a general instruction outlining how Mark would be handling the situation. Lester seemed to want the cops out of it for now. Mark had a feeling they wouldn't understand and somehow Lester would be judged for his father's sins.

It took Mark a few minutes to get upstairs. With little thought and less care he cleaned up the pig trail leading to the back door by tossing the loose magazines up and over the retaining wall that bordered the path. Mark was more discerning with the kitchen. He knew if he didn't clean out his breakfast nook he would regret it in the morning. Mark had enough to worry about with Sunday's impending trip to the mall.

The problem with cleaning up a formerly haphazard pile was that none of it had an actual place to which it could be restored. Each item or box had found its singular position in a pseudo-systematic fashion that existed only as it could at that time. Once that collection of happenstance imploded, there was no model from which to rebuild. Mark stacked half the crap back in the pass-through. The rest he bunched up in his arms and tossed down the basement staircase. The next time he was forced to enter the lowest and filthiest level of his home, the scatter-shot shit pile at the bottom of the stairs would be heaped on top of one of the basement's master heaps. For Mark there was method as well as madness.

After a seven minute wait at the microwave, Mark clomped upstairs with four Hot Pockets and two cold Toasted Lagers. He wasn't sure if Lester drank, but he had a hunch that turned out to be spot on. As he stepped into his room Lester was finishing both his second Hoptical Illusion and his 30th lap in Forza.

"Yo!"

"Oh, hey. Hope this is cool?"

Lester held up a near empty bottle.

"Yeah it's fine. I actually… why are you so filthy?"

Mark regretted the question the second after it was asked. It seemed impolite. Like asking an epileptic why they shook so much. But Lester was filthy. On display, under Mark's LED high hats, Lester looked as if he had rubbed dirt all over his body.

"'Cause I rubbed dirt all over my body. Let me get one of those Pockets."

Lester paused the game and grabbed a Hot Pocket and a beer.

"So what's with all the crap? Your mom a hoarder or something?"

Lester took a bite of the Hot Pocket with his left hand and at the same time with his right hand he capped his beer on the corner of Mark's desk. It was all very natural for him. Mark was astonished. Every action of Lester's appeared effortless: opening a beer, asking touchy questions, smearing dirt on his body, playing other people's video games, climbing trees, being shot at by his parents. There was no affect involved. Lester seemed to exist on a plane devoid of pretense. Mark at once realized that conversing with Lester was like talking to an imaginary friend when you were four. It was all truth and comfort.

Lester was vaguely aware of this comfort level as well, though he was in no position to analyze it. Lester knew if he concentrated on the structure of the moment, if he examined the reasons behind its sufficiency, its fluid form would tense and tangle. He felt good. He felt safe. Mark had come to his rescue when it mattered. He had let him into his disgraceful home. Lester was not going to ruin any of that with awkward conversation. He used his adrenaline and the alcohol to keep the moment lubricated, loose and alive. He needed Mark.

"Yeah, I asked first. What's with the dirt?"

Mark was feeling good, too. He didn't run from Lester's shotgun wielding father. He didn't call the cops. He protected his neighbor and let him inside his disgusting house. Mark deftly capped his beer on the lip of his desk and took a long swig. The suds went down easy. It was the first sip of beer Mark had ever enjoyed.

"I was tracking a buck and I didn't want it to smell me. I woulda took a shower, but my dad tried ta' kill me."

Lester smiled as he restarted the video game.

"You hunt deer now?"

"Always."

"Did you get one?"

Lester took a beat to look Mark over. He wondered just how much of "The Weasel" he could handle. He saw that Mark appeared to be both interested and kind.

"Nah, one day. So what's with the piles of shit? Fuck!"

Lester had crashed his Ferrari. He put down the controller and took another Hot Pocket off the plate. They were good. Truthfully, Lester was disappointed. His freezer was lousy with processed meat socks. He was hoping for some caviar or duck eggs or anything fancy that the other side ate. The beer was good. His dad only drank Bud Light.

"My dad died two years ago. He was with another woman when it happened."

"Ashley's mom?"

Everyone knew. Even the white-trash neighbor who just moved to town and had zero friends knew. Mark wondered what people would discuss if they were created as perfect beings. He assumed they wouldn't have a language. Just understanding nods amongst sunsets and silence.

"Yeah. It was all fucked up. She couldn't cope. She always had this hoarding thing in her. When my dad died she ran out of excuses and fully embraced the crap side."

Mark recalled a time when there was an excuse, when his mom had reason to avoid huddling in her own filth. Although the memories weren't pleasant they were less painful than his current situation. Mark remembered when his mom and dad fought. It averaged about three times a month and in the beginning it was mostly about her shoes. His father

had built her a shoe closet and it stunk. No matter
what he did to remedy the problem, the closet oozed
a lurking and wretched stench. It wasn't that Mark's
mom had a particularly bad foot odor; it was more
because she kept every shoe that she had ever owned.
Whenever Mark thought back, he remembered most
every fight that occurred between his mom and
dad was about her shit and the space it occupied.
Finally, his parents struck a deal. Mark's dad rented
his mother a premium storage unit. It was hers, and
only hers, to stock with anything she wished. The
deal had worked, Mark guessed, because shortly
after that all they ever fought about was money or his
father's prolonged absence from what was supposed
to be their family life.

Each fight sounded the same to Mark. It didn't
matter what they were yelling about. It could be
shoes, unavailability, or a bitchy remark made to one
of Mark's father's friends. All that mattered was that
Mark was powerless to stop any of it. No matter how
long or loud he cried and screamed, they would just
keep at each other. At times his parents would even
argue over the cause of Mark's tears. Blaming one
another for how Mark was responding, each saying,
"Do you see what you are doing to our son?"

The fights were always nasty. His parents would
yell and shout, well his dad would yell, his mom
would sit stoically until it was her moment to slide in
the knife. And when she did it was shrill and biting.
It was usually about Mark's grandfather and how

horrible and cold he was and how Mark's father was just like him. Mark's dad would fire back, blasting her alcoholic, convict of a father and her trailer-trash, piece-of-shit mother. Mark's dad loved to call Mark's mom a peasant. Early on Mark didn't understand this at all. The only word he knew that remotely sounded like peasant was pheasant. As far as Mark could tell, a pheasant was some kind of chicken.

During and after each argument Mark always felt badly for his mother because his father was so loud and animated with his vulgarities. He would bite on his knuckles and in a rage call his wife a "filthy cunt." After Mark was old enough to accept the inevitability of their battles he would sit at the top of the staircase and listen to his dad berate his mom with his throaty chortle, laced with spit and bile. Mark's dad would pace around the house for hours. Mark concentrated on his father's gravid footsteps and perceived the slight rumble of his wake. He would inevitably circle back to Mark's mother with a cruel remark garbled out of his knuckle filled mouth; always with the same intensity as the previous obscenity. It was as if each step through the house recharged his anger. It only ended when his father went to sleep or sometimes when he left for work. Those were the best fights. The six a.m. fights, because Mark's dad had to walk past his wife's odorous shoe locker to get to his ties. Mark's father would shake his mother awake so he could lean over her and scream at her face as she lay in her bed and prayed for him to die.

Each fight, the entire affair, always seemed so one-sided. No matter how angry Mark's mother became, she just could not match his father's thunderous intensity or his ability to insult.

That all changed in a single afternoon shortly before Mark's dad passed. Mark was gifted a glimpse of his father's frustrations and the reasons for his anger were made plain.

Mark's mother had been frantic for an entire morning. Her friend from high school, Donna, was visiting for the day and Mark's mom had to locate an old cheerleading outfit that she stored in the facility. Mark was forced by his mother to go to the garage and help her dig out the uniform. This ornamental relic that defined her glory days was probably the only item that Mark's mother had ever saved that held a residual function, even if it was only for an afternoon. When they rolled opened the large metal door that shuttered the inutile expanse, Mark's initial thought was that they should have hired help and brought a shovel, maybe a backhoe.

That was the first time Mark saw the beast, "it." The entire storage space was packed indiscriminately from floor to ceiling with bags, rugs, old furniture and new furniture, clothes, bolts of fabric, fish tanks, dog dishes... everything. It had found its Petri dish. A warm, dark room from which it could culture into what it would eventually become. They never found the outfit, accessibility was the one luxury Mark's mother failed to hoard. But for Mark, from that day until the time of his dad's death, his father didn't seem so loud and his mother seemed like some kind of chicken.

"Could be worse. She coulda bought an ice cream truck and a shotgun."

After chuckling at his own clever remark, Lester began his race anew. Mark noticed that Lester didn't like to use the brakes on his Ferrari. He just kept the car maxed out and took every corner at full speed. At first Lester was spinning out on each turn, but once he got a feel for the controls his strategy began to yield results. Right before he approached a corner he'd let off the gas for an instant, hit the turn, then pin it. He'd use his momentum to plow through the curve before straightening back out. It was sloppy, and his car would usually go off track a bit, but Lester continually made up ground with each lap. Lester had an unorthodox style with everything he did, yet it all seemed to work with fluidity and ease. Lester seemed less like a weasel to Mark and more like a squirrel leaping between the branches of two trees.

"Go take a shower. I'll get you something to wear. Thanks to Hoard-A-Beast, I have some clothes from a few years ago. Pretty sure I can still get to them."

Lester smiled. He paused the game and grabbed Mark's towel off its hook fastened to his closet door. He was about to leave the room when he thought of Mr. May.

"Mark?"

Mark had grabbed the Xbox controller. He took over Lester's game and attempted to mimic his break-neck approach.

"Yeah, bud?"

"So if you ever tackle me again, I'll fuckin' kill ya."

Mark's Ferrari crashed violently. He looked over to Lester, who was shoving a cigarette pack-sized hunk of hot pocket down his throat with a gluttonous smile. Before he swallowed the muddy pulp of cheese, pepperoni and baked dough, he made a suggestion.

"And get me something better to eat. Hot Pockets are straight up nigga food."

Lester grabbed his beer and closed the bedroom door. At that moment Mark couldn't figure out if he hated that he loved Lester or if loved that he hated him. He never had time to decide. Mark was distracted by his need to throw up into the empty garbage pail by his desk.

Chapter 50
Boundaries

Mark woke up in a panic. Lester slept on the floor at the foot of his bed. There were both empty beer bottles and dirty dishes dotted, like a domestic acne, around his room. Lester's clothes were lumped in a pile by the dresser. Mark's Xbox was spilling out of its cubby and his TV defiantly displayed a static blue screen.

Mark was dreading the walk with Lester back through his house. Without the moon, the cops, and the beer, Lester's presence in his home seemed excessive and inappropriate. Mark's ears began to ring. He felt his sheets chaffing on his skin. Mark was trapped in his own room by the deadly dual transgressions of sloth and gluttony.

Mark snuck out of bed, dressed and began to straighten up his desk. He did so quietly. At least if his space was clean it would show Lester that he and his mom had separate boundaries.

Mark and Lester had stayed in his room all night. They watched in the dark as the cops aimlessly tooled around Lester's back yard. They listened and laughed as those same officers knocked on Mark's front door. It was fun and exciting for them both. Mark hadn't enjoyed himself so much in his bedroom since the last time Umed slept over and they took turns masturbating to debased thoughts of Ashley. With the alcohol and the police it was thrilling at times. The laughter was non-stop. Lester was a one-man riot. He had a clever comment or comeback for everything. Mark's cheeks were sore from the smile he wore until they fell asleep.

Mark stole a peek at Lester as he slept. He had his shirt off and he was breathing steadily. Both his pale skin and contoured body were lost within Mark's cream-colored duvet. Lester looked peaceful.

"Maybe he could climb out the window," Mark thought to himself.

Mark was alphabetizing his Xbox games when he heard the scrapings of an indigent vermin-child clawing himself off the floor. Mark closed his eyes; he wasn't sure what this new reality would bring. Who would Lester be in the morning? What would their relationship be in the light of day?

Mark inhaled deeply and held on tight. He was afraid to let go. It was his last breath of retreat. His final sip from the still waters of a forsaken catacomb. As he exhaled, Mark turned to face the rest of his morning. His burden was both base and corporal.

Lester, the miscreant, was folding his blanket as he arched his back for a needed stretch. Mark, with a steady resolve that belied each of his desires, broke the silence.

"Hey."

Lester smiled.

"Hey."

"Listen, I gotta take my mom to the mall. What are you going to do, with your dad and all?"

Lester noticed the serious tone in Mark's voice. Worse, he sensed the regret. Mark's words were dripping with the same shame and remorse that his father's words swam in after he awoke from a prolonged and abusive bender. Lester placed the blanket on the bed and sat down next to it.

"Nothing."

"What about the shotgun?"

"Yeah. That was last night. Today won't have a shotgun."

"So you're going back?"

"I never left."

Mark turned his back on Lester to needlessly fiddle with the positioning of his television. He was having trouble looking Lester in the eye. And they still had to walk through the house together. Mark thought that maybe he should have allowed the bungee cord to remain fastened to his gate.

"Mark?"

"Yeah, bud?"

Lester smiled. He liked being called bud.

"All that shit downstairs. Fuck it. It doesn't matter. It's not real. Not to me, anyway."

With Lester's empyrean understanding Mark was released. In quick succession he respired three resonant gasps of air. Before he could circle back to his one friend, the only person in the school he never wanted to be friends with, Mark had to wipe tears from both of his eyes.

"I have some more Pockets and beer if you want to hang tonight."

Lester smiled.

"Sounds good, but it's a school night. I gotta ask my dad."

They both laughed. Lester helped Mark straighten up his room. They joked and laughed some more. Even without the beer or the danger their friendship felt real.

Lost in their camaraderie, neither Mark nor Lester had noticed Ashley through the slit in Mark's blinds. She wore a two-piece by the pool and she was beautiful.

Chapter 51
In for a Penny

The ride to the mall was taken in silence with one exception. Intermittently, Mark's mom would read a random sign aloud, something new, a business or an advertisement that had changed since the last time she and Mark went for a drive. There was neither a context nor a point to any of her articulations other than the existence of what appeared before her eyes. Every dispensable declaration stung Mark at his core. He couldn't help but echo each of her remarks with an audible sigh. For Mark the simple expulsion of breath from his mother's lungs was inherently fatuous.

Mark's mom spent the entire ride wearing a vapid smile comprised of merriment and wonder. Mark used the time to contemplate, among other things, if his mother felt the substance of the fat on her bones or if it, too, floated through a fabricated world of comfort completely disjointed from its weighted surroundings.

When they arrived at the mall Mark chose a space to the rear of the parking lot. He could have parked closer, but he wanted his mom to remember this trip as the imposition that it was. Mark's mom began to complain. She had her bulbous arm extended and her pudgy finger pointed toward an empty spot near the food court. She uttered the sound "mmm" before cutting herself off. She instead began the separate struggle of unbuckling her own seat belt.

Even with the passenger seat tracked back to its limit, Five-Chins McGee barely fit into her own car. Mark watched his mother in disgust as she contorted her billowing body in search of the latch that was nuzzled between two folds of hip fat. Mark had already assisted her in, buckled her up and would have to help her get out. If his mother could not perform this one small service for herself, Mark decided, he would crack the windows and leave her in the car while he went to try on clothes at Zumiez. Only after his solo shopping excursion would he drive his mom home without her precious Country Cousins. Mark frowned when he finally heard the click. The seatbelt had whipped around her bulging torso and clacked itself on the passenger door window. Mark's mother was officially a farce of existence.

While crossing the parking lot Mark took a moment to take in his surroundings and size up his adversary. He noticed that the mall was unusually crowded. It was the first Sunday after the first week of school, and life's participants were urged to buy the things they hadn't realized that they needed until they saw that others did. Mark looked back to his plodding podge of portliness. Walking, his mother's current adversary, was getting the better of her. For Mark, her being was detestable. He wondered if the throngs of shoppers would work to conceal her hearty carriage or if they would serve as an outline, a highlighted border, to her unchecked obesity. Either way, Mark was resigned. "Fuck it," he thought. "In for a penny, in for a ton."

After the labored breathing, sweat and joint pain that accompanied Mark's mother from her Volvo XC90 to the front entrance of the mall, she made a decision.

"We need to go to the office, Mark."

"For what?"

"I'm not going to be able to walk through all these people. I need…"

"No."

Mark put it together before she finished her plea. "Mark…"

"No. We walk or we go home."

Mark's mother's visage, formerly a countenance of pleading, reverted to stone. There would be no more discussion. She was at the mall. They were at the mall. There wasn't much Mark could do about it.

"I'll meet you right here in a half-an-hour, sweetie. I'm going to the office."

They hadn't yet entered the building and Mark had already noticed a clamor surrounding his mother's presence. It was as if with each pound she slathered on her blobby frame, her gravitational field, one that solely attracted the gaping glares of strangers, grew stronger. Mark had already caught a few of the eye-wide smiles and an intentionally audible snicker. Yet Mark felt nothing for his mother. Most of his sympathy was reserved for the patrons forced to accommodate her presence. The rest was for himself.

Mark opened the door, entered Forrest Side Mall and let the door close behind him. He didn't look back. Fatty McWorthless would have to fend for herself.

Chapter 52
The Wrong Things

Fred condemned the mall. He hated everything about it: the parking, the waiting, the crowds, and the crap. Store after store of items that few people needed and even fewer people could afford. Most of all Fred hated that his children enjoyed the mall.

Fred wondered sometimes, he worried sometimes, what if his kids liked the wrong things? Not now when they were clueless because of their youth, but later on when they were their own men. What about college? Would they even want to go to college or would they despise both learning and those that were learned? If they were accepted to a university, would they join a fraternity? Fred didn't think he could like someone who joined a fraternity. Imagine initiating yourself, ingratiating yourself, to a bunch of children who believed being wasted was the end-all of being cool. What would Fred do if his own offspring fucked girls, even raped girls, for sport and status? What if his kids found God after that? What if after their drunken, date-rape, frat boy days they were all born again and in turn they hated both gays and birth control because that was what one needed to do in order to love God? What if they were rude to other humans or they decided that reading a book was a waste of time? What if they refused to recycle or hold open the door for the person behind them entering 7-11? What if they loved the UFC and reality television or took pleasure in other people's suffering? What if they never learned how to forgive? What if they lied and cheated their way through life? What if they liked professional sports? Fred wasn't concerned with the casual fan who enjoyed the Super Bowl or a good playoff run, but what if his kids actually cared if one random team won or lost vs. a second random team? What if his own children became inconsolable because number twenty-three struck out in the bottom of the ninth or fumbled the ball on the one yard line in the fourth quarter? And the reason they fervently cared one way or the other was because either of the two teams played half of their games sort of within driving distance from where they lived.

Fred remembered when he was a child at his grandfather's house on any given Sunday afternoon. Granddad would be watching the Royals, living or dying with each pitch. Any pitch that wasn't either a strike or an out for the opposing team would be met by his grandfather with an expletive in kind. If the Royals lost, Fred's father told him, "Don't even try and talk to grandpa." If you did, you would be met with a "Fuck off!" or even the back of his hand. There were one-hundred and sixty-two games a year. Even the good teams lost nearly half of them. And this man, a man who gave Fred twenty-five percent of his genes, a man who lived for over half of a century, would be outright nasty when George Brett's team failed to best the Cleveland Indians in a preseason exhibition.

What would Fred do if any of his children behaved like that? Could he be proud of anything else about them if they were subtly racist or misogynistic, or worst of all, entitled? Fred didn't think he could stand any three kids, even his own, if they felt that the world and its inhabitants owed them anything.

Fred tolerated the mall. He bought his boys what they wanted, within reason. Then they got the speech. The lecture about respecting themselves and respecting others. They would need to read before they went to bed, by themselves and for an hour. And no, no matter how much they begged, they could not have a team jersey. Fred's children would not wear another man's name on their backs.

During his concourse meanderings with his kids in tow, Fred noticed Mark waiting on the Auntie Anne's pretzel line. Fred smiled; he enjoyed Anne's pretzels, too. Fred, on special occasions, liked to treat himself to one of her original knots double dipped in butter sauce. He never purchased the nacho cheese from Anne. There was a better cheese sauce served warm in a shot-sized plastic cup for fifty cents at the Steak Shack two booths down. Maybe the mall wasn't all bad all the time.

Fred wondered if he should say hi. He liked Mark. He was proud of Mark. He thought that maybe he could introduce Mark to his own children.

"Dad, we never went to Best Buy. You said…"

"Yeah, okay. You've got twenty minutes. We have to be here to meet your mother."

Even old, hard-assed Fred acquiesced to the demands of his whining children. Sometimes he was just too tired to climb to the top of his soap box. Other times he just wanted to hug them and never let them go.

Fred decided not to say anything to Mark. He supposed that Mark might not want to hear anything his UPS driver had to say. Mark spoke with Fred way too much as it was. Besides, Fred was tragically certain that he would catch up with Mark on Monday.

Chapter 53
A Unique Perspective

Larry T. loved the mall; especially on the weekend when it was crowded. He stood a head taller than each of its occupants. For Larry it was a unique perspective; that of a sea of people lost in themselves. Larry could wade in, witness, and still breathe his own air.

"Great game, LT!"

That was the other thing, Larry's celebrity. There were nine scouts at the game on Friday. The word was out, Larry T. was going pro. No doubt. Everyone in town loved it. It wasn't hard to spot the future star. He was bigger than everyone and he was black. Either or would do. Six-foot-five was noticeable. Being one of a handful of black teens in the area was just as obvious.

Walking through the mall, permanently seated in his genetically advanced perch, Larry was hard pressed to spot a single minority in the crowd.

They were all white. And they all looked up to him. Larry's father had not chosen Forrest Side by accident. He purposely threw his son into its bland, monochromatic stew. He needed his son to develop the taste buds necessary to digest its flavor. He wanted his boy to swallow and savor all of its success. His child had to respect and be respected by those in power, especially if he planned to dine amongst them. It was easy for Larry's family to be accepted. Even as an obvious outsider, Larry's father was a model citizen in both the town and the NFL.

During his entire hall of fame career John Thomas was constantly being commended for his professionalism and character. Every owner and advertiser that endorsed his enormous paychecks, without fail, told him as much with a smile. John wasn't stupid. He knew they were commenting on little more than him being a well behaved, non-threatening black man. But fuck them. He wasn't being polite to put them at ease. He was doing it for himself and his family and that wasn't even the entirety of his reasoning. JT was courteous and respectful because that's how people should behave. If he received contracts and commercials for functioning as a human must, then who was he to complain? His son was going to be a good person as well. Larry would be indoctrinated in dual disciplines of ethics and success. He was going to live and love them both. If the Thomases were the only black family in town, so be it. John was only living his life. He did not care to be judged by his neighbors, nor by those from his old neighborhood. John knew where he had come from and understood exactly where he was headed.

Larry had a slightly different take on his circumstances. He was fine wherever he went. Not because of who circled around him but because of who he was. Larry was smart, kind, and talented, and he deserved the admiration and respect that these traits demanded. Period. What he did not like was all the unnecessary approbation. What drove him particularly crazy was hearing an old white lady comment on how well he behaved or having a teacher single him out in class to affirm his remarkable performance on a test. Of course he was well behaved, he had character. Of course he received high marks in school, he studied his ass off. Ironically, the least authentic praise Larry received was for his athletic achievements. His talent was a given. He was presumed born with ability; a precious gift from his hall of fame father and Olympic medalist mother. The twenty-five hours a week he dedicated to his craft was considered ancillary to each of his singular skills. Both his daily toil and the monotonous grind were simply the actions any of us would take if we happened to be blessed with his glorious genes.

It amazed Larry T. how everyone around him, all the troglodytes, were expected to do well. No praise was heaped on them for saying "thank you" or for spelling the word "PERFUNCTORY". Half of them couldn't even dress themselves. Larry was surrounded by Wrangler-jean-wearing, Sketcher-shoe-footing mediocrity who felt the need to applaud his good-natured charm.

"Damn!"

Larry's bellowing baritone voice caused everyone within earshot to freeze in threatened expectation.

Mark's mom had not been looking where she was driving. She had been occupied by all the colorful advertisements draped around the mall. Most everybody had seen her and moved out of her way. The rest sensed her arrival, felt her enormity rolling up behind them. She caused a minor stir. Larry, a presence in his own right, did not feel the mobile mound creep up behind him until it had already driven directly into the back of his knee. He was more shocked than hurt. Larry could tell immediately it was nothing more than a bump. But any hit to his knee tended to give him pause for analysis. His body was his future and his future was that of predestined greatness.

"Oh, I'm sorry, dear. I don't drive these scootch-a-ma-hauls often."

Larry looked down at her with contempt. It was hard to look at Mark's mother in any other way.

"Don't worry about it, ma'am. It's crowded today."

It was difficult for Mrs. Brunson to see through the crowd from such a low vantage point. She was lost behind her size. It was hard for her to be taken seriously without being eye level to the world. Despite that, this gigantic, imposing man of otherness gave her his full attention.

"Wow! Such a polite young man. Good for you."

As she drove away and through the multitude that parted for her, Larry imagined hitting her in the stomach as hard as he could. He wondered if she would pop on impact and splatter her grossness all over everyone at the mall.

Chapter 54
A Matter of Degrees

Mark spent his first five minutes at the mall on a bench in the food court eating a pretzel. Surprisingly, he had yet to recognize a single shopper. Both Forrest Side and Lake Side were small towns, or at least they felt that way. The two towns were isolated by both the forest that surrounded them and the highway that cleaved them from their neighboring communities. You certainly couldn't know everyone, but there was barely one degree of separation between anyone and someone you knew intimately.

After a short bath in the public pool of anonymity, Mark chose to relax. He decided not to let any of it matter. As he took his first steps through the mass of mall rats, Mark thought of Lester and the ease with which he appeared to navigate his unconventional existence. Mark felt a knot in his stomach, a small pang, a longing for the company of his new friend. Mark missed Lester and fantasized about the scattered shavings of sarcasm, levity, and self-deprecation with which he would have spiced their mall-maddening exploits. On his way to GameStop, lost in his desire, Mark nearly overlooked a boisterous crew of Lake Side tweens. He didn't know them personally, they were seventh graders, but he had seen a few of the boys around town. Mark thought the tall, blond boy in the center of the group was Tommy Connely's little brother, Billy. Mark used to throw bombs to Tommy in junior high. The kid had hands like a bear trap.

Just to be safe, Mark kept his distance. He cut a sharp left into the main entrance of Macy's. The antiquated department store was large and sparsely populated. Mark planned to navigate one of its wide aisles into a shared corridor with GameStop. He wasn't going to buy a video game, but it never hurt to browse. Mark liked to peruse the box art and research any apps that he might download at home.

While Mark passed through Macy's young men's department he missed seeing Tommy Connelly meet up with his little brother. Mark probably would have chosen to wait in the car if he knew his old wide out was hanging around the mall. Unlike the weasel, Mark still had something to lose.

Tommy was a small detail from Mark's past. The two of them had gotten along well enough on the field, but they shared few hours outside of the white lines. Tommy was disappointed with their relationship, considering what a dynamic pair they made during their many trips to the end zone. He never admitted it, not even to himself, but he blamed Umed for hogging all of Mark's spare time. Tommy even went so far as to write the words "sand nigger" on Umed's locker with a black sharpie. It was a crime of circumstance that poorly reflected Tommy's conscious opinions on the subject. A mere childish prank that Connelly thought little of until an assembly was called the following week in which racial sensitivity was the headlining topic. This incident occurred only two days before Umed's parents decided to send Umed to an out-of-state boarding school. Another small detail in Mark's life.

Mark never made it to GameStop. He was distracted by a killer pair of Chucks prominently displayed at the top of a multi-tiered platform located in Macy's shoe department. The sneakers were black with red pinstripes and a gold star. By the time the shoe salesman admitted that they didn't stock a pair in his size, twenty minutes had passed and the remainder of Mark's spare time expired.

Chapter 55
A Good Deed

Mark's mom invested in all five of Hallmark's limited edition figurines. They were all so perfect. She even bought two separate Country Cousin collectables that she also noticed were perfect. There was a chance that Mrs. Brunson had purchased these same statues last year, but she couldn't remember so she picked them up just to be on the safe side.

Mark's mother was gingerly holding the bag of perfection in her left hand while using her right hand to steer her cart. She briefly considered putting over to Fabric Bonanza, but the store was on the second level of the mall and Mark's mother distrusted elevators. Plus, her time was running out and she didn't want to keep her boy waiting.

While scooting towards the exit, Mrs. Brunson noticed her well-mannered black friend chatting with a couple of girls over in the food court. In particular, he was openly flirting with a cute, giggly blond. With little thought and less discretion, she drove alongside the railing near their table.

"Excuse me, sweetie. I just wanted you to know that you have nothing to worry about. This young man is as polite as they come."

Mark's mom smiled at her own good deed. She had always excelled at random acts of kindness. Before the accident she liked to drop her little pleasantries all around town. Mark's mother had mastered the art of complimenting a woman's hair. She could routinely tell when a friend or even a casual acquaintance had recently visited the salon. She would often go out of her way to let complete strangers know how great they looked. Mrs. Brunson loved to offer her opinion, and those at the receiving end of her unsolicited sentiments, enchanted by her cast, would accommodate all that she had to say. Even into her forties, up until her husband's death, she was the prettiest girl in the room. Her opinion was commonly welcomed.

The group surrounding Larry T., both collectively and reflexively, lost it. Jared managed to spit a crispy nugget out of his mouth during a guffaw. The three girls and two of Larry's teammates were rolling in a fit of communal laughter. Larry never cracked a smile. Jared misread the situation and added his own little jab.

"Yo, Larry, exactly what did you do over the summer? I mean, baby's got back. But come on!"

Mrs. Brunson had failed to take into account the source of respect for her opinions. It wasn't her fault, she was gorgeous at birth. As a child, undevised voyeurs offered her their smiles as she skipped about the playground. From her teen years on, everyone she met thirsted for her acceptance and approval. There was no reason for her to try. Not when her presence alone made anyone near to her happy. Her opinions were craved as a sustenance derived from her attention. The relevance of her articulations didn't matter as each of her words were perceived as golden drops of honey. Now, with her beauty swallowed whole by the food that she ate, every sentence she spoke was either mocked or ignored. Her words were corrupted at their source.

Mrs. Brunson's eyes widened. Her smile warped into an open-mouthed frown. Her face flushed. Larry's face did, too. Mark's mom depressed the button on her scooter, but it didn't respond. Not many shoppers at Forrest Side Mall used the fat carts. Their maintenance record was spotty at best.

"What the fuck did you just say?"

Larry, now standing, towered. Mark's mom sat petrified. Larry's friends went silent. The girl Larry flirted with fought the desire to flee. Any shoppers within range of the disquiet had Larry's full attention. Mark's mother dropped her bag of hayseed collectibles, squeezed the scooter's yellow button and silently implored its wheels to turn. Over and over she flipped the gear switch and depressed the accelerator. Over and over the machine failed to respond. Sweat did find a way to stream down her back.

"I'm sorry. I was just… this thing won't move!"

Larry hopped the iron fence that cordoned off the food court. It was hardly more than a normal step for him.

"You was just helping out the nigger boy, right?"

There it was, that word. From the moment she bumped Larry's knee, it had consumed her being. Its guttural intonation had spouted from her core, flooding her body and soul. She was terrified of that word. At times, she refused to acknowledge its existence. The irony in her current situation was that Mark's mother was proud to admit that she had never uttered that word in her life. Not once. Even in college, when all of her friends regurgitated it regularly.

"I didn't say…"

"Nah, nah you didn't say anything. You just scooted your fat ass over here-"

Larry's teammate George had never seen this side of his team captain. It scared him. He was compelled to intervene even through the fear.

"Yo, Larry, chill out, man."

"No, fuck that."

Larry's eyes remained fixed on the separate institutions of obesity and ignorance before him. He was unwilling, perhaps unable, to discern a border between them. Larry watched as its vehicle remained unresponsive. He rejoiced as its burden frantically twisted and turned its bloated head.

"Fuck it. Fatty-three-ass scooted herself all the way over here to make sure this pretty little white girl felt safe. Why the fuck does she need your fat-ass approval to talk to me? You fat, worthless fuck."

A crowd began to assemble. Fred and his boys were waiting for their mother's nails to dry in the balcony above the food court. He had noticed the tumult below. Fred recognized Larry. Everyone did. Even from where Fred lived across the highway, Larry was a known entity. At first, Fred failed to recognize the overweight woman. The moment he realized who she was, Fred's jaw dropped. It was Mark's mother. Mark, who Fred recently spied buying a pretzel from Auntie Anne. Fred hadn't seen Mark's mother in a while. It was only once, about six months and seventy pounds ago, but even then she was the fattest person he had seen in real life since renewing his CDL at the DMV.

Fred scanned the crowd for Mark. He found him two kiosks down, heading in the direction of the food court.

"Mark!"

Fred yelled loudly. His children were frightened.

"Dad, what's going on?"

"It's okay, Dave. Just… Mark!"

Fred's voice was thunderous. Nearly half of the shoppers on the lower level of the mall looked up to him. Mark took notice of Fred and promptly lifted his hands and squinted his eyes to gesture, "What the fuck?"

"Don't move!"

Mark was confused. He scanned the concourse and spotted a mass of shoppers bunched up and bearing witness by the tables in the food court. Fred grabbed the nearest woman who happened to be walking by.

"Listen, these are my kids. Please stay with them. It's an emergency."

Before the confused patron could respond, Fred had left her alone with his three children. The nearest escalator was in the opposing corridor around the back side of the dining area.

"Daddy!"

Fred's kids were worried. He had no time to explain.

Mark hurried towards the commotion. He had assumed his mother was dead. As he jockeyed himself through the spellbound audience, Mark was overcome with disparate emotions. Relief was not among them. He worried most about the spectacle involved in removing his grotesque mother's tremendous, dead body from the food court at Forrest Side Mall.

Chapter 56
Mark's Avatar

Once Mark broke through the crowd, he was immediately both relieved and perplexed. Mark's mom was on her scooter and she was alive. She looked frightened.

"Fatty McWorthless. That's all you are. That's all you'll ever be."

From inside the loop of the crowd Mark heard Larry T's resonant voice rank on his mother. The star athlete of Forrest Side High, a minor celebrity, was calling Mark's near disabled mom his favorite pet name for her. A personal name that Mark reserved for special occasions to inflict intolerable pain on his forebear. He walked with certainty towards them both. A thought never crossed his mind. Mark's fist raced toward Larry's nose with everything he had in him. Everything.

Larry's nose exploded. Blood spatter reached the crowd. Before Larry could react, a fierce left caught him just to the side of his right eye. It shook his brain. Larry lost consciousness. He fell to the marble floor with all that gravity brought to bear against his mammoth frame. The thud of his head bouncing off the stone set echoed throughout the food court.

On instinct, through the shock, Larry's friend and teammate, George, jumped the small gate to protect his idol. Mark had none of it. He caught George with an uppercut to the jaw. Three of his teeth shattered when George's bottom molars were forced up and through his top ones. The onlookers were stunned by both the sight of the two bodies lying on the floor and by the force of will that sent them there.

Mark's mom struggled to get out of her cart. None of the bystanders knew how to react. Mark didn't hesitate. He quickly straddled Larry's prone and lifeless body and preceded to unload on his face, alternating rights and lefts, with all of it. Most of it was from his father. Some of it was from Ashley and a bit more of it was from Todd. The rest of it, the furious part of it, was from his mother, Fatty McWorthless.

Larry's eye socket cracked with the fourth left Mark threw. The next punch might have killed him. It never came. Fred forced his way through the audience, dove into Mark and tackled him to the floor where he struggled to keep him pinned down.

Fred heard his kids screaming for him from the railing on the second level. In that instant he both feared for and loved his children with everything in his heart.

Fred, on the verge of losing his leverage, experienced the onset of panic that preceded all intended chaos. Mark was a shoulder thrust away from freedom. Fred screamed Mark's name two inches from his face. Mark stopped his struggle completely. He went limp and looked Fred squarely in the eyes. Fred caught his glare, for an insufferable moment they shared the intimacy of lovers. As Mark came into being, Fred noticed that there was nothing there, nothing except the structure of human flesh. It was bare and disjointed, without makeup. There was richness in only the raw truth of the experience.

"Fred, I'm gonna kill that nigger."

Before Mark could begin his struggle anew, a feral right cross stung his temple. Inside of an uncontrollable blur Mark was dragged to his feet and tossed into the crowd. Mark's large, flailing body bowled over three bystanders on impact.

Fred didn't know why he hit him. He never thought that he could hurt Mark. Was it because Mark had whispered such a horrible word? Or was it because he threatened the life of another human being? Fred wasn't sure. All that he knew was that Mark meant them both.

"Go home! Now!"

Fred turned his back to Mark and went to check on the unconscious boys. Mrs. Brunson's opportunity had finally arrived. She could partake in the moment and be useful. From her cart, without having to move, she could comfort her son.

"Oh, Mark! Come here, baby."

She held her arms open wide and turned towards Mark with her ass firmly rooted to the seat of her scooter.

The punch by Fred did little to curtail Mark's determination. He was still focused and ready to kill Larry T. It was his mother's voice that engaged his sanity. He looked at her. She was crying. She was enormous. She was worthless.

"I don't love you, Mom."

Her face dropped along with a painful moan and tears. Fred spun his head from comforting the unconscious boys to watching Mark push his way through the crowd. He witnessed Mark leave and felt pity.

Tommy Connelly was watching Mark leave, too, though Tommy didn't actually see Mark. All that Tommy saw was Mark's avatar, a two-inch, digital representation of Mark walking away from his distraught mother. That Mark was trapped on Tommy's phone. Tommy owned that Mark. Tommy put that Mark in his pocket and smiled.

Chapter 57
That's Why

Tommy's recording went viral within minutes. The violence was too savage. The slain monster was too great. His video was the lead story on the six o'clock Sports Center. Tommy had captured the engrossing scene in its entirety. Well, from the beginning of what Larry said anyway. What Mark's mom had said leading up to the fight was up for debate. Not only that, it didn't matter. It wasn't recorded, so she might as well have said nothing at all. Her role as victim was now a matter of record. Tommy's video caught nearly every horrific word articulated by Larry to this pathetic woman. It did not look good for the Forrest Side superstar. Even if Mrs. Brunson had called Larry the N-word, which wasn't believed to be the case, she just looked too fat and helpless cowering under his monstrous shadow for it to matter.

Tommy, absent media credentials, was savvy enough to edit out what Mark said to his mother before he left. He intuitively understood that without Mark disparaging Larry's prey, the video was less complicated, more black and white. In turn, Mark came off at worst as a sympathetic figure, at best as a monolithic hero. On social media he was lionized. The hash tag #niggerslayer was trending. The country had been waiting patiently for its Uncle Tom to fall. Mr. Thomas was not willing to oblige, so they shoved his son off a cliff.

John Thomas handled the situation with both tact and acuity. His first move was to view the video in its entirety. He watched it until it made him gag. He replayed it until he memorized every insult uttered and he felt every punch thrown. He wasn't sure what disgusted him more, his own blood brutally humiliating a fat, pathetic woman on a motorized scooter or his cherished offspring being brutalized and humiliated moments after.

Next, he spoke with his son in the hospital. Of course, Larry couldn't remember the incident, but he did recall an obese woman on a scooter patronizing him in the mall earlier in the day. John was able to fill in the rest of the story after talking to Larry's chicken-shit friend Jared. Mr. Thomas concluded that the fat woman deserved it. Maybe not exactly what she received, but something. She was belittling and a buffoon. Her remarks, though arguably well intentioned, came from a disgusting institution. The problem was that Larry deserved it, too. It wasn't hard to imagine how John would have reacted if he were Mark and his already defenseless and pitiful mother was being torn apart in public by someone who seemed to have it all.

John remembered Mark from junior high football. As a favor to the local coaches, he would attend a few games each season and lend his expertise. He was impressed with Mark back then. Even at the age of twelve, Larry's father bore witness to Mark's talents and sensed his potential. John was impressed with Mark now, too. He only allowed this internal praise for Mark to register after he got word from the doctors that his son would recover completely. Larry's eye socket did have a hairline fracture, but there wasn't any damage to the eye itself or the soft matter behind it. He was concussed, but only mildly. And truthfully, his son needed it. Larry hadn't taken a hit in his entire life, physically or otherwise. He had been spoon fed talent, praise, and the notion of potential from birth. John's son needed to know what it felt like to be brutalized whether football was to be his chosen profession or he decided to merely exist as a black man in America.

John Thomas was awed by all of Mark's recorded actions. He realized that Mark caught his son off guard and if Larry had expected Mark, events might have played out differently. But one could not argue the fact that Mark took total advantage of his advantage. Larry never had a chance. John was also inspired by the knock-out blow given to Larry's friend George in the midst of his son's beating. George had the drop on Mark. Mark was distracted by Larry in the same manner that Larry had been distracted by Mark's mom, yet Mark didn't miss a beat. One savage uppercut, practically a reflex, and Mark became an Internet god. What was truly astonishing, what the video failed to capture in detail, was that George was a tough bastard in his own right; two hundred plus pounds on a six-foot frame. He was all muscle and guts on the football field. Before the fight, George was a starting linebacker being aggressively recruited by division-one schools. After the beating he was on injured reserve for six-to-ten weeks with a shattered jaw.

John's true brilliance came at the press conference. He was clear, concise and unequivocally apologetic. He never mentioned what Mark's mother either said or did leading up to Larry's belittling remarks. Only that she inadvertently offended his son and that Larry had overreacted. Attempting to justify or in any way mitigate what Tommy's recording showed - it wasn't worth it, according to John. Imagine trying to explain to white America what it meant to be patronized by a disabled fat woman in a muumuu. She had given Larry a compliment for Christ's sake. How could any of this be explained, and in a seven second sound bite, to a public that already had a finger in its ear?

John Thomas won over the nation when he announced that he and his son both agreed that Larry got what he deserved. John said that he never condoned violence and that it was never the only option, but that both he and his son were hard-pressed to imagine themselves behaving differently had the roles in the fight been reversed. It was the truth, part of it anyway, and the public gobbled it up. It was as if a prized steer voluntarily stepped on the grill and begged to be charred in front of a famished audience. After the press conference John was viewed as a man of true character and purity. He closed his remarks by stating that no charges would be pressed and that he would be footing all the bills for George's surgery and rehab. He had tried to contact both Mark and his mother, but they had so far been unreachable. Finally, John Thomas assured everyone that this kind of unacceptable behavior would never happen again. His performance was flawless from script to falling curtain.

Later that night, John was contacted by a representative from McDonalds. He was offered a multi-year, global advertisement deal to be their spokesperson. They presented him a ball pit full of money to endorse their hyper processed beef patties and pink nugget sludge. He refused the offer without deliberation.

John's agent stopped by the house a few days after the opportunity was discarded. In order to make sense of what she perceived to be objective reality, she needed to look her client in the eye and ask him why he turned down such a substantial amount of money from a former employer. John took a moment before responding. He would only explain this to his employee one time. If the question was ever asked again about this situation or any other like it, he would be looking for new representation.

"Because fuck them, that's why."

Chapter 58
Cud

Mark tramped his way home from Forrest Side Mall. He stuck exclusively to the winding back roads. The meandering trek took him nearly three hours. Mark figured he'd leave the car for his mom, but that plan backfired when twenty minutes into his walk he remembered she was too fat to fit behind the steering wheel. That and he had the keys to the car in his pocket. He had no idea how she would get home and he didn't care.

Mark wasn't entirely aware of what was happening with the Larry T. incident. His phone blew up after the first hour of walking, but its battery ran out of juice before the extent of the buzz he had created crystallized. He had received a hyperlink to the fight and a few texts from some crazed fans at school along with a voicemail from the local newspaper. Mark viewed Tommy's video on a continuous loop until his phone died. Had it survived three minutes longer, he could have listened to a message from someone claiming to be a reporter for ESPN. Mark wasn't sure how anyone got his number. As far as he knew the only list of contacts that bore his digits was attached to Kim's cell. He supposed she told a friend and from there the knowledge spread like the Rotavirus during a mid-winter birthday party hosted at Chuck E. Cheese. Mark could only imagine what Ashley thought of the fight. He was officially "the man" and there was nothing she could do about it. Fuck Ashley.

When Mark turned the corner that led to North Dunton Avenue he spotted two news vans parked in front of his house. Mark was exhausted. He was in no mood to be interviewed. Mark made a quick right at the corner leading to Lester's court. He decided to cut through his neighbor's yard and slip through the gate to access his property and then enter his house through the back door. As he approached Lester's derelict home, Mark noticed a fresh skid mark arching out of his driveway. The ice cream truck was still MIA. After taking three steps onto Lester's front lawn Mark heard the hiss of a weasel emerging from its wooded sanctuary.

"We doing the Pockets and beer, or what?"

"Not tonight, Lester."

"What the fuck? I thought we had a date."

Lester regretted his words the moment they were spewed from his ferine mouth. His compunction thickened as he bore witness to Mark's lowered head and slumped shoulders. It became painfully clear to Lester that Mark was already dealing with someone else's bullshit.

"Go back to your forest, Weasel. I don't have anything for you."

Mark's words stung at his heart. Lester's dad was gone. He had received Mark in exchange and now he was gone, too. One wise ass remark and Lester was left with no one. Without his father's monthly phone card Mr. May would soon be lost as well. Lester thought about knocking out Mark right there and then. Lester warned his neighbor not to tackle him anymore. He had assumed Mark understood that a verbal assault was also grounds for an ass kicking. Instead, Lester did nothing. What good would it do? What good did anything do? Ever?

Lester dropped to his knees. Hunger panged his forsaken belly. Shame bubbled up from inside his hollow core. Lester ignored both the bird on his shoulder and Mookie Fuckin' Wilson as regret passed into rage. Lester dreamed of jamming fistfuls of bacon into his mouth at his failure of a father's pleather-bound kitchen table. Lester thirsted for his dad's sinewy hands to scrape for his innocent eyes as he gnawed at the underbelly of a butchered hog. Lester longed for the presence of Mr. May at the head of his father's hinge-legged dining ledge. Lester would listen politely as his benefactor preached good manners and self-restraint. He would allow his father's nails to scrape at his cheeks and Mr. May's pedantries to burrow through his undersized skull and into his poisoned brain before grabbing both of them by the throat and wresting each of their spineless backs to the vomit-stained hardwood floors. While Lester crouched over their prostrate and helpless bodies, a mixture of saliva and grease would ooze down his jowls and drizzle their pursed lips before he leaned in to force feed the masticated cud into each of his fathers' vile mouths. He would fill their bellies with sulfites and pig fat until they were content in their place as both fools and false prophets.

Coinciding with the drop of his first tear Lester, felt a strange sensation near his hip. Lester pawed for the phone as it sang and danced in his frayed pocket. Released from the forest's protective canopy, Lester had received his first ever texts. There were twelve in total, and they were all from Kim. Lester had been in the woods all day, hunting and gathering. He knew nothing of the beating Mark had put on Larry T. He knew even less about the suffering of others.

Lester smiled and cried as he knelt at the foot of the forest and read each sublime word aloud to both himself and his natural mother. Initially, Lester's conspicuous joy stood in stark contrast to his understanding of the text. With his first pass he noted only an indecipherable scattering of transcribed celestial characters. As he read each text a second and then a third time, a narrative formed outside of his own inconsequential being. It was a story of betrayal, violence, and redemption, an amazing tale whose details mattered little to Lester other than the unassailable fact that he was a tiny part of it all.

Chapter 59
Consumed

After shouldering open the back door, the first of Mark's senses to be assaulted was his hearing. His mother's TV was offensively loud. The noise pollution was nearly as maddening as the material pollution. Shortly after Mark let out his habitual sigh and a wince, he realized the significance of the cacophony - she had found a way home. Mark's mother had entered the car of another human being. That car had comically tilted to one side when she sat down. Someone actually helped to wedge Mark's mom in and out of their car, someone who didn't know her, someone who didn't love her. Mark was consumed with guilt.

Mark chose not to say anything to his mother and thankfully, assuming she had even heard him enter, Mark's mother chose not to speak with her son.

Mark sneaked past the hallway leading to her room. He squeezed his way into the only unburdened nook near his living room window, inched the curtain aside and stole a peek at the front yard.

There were now three news vans parked outside. Mark wondered what would happen if a reporter finagled a camera into his home. For the seconds that he focused on this possibility, the anxiety involved was nearly paralytic. A noxious quiver emanated in his gut and trembled its way towards his extremities. In a moment, he was able to regain his composure. Like each unnecessary human institutions: war, hunger, slavery, corporate ruin, pollution, antisemitism, misogyny... If one lets it go, chooses to ignore all of its implications, none of it is real. Mark shut the curtains tightly, checked the locks on the door, left the lights off and dashed to his room. As far as Mark was concerned, the news vans ceased to exist and sex trafficking remained a localized problem involving women who made poor life choices.

Mark's cell had died. He wanted nothing to do with either his computer or the television. He checked the home phone after noticing it was in use. There was no one on the other end. Mark supposed his mother took it off the hook to stifle the endless barrage of calls. Mark, at once, felt the burden of cognition and recognized that his salvation lay under the covers of his perfectly dressed bed. Mark kicked off his shoes and stripped down to his boxer briefs. He crawled under the blankets and allowed the cold, fresh linen to caress his wearied frame. In the thirty seconds before he fell asleep, Mark relived the perfect spirals he threw to Tommy Connelly and the clarity that preceded their depth.

.

Ashley had burrowed herself deeply into her own bedroom. She was all over the internet. Mark was all over the internet. She was crying. Ashley could not be consoled. Her father stopped trying. He had some issues of his own to confront. He couldn't believe how fat his friend had become. He hadn't spoken to Karen since the funeral. After his wife died Ashley's father threw himself into his work. He kept late hours nearly seven days a week. The house where his former best friend lived was of little concern to him. He had heard rumors of what Mark's mom had done to herself but chose to ignore or maybe revel in them. It was one big mess.

.

Lester had his own emotions to contend with. He had masturbated twice to Kim after reading her texts. He had called her, and she filled him in on all she knew about Mark and Larry. They planned to meet the next day during lunch and talk some more. Lester thought of Mark and how he reacted to his comments earlier. He forgave him; he wasn't happy about it, but he understood. Lester thought of Todd before he went to bed. He thought of the south gym and the pipe. Lester knew none of this was over. He was supposed to give Mr. May a call but decided on his own that it wasn't necessary. After chafing his uncircumcised foreskin a third and final time, Lester was finally satisfied.

Chapter 60
Euphoric

Mark woke up abruptly and with the overwhelming feeling of dread. The sensation compressed his lungs, surged up and through his throat, finally settling in his mouth with what felt like a ringing in his teeth. He needed his dad, badly. He needed his mom even more. He had no idea how to find her. She was lost inside of herself.

Mark grabbed his phone from its charging base and plowed his way downstairs. He slid aside the drawn curtains in the living room and took a peek at the outside world through the tiny sliver of unobstructed pane. One news van remained. Mark's phone vibrated itself back to life. After a cursory glance at the screen, Mark choked on his own saliva. There were three-hundred-and-seven unread texts and forty-two voicemails. It was too much, all of it. Mark was an instant from deleting the ream of messages en masse when the second to last text poked his eye. Mark had few contacts stored in his phone, so he was forced to ignorantly touch the random set of numbers on his screen. The text read:

if you come to school, it's on

The warning was digitally signed by Todd. Mark exhaled before laughing to himself. Mark had forgotten about Todd. He hadn't thought about him once. Not since Saturday's football game or maybe when he had hung with Lester.

Lester? What horrible thing had Mark said to Lester yesterday? He had gone straight for the throat. Mark called him a weasel. He would have to make that right. Mark needed fix the relationship with his mother as well. But that would all have to wait. First, Mark was going to take his life back from Ashley.

The events of the previous day had taken their toll on Mark's body. He had slept for nearly fifteen hours. He was already over two hours late for school. Mark took a brief shower, brushed his teeth and shaved. He dressed quickly, ignored his reflection in the mirror and ran downstairs. When Mark passed his mother's room he considered stopping in to give her a hug and an apology. But he didn't want to see her. He didn't want her to see him. What would one even say? One thing at a time. Mark tripped out of his front door the same moment a second news van pulled up to the curb at the end of his driveway. Both vans emptied as reporters and camera men converged on their prey. Mark noticed two of his neighbors across the street peering out of their windows. They were all lying in wait.

Mark ran swiftly past both the cameras and the questions. He opened the passenger side door to the van that had just arrived and hopped into shotgun.

"Get me to school. We can talk on the way."

The van was from Channel Seven, ABC News, and the reporter had a ton of questions. During their drive she asked about his mom and how she was feeling. She asked if he planned on joining the football team. She asked Mark if he spoke to Larry or his family and if he was worried about any type of reprisal. Mark refused to answer a single question. He told the reporter to get him to school and that he would give her an exclusive at the end of the day.

As the mobile news station idled its way towards the main entrance of the high school, three security guards were dispatched. They were in the process of shoeing the vehicle away when Mr. Busby, the head of security, noticed Mark exiting the van.

"Oh. Hey! Mark-my-man. You ready to take some snaps again or what?"

Busby was the offensive line coach for the varsity squad. The O-line that was torn apart by Larry T. Mark didn't respond. He just threw Buzz a generic head nod and broke for the perceived safety of the school.

Mr. Busby allowed the news team to drop Mark off, then insisted that they leave. Before driving away the reporter called after Mark, reminding him of their exclusive. Mark didn't like to lie, but he was certain that he would not be speaking with anyone from ABC News any time soon.

Mark traipsed towards the main entrance of Lake Side High School. For a moment he considered turning around. "Maybe," he thought, "an interview wouldn't be so bad." Mark adjusted his jeans, stole a look at his Chucks, then reached for the lobby doors. A bell blared over the school-wide intercom.

Fourth period had ended. An imperceptible amount of time had passed before the hallways clotted with students. Danielle Hawkfield noticed Mark first.

"Holy shit!"

Amy Valenti was the first to scream his name. Seconds later, Tia Michael kissed him on the cheek. Random schoolmates started patting him on the back. Lisa, a tiny freshman girl with average grades and port wine stains around both ears, forced her way under the swarm, and grabbed a hold near the crotch of Mark's pants. Mark let go of his remaining insecurities and shoved his way through the crowd. He began his march upstairs to the senior locker banks with his fans in tow. Principal Dunn, doing nothing to curtail the insanity, stood outside the main office and held up his hand for a high five.

After a few strides into the Language Arts corridor Mark couldn't help but smile. All of the attention reminded Mark of his second game of the season in eighth grade against Forrest Side. Lake Side scorched their rivals twenty-one to nothing. Mark insisted on playing the entire game on both sides of the ball. The celebration after the victory was invigorating. He felt that now, in the halls. Mark never wanted it to end.

Todd heard the tumult before the boisterous mob had reached him. He knew what it was. He knew what it meant. Todd looked to Ashley. They had been sharing a quiet moment at his locker. She saw the fear in his eyes, turned and walked away. Todd couldn't stop her. He didn't know how. Todd had texted Mark late in the morning in the hope that Mark would be frightened and stay home. It was a last-ditch effort inspired by the fact that Mark had already missed the first three periods. It was cowardice and it consumed Todd.

The crowd stopped as Mark did. They saw Todd as Mark did. This was everything they ever wanted. The portended fight between Mark and Todd was a constant buzz all over social media. No one gave Todd a chance.

"The pit, at lunch."

Todd didn't know what to say. No one said anything. No one took a breath. After the time it took him to swallow and scan the crowd, Todd gave it his best shot.

"Why don't we do this right now, pussy?"

Todd's reaction felt hollow and scripted. It was like watching a bad indie movie. A poorly contrived film cast with actors found on Craig's List. Mark smiled.

"The pit. Sixth period."

Mark turned and walked away. He had already won.

Chapter 61
Super Star

The rapturous atmosphere on campus in which Mark had been enveloped turned hostile. Mark's classmates were poking and prodding him with their interest. As soon as he dug some space for himself, more students would fill the void like beach sand pulled from a hole by the clumsy hand of a toddler. They wanted to know where he learned how to fight, if he was going to join the football team, if he wanted to hang out. A few of the students had enough sense and empathy to inquire about Mark's mom. Mark appreciated their concern, but it annoyed him that his peers knew he had a mother.

Mark's homeroom teacher and the football team's defensive coordinator, Mr. Bradley, reached out of his classroom and threw an arm around Mark's shoulder.

"You coming to practice today? You put in your two weeks and Jacko will give you the top spot."

Mark didn't have an answer for Mr. Bradley. Not then, between fourth and fifth period, while being groped and molested.

Mark was finished with Lake Side High for the day. He had a fight and a show to worry about that required all his focus and attention. Besides, Mark didn't want to be handed the "top spot." He intended to earn his position with the letting of his blood and guts at the base of a filthy ditch.

"Okay, break it up. The bell rang two minutes ago, children."

Mr. Busby had arrived. Buzz had the three physical attributes needed to authoritatively command a bunch of entitled teenagers. He was big, bald, and black. The three B's of bossing around a bunch of brats. That was all that it took. At the crack of his voice every student, and teacher for that matter, had his full attention.

Mark used the discomfort created by Mr. Busby's presence to locate the closest lavatory. Upon entering the bathroom, Mark, without pause, marched to the nearest open window, hung himself over the sill and dropped the ten or so feet to the grass below. There were four boys in the bathroom, recording each other, as they attempted to flip half empty Poland Spring bottles on to the lip of a sink. The video they filmed and forwarded of Mark pulling a Spider-Man solidified his pre-fight status as a legend.

As Mark distanced himself from the school, dozens of students in the classrooms facing the soccer field huddled around open windows to watch. Michelle, a waif junior with shoulder length blond hair and an aunt who liked to touch her nipples as she slept, yelled that she loved him. She meant it. Leslie and Chloe, two senior girls on the color guard who shared a musky odor, pressed their bare breasts against the window in the girl's lavatory. Mark never turned around. He refused to acknowledge any of his peers' gestures of surrender.

Kim sat by herself in the back of math class. Several of her classmates stood and gaped across the empty field to watch Mark as he strutted towards the pit. Ms. Petry initiated the impromptu awe-fest by running to the window and announcing to the class, "I think that's him!" Kim had only looked for a second when the commotion first started. He was so far away.

While the class exchanged fabricated stories and gushed over their superstar, Kim took out her phone and looked over her contacts. There weren't many, it only took one slide of the thumb to scroll to the end of the list. After a few flicks both up and down, she randomly laid her thumb on the screen. The scroll stopped and her finger rested on both the "e" and the "r" at the end of Lester's name. Kim palmed her phone and read his name, voicing both syllables just under her breath. She put her phone away, exhaled deeply, and smiled just the same.

Chapter 62
A Tiny Nugget

Ashley left Lake Side High before Mark did. She just couldn't be there anymore. The combined smells of floor wax and cafeteria food along with the sound of impetuous children and the sight of warrantless joy were intolerable. She grabbed Matt in the hallway by his locker and dragged him to his car. Matt refused at first, he never cut class, but Ashley refused his refusal. She was going home and Matt was taking her. The ride to her house was quiet. Matt knew not to push anything with Ashley when she got in one of her moods. He hadn't known her long, but he could always tell when she was dealing with her mother. He felt for her. Five minutes into the drive Matt realized he could probably avoid a cut slip if he told his guidance counselor that he was helping Ashley cope. Matt stopped worrying and began to relax.

"You wanna smoke?"

Ashley didn't respond. She just kept out the window. Her mother was dead. Her father was heartbroken. Todd was useless. Mark was a star. She was confused. Ashley was having difficulty recalling why she needed Mark to suffer. She missed him. She remembered that she had loved him. It was two years ago, it was junior high, but it was love. She had loved Mark. Her father had loved her mother. Her mother had loved Mark's dad. She had felt the love then as clearly as she felt the pain now. Matt pulled his reef blue Passat into Ashley's empty driveway.

"Do you need me to come in? 'Cause I can still get back before the period ends."

Ashley was about to say no. She didn't feel like dealing with Matt's inevitable snark. But something caught her eye before she told him he could leave. It was Mark's house. Fred was dropping off four large boxes, but that wasn't it. Fred was a fixture. What caught her attention was the empty driveway. There was always a company lease parked in front of his garage. She wasn't sure of its significance but maybe with Matt's help she could figure it out.

"No. Come on up. My dad's not home. We can fool around a little."

Matt laughed. He wondered how many boys in school, in the world, would outright murder to hear Ashley speak those words. The funny thing was that Matt had jerked off to a similar scenario the night before. But he wasn't in Ashley's driveway, he was in Mark's. Watching Mark kick the shit out of Larry T. was impressive. It got into Matt's head, his imagination.

Matt watched Ashley glide up her walkway and enter her home. Even though Matt had not agreed to stay, Ashley never turned to confirm his intentions. She just walked into her house and left the front door open. Matt wanted nothing to do with her body. He didn't care what her underwear looked like. Still, she owned him all the same.

Matt exited his car and stretched as he looked up at what he hoped was Mark's bedroom window. It was closed and the blinds were drawn. He wondered what Mark's room looked like. Knowing something like that, a tiny nugget of a detail, worked wonders for one's imagination.

Chapter 63
Done, Empty

Mark strode with confidence past the soccer fields towards the pit. He wasn't scared. He was done. He was done with Ashley and Todd. He was done with his mother. He was done with all the yard work. He was done with hiding from his life. Mark focused on the pit. It was his redemption. A thirty-foot plunge down into the earth, he would give or take a few lumps before ascending the slope reborn.

There was a hole cut into the fence that bordered the far end of the school yard. It was a triangular cleft that widened as it neared the ground. Mark had to crouch and turn to enter the opening, but he never slowed his pace. Mark wondered how long it would take for nearly half the school to get through the cut-out in the fence one student at a time. Maybe some of his classmates would travel the long way around, behind the bottle factory, and down the unpaved road that led to the sandy ditch.

A few steps beyond the fence Mark was reminded of his summer time adventures in the forest with Umed. The trees that surrounded him were stout and lush. The verdure that bordered each of his steps down the soil-rich path was green and vibrant. Umed was now in his past but the fall, barren and still, remained in Mark's future.

Both the path and the woods ended where the sand that composed the perimeter of the sump began. The rear entrance to the pit was nearest to the path. The drainage ditch was uniform all the way around with the exception of two sets of double swing gates at both its east and west ends. At the end closest to Mark the gates were locked. There was another cut out in this fence beside the corner post that Mark chose to avoid. Instead, he strolled along the outside of the enclosure toward the structure's front entrance. The chain and lock for the front gates had disappeared a few summers back. No one bothered to replace them.

Mark ran his fingers through the links in the fence as he walked. When Mark neared the unlocked gates, he paused to peer down into the crater. The man-made construct was suffused with nothing. Its existence seemed unnecessary, even gratuitous, like a salad fork or lust. Mark turned his back to the empty pit and walked across the sand-lined road and into the woods that resumed, bloomed in full, on the other side of the curb.

Chapter 64
Adventure Awaits

Ashley's house was spacious, beautiful, and despoiled. Crossing its decorative threshold provided little solace and even less joy. To Ashley home meant nothing more than a sterile place to bleed.

After entering her two-story colonial Ashley had a mild episode. Her light began to dim and she lost her balance. Ashley was stuck in an oscillating atmosphere derived of mud and sheetrock. Her existence was dispassion. Ashley had no idea what to do with herself. After regaining her resolve she dropped her backpack in the foyer and went straight upstairs to her bedroom. She kicked off her shoes and crashed on the bed. Matt called up after her.

"Ashley?"

"I'm up here."

Ashley was anxious and confused. She felt her hand rubbing her stomach just below her belly button. She needed to clear her mind.

Maybe, she thought, maybe Matt could help her out. How gay could he be?

Matt entered Ashley's room with a glowing smile. He was getting used to his impromptu break from ELA.

"Your dad is hot."

Matt failed to notice that an insanely gorgeous woman was splayed out on her bed. Matt had noticed a picture of Ashley's father with the rest of the family photos lining the staircase. Ashley let go of her belly.

Matt skipped to the window overlooking the pool in Ashley's back yard. He took a pull from his pen. Matt preferred his THC in vape form.

"Is it heated? You wanna go swimming?"

Ashley didn't respond. She didn't want to go swimming. She wanted to hug her mother. Matt watched as his exhaled vapor rolled up and bellowed off the window pane. When it cleared, he scanned the surrounding vista.

"Ewww. Who lives there?"

Matt was referring to Lester's house. There was a large oak tree blocking most of the offense, but you could still make out the crap strewn about the back yard beneath its branches. The view would only regress in autumn as the great oak's veil of leaves surrendered to the season. Ashley's father had already called the town twice. Nothing had changed.

"It's the Weasel's. He likes to burrow around in his own filth."

"Does he burrow over here?"

"Ewww, no! Never."

"So what's with the gate?"

"What gate?"

Ashley leapt out of bed. Her mind would have to stay cluttered for at least a few more minutes.

She joined Matt at the window, purposely leaning into his long and slender frame. In the corner of Ashley's yard by Lester's oak tree the double gates were ajar, creating an access way connecting all three properties. The gates hadn't been opened in two years. A bungee cord had kept them secure.

Ashley had fond memories of the gates in the corner of her yard. They were the fulcrum to her friendship with both Mark and Umed. Nobody had used either of the passage ways since her mother had died. Ashley was never mad at Umed, but without Mark as a go-between, Umed and Ashley's relationship strained and eventually withered away. As Mark grieved, Umed made new friends. At the start of ninth grade his parents sent him to a boarding school in Seattle. The gates remained shut for almost an entire year. They were eventually bungeed closed by Mark after the latch on Ashley's fence rusted off. Umed's family moved back to India and the gates became little more than unnecessarily hinged sections of fence.

But why were they opened? And what happened to Mark's bungee cord?

Before Ashley could finish one thought, a mess of others flitted through her mind. Mark's mother's car was not in the driveway. Mark's father, like Ashley's mother, was dead, but where was Mark's mom?

Ashley pulled the phone from her back pocket. She looked Matt directly in the eyes with bemused anticipation.

"You wanna go on an adventure?"

Matt may not have wanted to fuck Ashley, but her enthusiasm was intoxicating. He took a long pull from his vape pen before responding.

"Ashley, sweetie… always."

Ashley grabbed Matt's wrist and dragged him toward the stairs. She wasn't confused anymore. She had finally put it all together: Mark's disgustingly fat mom, the twice-daily UPS trucks, the thrice-daily pizza deliveries, the intermittent glances she stole into Mark's garage, the permanently drawn blinds, the constant yard work, Lester.

Ashley hadn't been this happy in over two years. In her semi-euphoric state she tripped and nearly tumbled down the stairs. Matt grabbed the railing just in time to stop them both from rolling head-over-heels to the landing below.

"Whooaa! Relax, Ash. Adventure awaits."

Chapter 65
Through the Trees

Ten hardy steps into the thicket lay an old, cement-cast irrigation pipe. It's diameter was twice the width of an average high school boy. Over a century ago it was used to bring fresh water down from the mountain to the residents that lived at its base. Today the pipe's main utility was as a seat to smoke weed on while hanging in the woods. That, and the track team liked to initiate their freshmen pledges by forcing them to belly crawl through a fifty-yard stretch that was still mostly intact down by the lake.

Mark sat on top of a length of pipe where two casts met. At the opposing ends of either section there was a square cement collar. The collars were fastened together with four two-foot bolts, one in each corner. From his purchase, which he shared with an abandoned pack of Pal Malls, Mark had a perfect view of the pit.

The first two students to breach the wood at the rear of the pit were Lester and Kim. Mark's stomach sank. He had been a horrible prick to both of them. Mark tried not to think about it. He just watched as they passed through the cut-out closest to the path. Lester stopped and let Kim walk through the opening first. She giggled before getting her shirt caught on an exposed link. Lester snorted as he released her sleeve from the metal barb. They both ducked inside and took a seat with their backs up against the fence. They were laughing. Mark couldn't hear what they were saying, but they seemed to enjoy each other's company. Mark smiled.

Their moment abruptly ended when a second group of students exited the path. Five more kids tucked themselves into the hole and stood sentry at the edge of the pit. From there the migration was relentless. Mark could hear the crowd as it approached in an endless line, two and three abreast, trudging down the path. A few of the kids were chugging cans of beer as they arrived. More students were walking down the unpaved road that began behind the factory. They had driven their cars around to the factory's parking lot to avoid the bottleneck at the back of the field. Many of them had beers, too. The lucky collection of students with four-wheel drive vehicles drove the sand-filled road right up to the gates. Tufts of smoke loitered above a small subset of students using the event as a reason to get lifted. Half of the school, those without sixth period lunch, were risking an afternoon in the pink room to witness the fight. It was a dense, fluid mass of mirth and good cheer.

It took fifteen minutes from the moment Lester and Kim appeared for the crowd to completely occlude Mark's view of the pit. He could see only the backs of the students lined up by the front entrance across from his wooded sanctuary. There wasn't enough room around the pit inside the enclosure, so some students, mostly freshmen, had to select a spot outside of the chain links. A few did their best to hang on to the top of the fence to secure a better angle.

At minute sixteen Mark heard the first of the visceral screams. Todd had made the trip. He took the back way through the soccer field. Mark did not see him arrive, but the cheers were unmistakable. Mark's heart jumped a bit.

The crowd near the rear cut-out did their best to part for Todd. A few fell into the pit before landing on their asses to stop the slide. They were quickly helped back up. No one was allowed into the pit except for the two combatants. The students near Todd were cheering and patting him on the back as he passed by. "Kill 'em, Todd" and other random stock phrases were flung from the mouths of insatiable onlookers. Not that everyone around Todd was in his camp. Even a few kids on his own football team were rooting for Mark. But it seemed the right thing to say to someone getting ready to suffer for the sake of entertainment.

When Todd took his shirt off, the crowd lost it. The roar was resounding. Mark was ready. He jumped off the buttress. He didn't want Todd in the pit too long, either psyching himself up or rubbing on his nipples. Mark's plan, though not very tactical, had always been to hit him fast and hit him hard. Mark took one step from the pipe toward his opponent when he heard the boos overtake the cheers. There were cries of "bullshit" and "pussy." The students who couldn't see into the pit nor the source of the foul were clamoring for information. The crowd was angry. Mark needed to know why. He dashed from the woods to the back end of the audience. No one noticed him until he began to fight his way through the mass to get to the front gate.

Little Houseman, a dandy of a freshman with a helicopter for a mom, who also happened to be one of the 1.5% of American teens with a bedwetting problem, took one of Mark's shoulders to the back of his head. Before the indignity over the shove set in, and Little Housman was always indignant, adrenaline rushed to his vocal cords.

"Kick his ass, Mark!"

The nearby students picked up on Houseman's cheer and began to scream. Others in the crowd heard these screams and began screaming in kind. They knew it had to be Mark.

It was now obvious that the original cheers for Todd were all for the show. They were not excited to see Todd, they weren't rooting for him, nor were they on his side. They just wanted to witness Mark's opponent enter the ring. The screams for Mark were ear-popping. A group of girls, three juniors and two sophomores, all cute, all carrying the human papilloma virus and all toeing the precipice of the pit, pulled up their shirts and yelled, "We love you, Mark." The screams grew louder. With the reverberations a dozen more students fell over the roving edge of the sandy maw before being hastily pulled back up. The chain link fence was buckling under the weight of its teenaged carriage. They all wanted this. They all seemed to need it. Their excitement bordered on frenzy.

When Mark arrived at the rim of the pit he understood the clamor. Todd stood bare chested in the center of the sump flanked by both Victor and Steve. They had their shirts off, too.

Chapter 66
Fulfillment and Bliss

Todd was staring up at Mark with a crooked grin. He had no shame. He wasn't about to take a beating on film. And this fight would be filmed. The crowd was less a mass of people than it was a collection of tripods supporting their cell phones. Todd would not take a public ass kicking when he had the Lake Side High football team at his disposal. Todd knew he would lose some face but not as much as if a sophomore, and a potential understudy, smacked the shit out of him in front of half of the school. Todd knew the only thing worse than that would be if he hadn't shown up for the fight at all.

Mark searched the crowd for help from his roost at the lip of the pit. It was a futile endeavor. Mark had no friends, no buddies willing to take a beating on his behalf. He half hoped to see Umed pop out of the rank and file without a shirt and wearing one of his father's ties as a band around his head.

Like when they played army as kids pretending to kill insurgents from the Peshawar Region. Mark did find one formerly friendly face, one that recently committed to having his back, but not one that would make eye contact with him. Jason had wormed himself into a ringside seat. His head was slung low to hide the pus on his face. The din of the crowd messed with his hearing aid. The mound in his chest made it difficult for him to swallow.

Without a supporting cast, Mark had to fend for himself. Turning back was not an option. Mark understood that the price of repurchase invariably carried the cost of the original sale. Mark tore off his shirt and hopped down into the pit. Cheers, screams, and a collective fist-in-the-air shook the arena sand. Mark was a total badass, a #niggerslayer with balls of steel. Even Todd's heart palpitated when Mark took that first shirtless step.

The reality was that Mark held no chance. He wasn't a protagonist heading to incapacitate mindless henchmen in an action movie. Although Mark liked to fight, and he was good at it, he was not a highly trained martial artist. He was walking toward three kids his own age and for the most part his own size. Three kids who had brawled before. Three kids who, week in and week out, left it all on the gridiron. He could probably take any one of them head-to-head on most any given afternoon. He could just maybe get lucky against any two of them if the pugilistic gods afforded him a miracle knock-out blow. Against three of them the odds became insurmountable. Mark figured he would get one punch in on Todd before his boys jumped him. Mark would then duck and cover and wait for the crowd to intervene in the carnage.

Mark had already won the moment. Todd stepped into the ring with extra muscle. It was just a matter of Mark taking his lumps and earning his spot as Lake Side's resident silverback. Mark was confident that the self-appointed moderators, as per pit protocol, would quickly break up the lopsided affair. The beating wouldn't be that bad, but damn, Mark wanted a V on this one.

When he was halfway down the slope of the pit, Mark heard the crowd's collective gasp. He looked up and saw Lester strutting down the opposite sandy slope without a shirt. He was impressive to look at. Zero body fat, no bulk, just sheets of tightly compacted muscle cut from an iron cast. Kim was standing at the far edge of the sump, holding back tears.

The hyper-stimulated audience didn't know what to make of Lester entering the mix. Most assumed he was headed down to join the already numerically superior "bad guys." All they knew of the Weasel was the incident in the cafeteria, the incident that set everything in motion, the incident where Mark and Lester were on opposite sides. Besides a couple of beer bottles thrown in his direction no one interfered with Lester's descent. Anyone who jumped in on Mark's behalf would chance a rumble versus the only kids in Lake Side used to mixing it up. Todd was the toughest kid in school and he had the entire football team at his back. The only assistance Mark was going to receive from his classmates was vociferous disapproval and a few errantly thrown IPAs.

Mark was proud of Lester. He didn't expect much from him. Sure, Lester worked over his drunken father something fierce, but the three boys in the pit were in their life's prime and they had an average of sixty pounds on the Weasel. Maybe Lester could keep Steve busy for a few minutes while Mark tried to work Todd and fend off Victor. At least the beatdown would now only consist of eight limbs.

Lester reached Todd first.

"What's up, shorty? Comin' to get some licks?"

Lester did not acknowledge Todd. He instead bounded past the Prince of Lake Side High and put his fist through to the back of Victor's throat. Victor slumped like spilt milk down to his hands and knees where Lester kicked him in the face. Vic's head snapped back. Lester's stolen Salvation Army hat fell to the sand. Lester liked Mark and he was happy help him out in his time of need. But what was happening in the pit was just as much for himself as it was for his neighbor. Fuck Mr. May.

Todd didn't know what to do. Mark was breaking towards the action. Steve was freaking out. This was supposed to be a sealed deal. The previous night, as a contingency after Larry T. was practically lynched at the mall, Todd called his teammates to secure their oath. He assured them that everything involving the pit would go down smoothly. Steve had even broken his no-shaving rule to look good for the show with his shirt off. No one but Mark was supposed to be hurt.

Lester bent over and scooped his Marlins hat from the sand. He put it on backwards and lifted his arms to the audience. Like a lion. The roar of the crowd was deafening. Mark ran up and stood alongside his friend. He would have hugged him if it was acceptable to do so.

Victor was on the ground, teeth dribbled out of his mouth along with gobs of blood. He was done. The entire school learned all at once not to underestimate the Weasel.

Lester turned to face both Todd and Steve. Todd had something to say, but it lacked both certainty and menace.

"You're dead, little man."

Lester ignored Todd's empty threat and broke for Steve. Steve attempted to get out of his way in order to regroup, but Lester was too quick. It was always tricky to fight in the sand. Your feet sunk with each step. Your reflexes dulled as your body adjusted to the shifting soil. Not for Lester. With his size, weight and speed he seemed to glide above the grain. His weaselly little body was crafted to brawl in the pit. Lester landed a right cross, followed by seven sharp punches landing true to Steve's face. Every muscle in Lester's body worked in unison to pack each blow with all the strength Lester's core had to offer. Steve was out cold by the fifth punch. The sixth was a left uppercut that kept The Beave's freshly shaved body vertical for the single instant needed for Lester's right fist to land square on the bridge of Steve's nose.

Steve's limp body collapsed into the sand. The crowd watched as streams of blood pulsated from his now misshapen nose. Some in the audience were forced to look away as pools of crimson filled the divots surrounding his maligned face.

Todd looked up to the rest of his team. They were stoic, motionless, waiting for their leader to emerge. Lester took a seat in the sand between the prone bodies of both Victor and Steve, then gestured to Mark for his turn to begin. It was Todd who didn't waste any time. He knew he had only one chance to end this in his favor, one chance to save his spot on the football field, one chance to be with Ashley.

Todd pounced on Mark with everything he had. Mark was ready. He went under the right hook and caught Todd in the obliques. The powerful, precise punch knocked all the breath out of Todd's body. Pain and pressure plied his lungs. He was forced down to his knees, defenseless. Mark grabbed Todd's hair and pulled his contorted face skyward for everyone to witness. Mark took his free hand and mushed Todd to the ground. The audience lost it. Not only was Mark an absolute badass, he was profuse with mercy.

In an orgy of fulfillment and bliss, the crowd plunged into the pit.

Chapter 67
What's Inside

The first phone to vibrate was Mark's. Amongst the maelstrom he failed to notice the rumbling in his pocket. The students of Lake Side High were elated and initially nobody cared about their beckoning phones.

Jason was the first kid at the pit to watch the video. He had not seen the fight. As Mark marched towards unspeakable violence, Jason limped his way back through the crowd. The going wasn't easy. Nearly every student he passed on his way out gave him grief. A few of his classmates questioned his navigational aptitude. Jason decided to forgo exiting through the front gate and instead he struggled to hop the nearest section of fence. By the time the action in the pit had ended Jason was already sitting on the pipe. He knew nothing about Lester nor the fight's eventual outcome. All that Jason knew was the torment of being worthless.

When Jason first screened the video, all of that angst was swept into a void. As he scrubbed it for a second viewing, that void was filled with peace.

Mark's mother was on her bed, topless, eating a cheeseburger. Her enormous breasts were splayed and tucked between her armpits. She was surrounded by crooked shelves, bare drywall and unimaginable filth. The floor was carpeted with condiment-stained food wrappers, tattered cardboard, and sorted trash. But what made the video, what transfused unfettered joy deep into Jason's soul, was the noise Mark's mother made upon being discovered. Even with the spotty, filtered sound that his hearing aid provided, what Jason heard filled him with glee. It started as an inaudible hum and crescendoed with a throaty moan. A sound not unlike one a deaf person would make in the face of grave danger. Jason appreciated the irony and giddily forwarded the link to all his contacts. Not that it mattered. Matt had nearly everyone's number in the school stored on his phone, and they all received the attachment.

One person at a time, the raucous crowd quieted as they watched and shared the video. It was an odd brew of emotions, and Mark picked up on it immediately. Moments prior he had been in the middle of a mob that wanted to be inside of him. His classmates were touching him and cheering for him as if he had single-handedly won the Super Bowl. Mark was struggling to find Lester when he sensed the change in mood. Wherever he turned, he witnessed silent groups of students huddled around their phones. Some were obviously disgusted by what they had viewed. Others giggled politely. Even more laughed uncontrollably. The one trait they all shared after screening the video was that they looked at Mark when it ended.

Mark felt his phone vibrating incessantly in his pocket. The post-fight cacophony had quieted. A chorus of laughter and snide comments filled the muted soundscape. Mark was determined to locate Lester, his friend, as the celebration spiraled into despair.

Mark found Lester sitting in the sand with Kim. They were watching the video together on Kim's cell. As he approached, they both raised their heads. Lester could not look Mark in the eye. Kim was visibly shaken. Her voice trembled some as she spoke.

"Don't watch it."

At that moment Mark realized he hadn't seen Ashley since the scene at his locker. His mind went straight to his unfinished koi pond. He grabbed the phone from his pocket. Mark scanned the text, titled simply:

whats Inside

It had been forwarded forty-four times by unknown contacts. This was a special type of redundancy practiced by acquaintances that found comfort in sharing tragic news.

The crowd around Mark was silent. There would be an encore to his historic fight in the pit, and the anticipation was greater than that of the main event. Mark opened the attached link and pressed play. The video began with a view of Ashley's bare feet as she readied the camera. From there she turned a knob and carefully cracked open the back door to Mark's mother's makeshift bedroom. Ashley then slipped her phone into the crevice and slowly panned the camera through the crap-infested space and around to Mark's topless mom eating a broiled beef patty off her own bare chest.

Mark dropped the phone to his side and stared at Lester as his mother's zombie-like hum floated through the now silenced pit. When the moan ended, Todd's comment hit clearly and with bite.

"Someone better milk that cow before she bursts."

Todd's breath had returned, and with it came his essence. Many in the crowd laughed, some with restraint, some with genuine delight.

The rumors about Mark's mom had been circling through the community since last Christmas. Her coming-out party at the mall confirmed her fall from grace. Mark's fight with Larry overshadowed anything that could have been said about her in public. Regardless, the feelings of contempt and disgust for Mark's mother ran deep.

Mark ran through the crowd, leveling anyone who wasn't quick enough to get out of his way. Paul, a junior with a skin fade and a burgeoning addiction to online pornography, had his head down, watching the video when he caught a forearm to the face. The crowd parted while Mark scrambled up the slope. When he neared the sump's rim, the sand beneath his feet avalanched and caused his feet to slide. He was frozen on the side of the pit as his limbs flailed wildly. A few kids in the audience laughed, while others averted their eyes. Mark's tail-tucked escape was agonizing to watch. Mark exited through the front gate. He stumbled a bit on the cement curb before regaining his balance, then he trudged along the sandy road before scurrying into the underbrush.

Once he entered the forest, Mark found his footing. He reached the pipe with four large steps where he paused to collect his bearings. With one foot on the cement cast and the other on the ground, he exhaled. As he did, he felt a tide of emotion knot up under his ribcage. Mark's vision blurred as the blood rushed from his head. In that instant Mark heard and saw nothing. He held out his arms to steady his gait. Mark was whisked back into the moment by the acrid smell of cigarette smoke. He turned and saw Jason sitting on the buttress, watching him, pulling hard on a filter-less Pall Mall.

Mark stepped over the pipe. When he reached the other side he heard Jason speak. His words were clear and true, without a hint of his disability.

"You're not a good person, Mark."

Mark turned to his former charity case in disbelief. He witnessed Jason's black eyes ignite as he again pulled hard on his cigarette. Jason let out a huff and a small smile before exhaling a thick ream of smoke from his lungs, obscuring his face with a veil of grayish blue.

The smoke cleared and Jason held his phone face out, up in the air, beside his head. He coolly flicked his cigarette aside, brought his now burden-free hand around to the phone's display and touched play. The clip started at the same instant Mark's mom began to moan. Jason (sort of) listened with a smile. A bewildered Mark took a step towards this strange boy, whom he did not recognize. His hands were made into fists. Mark stopped in his tracks as Jason began to mimic his mother's pain. His disability was back as he voiced her groan, pitch perfect. The imitation was pure, golden until its pointed end when Jason spoke again, both clear and true.

"None of us are."

Before Mark could react, Jason stood up and turned his back to him. He hopped the buttress with relaxed ease. His gaze was fixed forward as he walked up the pipe toward its source in the mountain. Jason echoed the fat woman's moan as he strolled, one foot in front of the next, above the abandoned cast.

The end.

Epilogue
Shared Universe

It was three hours before Mark, both weary and bare-chested, found his way out of the forest. He had played in the woods his entire life. He and Umed practically lived within its branches the summer between seventh and eighth grade. Ashley was a frequent house guest of theirs. Mark knew the forest near the pit connected to the woods behind his home. It just took him a short while to locate the right path. He hadn't cut the trail in two years. He had no fear of getting lost. It was just a matter of finding his old footsteps.

When he stepped out of the forest and into the street in front of Lester's house, Mark was forced to shade his eyes. The firmament was bright, astoundingly blue and beautiful. Even Lester's near-condemned home looked quaint under the late summer, mid-afternoon sky. As his pupils thinned, it struck Mark that the ice cream truck had yet to return. Mark decided in that moment that Lester would move in with him. At least for a little while; until his dad got back, and maybe longer still. Mark would clear out one of the rooms upstairs. He would buy Lester clothes and feed him breakfast. The Weasel deserved at least a dash of material comfort. Mark could provide it, so he would.

He thought about cutting through Lester's yard, through the old double gates, but decided against it as he crossed the road. The bungee needed to be fastened, Mark wasn't in junior high anymore, Umed was gone and Ashley was close to the worst person in the world. He didn't hate her, though. Mark realized that on his walk through the forest. He was past the hate. What Ashley did to his mother was repugnant. The amount of turmoil in the soul of another human being needed to carry out something so disgusting was literally pitiful. He felt badly for her. He hoped she could get some help. In the meantime, he just wanted her to go away.

Mark had his head down when he turned the corner alongside Lester's property. He had taken a few steps up the block when he noticed Ashley sitting on the curb. Ashley lifted her head from its cradle in her chest and looked at Mark. An unbroken string of tears streamed down both of her cheeks. Mark was unable to move. A tide of conflated emotions consumed his body. A wellspring so powerful that neither feeling, love nor hate, held any significance. The only concept that registered at all within Mark's being was that of inevitability.

Mark began to cry. He missed his father. He missed Ashley's mother. He missed Umed, and he missed his own mother. He missed Ashley. He missed being able to touch her and laugh with her.

He missed the level of comfort that used to surround his life and everything in it. He missed being himself. Mark was sobbing uncontrollably. He fell to his knees in the middle of the street. Ashley crawled over to him. She hugged him and cried in his arms.

"I am so sorry, Mark. I love you so much."

Mark hugged her back as he cried. He spoke through his tears.

"I've always loved you, Ashley. Always."

They stayed that way, weeping in each other's arms. They didn't move. No one disturbed them. When their tears ran dry, they continued to hold each other up as the sun slid westward across the cloudless sky. For a brief instant Mark felt that his father's death was worth the moment he was living right there and then. He quickly buried that notion behind everything else in his mind.

As his thoughts coalesced, Mark heard the unmistakable laugh of a weasel, the laugh of the Weasel. He pulled himself away from Ashley and opened his eyes. Lester was around the corner at Mark's house. Mark heard a strange chorus of disparate sounds emanating from his front yard. He heard Mr. Hutch, his father's foreman, giving instruction. He heard trucks backing up and the sound of metal being knocked around. Mark realized that these noises had been the backdrop to his and Ashley's entire reunion.

"What's going on over there?"

"Mark... My dad saw the video."

Mark stood up. He remembered his mom. He remembered that he loved her. Ashley rose from the pavement as she spoke.

"He was so mad at me."

She looked down at her bare feet. They were filthy.

"He actually hit me."

Mark looked at her with genuine concern.

"Are you okay?"

"Yeah. I don't even... I... I couldn't feel much at the time."

Mark overheard Mr. Hutch doling out additional orders, this time in Spanish.

"Wait. I don't understand. What's going on at my house?"

"He didn't know. No one knew about your mom. He..."

"What?"

"We all knew she gained weight. But the stuff. I mean we knew there was some stuff, but we didn't... You hid it all so well, Mark. We didn't know."

Mark walked passed Ashley toward his home. He needed to be with his mom. Ashley grabbed his arm and stopped him.

"Ash, I have to see my mom."

Ashley pulled him close and kissed him hard. She clutched his hand and placed it on the front of her pants. Mark melted. The kiss lasted long enough for every one of Mark's electrified blood cells to run two full circuits around his elevated form.

"I have to see her."

"I know."

Still clasping Mark's hand, Ashley led him around the corner. Once past the last section of picket fence, Mark inadvertently gasped as his eyelids merged with the folds of his brow. He witnessed his mother in the front yard sitting on a blanket with Ashley's father. They were watching Lester deftly perform repeated front flips and cartwheels on the grass. Ashley's dad was laughing so hard that he struggled to catch his breath. Behind them, two dozen of Ashley's father's employees were unloading the contents of Mark's house into three forty-yard dumpsters. The workers were oblivious to the pig trails they stamped into Mark's perfectly manicured lawn.

Lester noticed Mark first. He nixed the parlor tricks.

"What's up, superstar?"

"Hey, Weasel."

Ashley's father jumped to his feet and ran over to both Mark and his daughter.

"I'm so sorry, Mark. I'm so embarrassed for what my... what she did to you."

Ashley looked at the ground. Mark smiled.

"It's okay, Mr G. What's all this?"

"It's my guys. Well, our guys. They're cleaning out the house. But don't worry, we're not throwing anything away."

"Ha! No worries. You can burn everything for all I care. But what about Mom?"

Ashley's father smiled for the first time.

"It was her idea."

Mark looked at his mother. She was impossible to miss as the only amorphous blob propped up near the stone walkway. She was tearing up and smiling as her white knuckles served to garrote her favorite Country Cousin figurine. Mark turned back to Ashley's father.

"What are you doing with it all?"

"We're going to take it to the yard. You did such a great job storing everything, and for a hoarder your mom had pretty good taste. We're planning the biggest garage sale ever. Even at a buck an item, we're looking at tens of thousands of dollars."

Mark's cheeks went flush. He wasn't sure if it was due to shame or relief.

"Your mom wants to throw a block party with the money when she gets out of the hospital."

Mark ran to his mother. He practically tackled her to the ground. He told her that he loved her and they cried together.

Later that night, Mark and Ashley sat in the lounge chairs beside Ashley's pool. Lester was upstairs in Mark's house setting up his new room. If he had glanced out of Mark's window five minutes earlier, he would have caught Mark with two fingers down Ashley's bathing suit. They had been apart for so long. It was difficult for them to keep their hands off one another.

When they did find the strength to abstain from touching each other, their time together was effortless. Mark was looking up at the starlit sky. He was satisfied. Ashley was catching up with her phone.

"Oh my god!"

"What?"

"Fifi tried to kill herself."

"Who?"

"Fifi Diaz."

"Oh, what happened?"

"She swallowed a bunch of pills."

"Is she okay?"

"Yeah, I guess. She's at the hospital."

"Good."

At that moment, under the canopy of our shared universe, Mark did not understand why anyone would attempt to take their own life. How could it be that bad? Mark could not imagine a single reason. Everything in the world was perfect. Everything was just so utterly perfect.